M000228712

GHOST
DETECTIVE

A MYRON VALE INVESTIGATION

GHOST
DETECTIVE

A MYRON VALE INVESTIGATION

SCOTT WILLIAM CARTER

FLYING RAVEN
PRESS

GHOST DETECTIVE

Copyright © 2013 by Scott William Carter.

Published by Flying Raven Press, July 2013.

All rights reserved, including the right of reproduction, in whole or in part in any form. This book is a work of fiction. Names, characters, places and incidents either are products of the author's imagination or are used fictitiously. Any resemblance to actual events or locales or persons, living or dead, is entirely coincidental.

FLYING RAVEN PRESS
4742 Libery Rd. S #382
Salem, Oregon 97302

For more about Flying Raven Press, please visit our web site at
http://www.flyingravenpress.com

ISBN-10 0615831273
ISBN-13 978-0615831275

Printed in the United States of America
Flying Raven Press paperback edition, July 2013

For Sarah,

the best sister

a guy could have

Chapter 1

THE FIRST TIME I met Karen Thorne, I'd just clicked yes on two tickets to Honolulu for the holidays. Nonrefundable, of course.

In the throes of one of her periodic funks, Billie had stepped out for a walk—the rain always made her extra restless—and I was alone in the musty closet my landlord had advertised as office space so he could charge me office rates. As the dreary Portland afternoon slipped into a dreary Portland night, I'd forgotten to turn on the desk lamp, so the pale glow of my monitor was the only thing warding off the growing darkness.

When she opened the door, the glare of the exposed bulb in the hall made me squint. She was visible only as a silhouette—and a hell of a silhouette it was. I caught a hint of blond in the shadowy curls of her hair.

"Are you Myron Vale?" she said. A husky voice. Right. Why wouldn't it be? The voice had to go with the bombshell figure.

Faintly, from down the hall, came the off-key singing of people without any musical ability whatsoever attempting to belt out hymns. Their door was probably open again, but it wouldn't have mattered even if shut; our worthless doors were no better than cardboard. I just kept hoping the Higher Plane Church of Spiritual Transcendence would finally gather up enough gullible sheep that they'd be able to upgrade to a different location.

Either that or they'd give up all their nonsense and accept the truth that I knew better than anyone: Dead or alive, none of us were going anywhere.

"Whatever you want, I can't help you," I said.

"You're Myron Vale?"

"I'm leaving on vacation."

"Myron Vale, the ghost detective?"

"Please don't call me that."

"I want to hire you," she said. "My name is Karen Thorne. It's very important."

"It's Hawaii," I added.

"I can pay you."

"Did I mention it's Hawaii?"

"I can pay you a lot. I'm—I'm very rich, Mr. Vale. I wouldn't even be here, but they tell me—they tell me you're the person to come to for ... for my situation."

So much for the husky confidence. She'd started to come off like a little girl who'd lost her lollipop.

The rain, picking up its pace, pinged like marbles on the metal roof. The red neon glow from the bar across the street pulsed on my cracked window, rivulets of water dribbling down the glass like red wine. Inside my office it was quite dark, but outside, the sky contained the last gasps of dusk, lavender clouds over a gray horizon. I took one last longing look at my monitor—a happy couple holding hands on the beach, bodies tan and glistening, two margaritas on the bamboo table—then rose with a sigh from my swivel chair.

A little too fast, as usual. There was the familiar wooziness as the blood rushed to my head—and then, faintly, that dull throbbing at the front of my skull, white and bleak, a discomfort on the edge of nausea, in that sacred place where the .38 was lodged in my brain. I'd never had dizzy spells until the shooting. Of course, lots of things changed after the shooting. Everything, really.

"Are you all right?" the woman asked.

"I'm fine," I lied, steadying myself with a hand on my desk. The world was still tilting, but I wobbled through the darkness toward her anyway. Male pride could motivate a man to do many things.

On my way, I flicked on my desk lamp.

The woman in my doorway more than fulfilled the details my imagination had furnished to her silhouette. She was tall, taller than Billie—at least in her white heels—and she had the kind of curvy, womanly figure that was once the ideal before the runway popsicle sticks got plastered all over the fashion magazines. Her skin was slightly on the pale side, which made her sultry red lips look all the brighter. There was a pair of oversized white sunglasses in her hair, a lacy white shawl over her shoulders, and white pearls around her neck. Her dress was a sleeveless lavender number that matched the handbag she was clutching against her ample bosom. Her *very* ample bosom.

Sexuality oozed out of her every pore. When she blinked at me, her eyes a liquid green, I could almost feel her long eyelashes brushing against my face. Easy, Myron. You're a married man.

"You're—you're not what I imagined," she said.

"You were expecting someone taller?" I replied.

She flicked her hair over her shoulders, so much hair, so golden and curly, a single subconscious act probably capable of bringing armies of single men to their knees. "No … Just, I don't know, more Yoda-like, I guess. Wizard of Oz. Something like that. You've got quite a reputation." She smiled weakly and fidgeted with her handbag. "Mr. Vale, I've—I've come a long way. I need you to find someone. I'll pay whatever you want. Double your rates. Triple even. This man, he's—"

Before she could finish, I put my hand on her chest.

Her face reacted in the predictable way—a flinch, eyes flaring wide, those big red lips forming an even bigger O. Her chest, however, didn't react to my touch at all. In fact, my hand passed right through her, feeling only the slightest tingling chill as it disappeared into her body and came back out again.

"Now we can talk," I said.

A blush spread up her chest and neck to her cheeks, a bright pink wildfire raging across all that pale skin. She touched her chest, her own hand solid to herself, of course, and took a few quick breaths. I thought she might pass out, but she only wobbled a little, swallowing hard, glaring at me. Outside, an eighteen-wheeler rumbled by on Burnside, splashing through the puddles.

"Are you always this forward when you meet a woman for the first time?" she asked.

"Only the dead ones," I said. When her face crinkled—most ghosts, especially the recently deceased, hated to be reminded that they were no longer among the living—I quickly added: "Sorry. I just had to be sure. You did open the door, you know, rather than walk through it. Not many ghosts can do that."

"Oh," she said, her face softening, more sympathy there now than shock. "I just thought, you know, opening the door would make you more comfortable. Since you're, well, you know … You mean you can't tell by looking?"

I shook my head.

"Oh. That must be—um, hard. In your line of work."

"And what line of work would that be?"

"You know. For a ghost detective."

"Again, I'd rather you not call me that. I'm just a detective. A licensed private investigator, actually."

"But you do work for ghosts?"

"I work for all kinds of unsavory types." When she stared blankly, I sighed. It was no use. "Yes, I sometimes work for ghosts. It pays the bills. And yeah, not being able to tell the difference makes it challenging. Now what can I do for you, Mrs. Thorne?"

She still hadn't quite recovered from my otherworldly feel-up, biting down on her lower lip, kneading the beads on her handbag, whatever was left of her confidence having evaporated when I'd confirmed her non-corporeal status. I felt bad that I'd done it, but it wasn't like I had a choice. When Billie wasn't around, I had to take matters into my own hands. Literally. It was either that or lose everything.

"Do you want to sit down?" I asked.

"Um, all right."

I directed her to one of the two padded office chairs across from my desk. Rather than return to my desk chair, a more imposing position, I took the seat next to her. She perched with her legs pressed close together, handbag in her lap, our knees nearly touching. I was still just humoring her. I had no intention of taking up the case, but she probably deserved more than a casual brush-off.

"You said you wanted me to find someone?" I prodded.

She cleared her throat. "Yes. As I said, Mr. Vale—can I call you Myron?"

"It's either that or Vincent, I guess."

"Vincent."

"It's my middle name."

"Oh, well, if you would prefer I call you Vincent—"

"I wouldn't. Not unless you're my mother back from a pretty incredible face-lift, because I have to say, you don't look anything like her."

"Oh."

"And I only let her do that because she used to call me Vinnie," I said. "Drove me bonkers, but I never said anything about it until she passed. Always figured she wouldn't live forever, so why make waves, right? She'd always wanted my first name to be Vincent just so she could call me Vinnie, who knows why, but Dad had insisted on Myron after some friend of his who died in 'Nam. Of course, then things changed for me—and when I realized that she was going to go on calling me Vinnie for eternity, well, I put my foot down. Told her to call me Myron like everyone else." I knew I was rambling, but it seemed to be putting her at ease.

"But you said she still calls you Vincent?"

"Right. That was a compromise. There's only so much my mother will listen to reason, especially now that she's dead."

She laughed, and it was a good one. Genuine. She wasn't putting on airs, which was the sense I got from her the rest of the time. She laughed with her whole body, head thrown back—a bone-rattling kind of laugh that would have woken up the dead if there was anybody left to wake.

"You're a funny man, Myron," she said.

"Tell that to my mother. All right, out with it. Who's this guy you're looking for?"

That sobered her in a hurry. The little banker's lamp on my desk cast a warm yellow glow in my otherwise sterile office, but it was a weak light, weak enough that I could still detect hints of neon red on her cheeks from the bar sign. Another truck rumbled past in search of more potholes, and when it passed, shifting the light and the shadows in the room for just a moment, no more than a split second, surely, the color of her hair changed. It was still blond, a vibrant yellow, no more transparent than it was before, really, but there was a different tint to it, a certain quality that set it apart, that gave it a more ghostly shade of gold.

Every now and then, if the light was just so, if the mood was right, if the stars aligned, whatever it was, I could *tell*. I could see, just for a second, the difference between the living and the dead. It gave me hope that one day all this madness would end.

"His name is Anthony Neuman," she said. "Or Tony. I always called him Tony." She looked like she was going to tear up.

"Husband?" I said.

She nodded.

"Living or dead?" I asked.

"Living," she said. "At least I think so."

"You think? When was the last time you saw him?"

"Three months ago," she said, and then she did tear up. The blurring line of her mascara strained to hold back the waterworks, and I thought, Oh no, it's all over but the crying, but then she battened down the hatches and shot me an angry look as if I'd insulted her somehow. "Actually it was three months, six days, and four hours ago, to be exact. I saw him ten minutes before I was murdered."

That got me to sit up a little straighter. While it wasn't the first time a client had uttered the word *murder* in my office, it was still rare. Of course, Vale Investigations had only been open for three years, but still. Finding a murderer was a hell of a lot more interesting than finding someone's estranged son or a dead Army buddy who had fallen out of contact.

Still, I wasn't planning on taking the case. Blue skies and warm sand still beckoned.

"Murder, you say?"

"That's right," she said.

"Do you know who killed you?"

She hesitated. "I think it was Tony, but I don't know for sure. That's why I want you to find him."

"Really? And you want to find him for, what, revenge?"

"I said I don't know if it was him. I'm hoping it wasn't. That's why I want you to find him."

"Why would he want to kill you?"

She swallowed. "For money, I guess. He didn't get any." When I raised an eyebrow to this, she went on: "I started to suspect, you know, that he might try something. I had this funny feeling. We'd only been married a few months, and he was acting strange."

"Strange? How?"

"Moodier. Edgy. I don't know, it was just a feeling. It was so vague that I didn't even tell anyone, but I—well, I changed my will. Made sure all the money went to my sisters instead of him. My plan was to tell him I'd done this, really for my own peace of mind. I figured if he knew, and if he stayed, well, then he really loved me." She choked on the words, swallowed, and pressed on. "I really thought he loved me, Myron. In fact, I still do. I think he must have been in trouble. I don't know. Maybe somebody else killed me as revenge for something he did and he's in hiding."

"How was it done?" I asked.

"Done?"

"Yeah. The method. Bullets, poison, what?"

She reacted as if she'd swallowed something sour. "You know, this is my life we're talking about here."

"Sorry. Just used to cutting to the chase. Comes from the old days when I was a cop."

She nodded. Down the hall, the singers were starting into another hymn. I felt my anxiety swelling. Billie was right. If I didn't take a vacation soon, I was going to become a murderer myself one of these days.

"Car crash," she said. "Somebody messed with my brakes."

"You sure it wasn't an accident—you know, car trouble?"

She glared at me. "Do you think I'd be here if I thought it was an accident?"

"Sorry."

"I was *there*. Everybody may think the reason I ran into that brick wall was because I'd had too much to drink, but I know what happened. I know how the car just started going faster. For no reason. And it was a Bentley! Brand new!"

"A Bentley? What kind of money did you come from anyway?"

"Come from? What, a girl like me can't just earn it on her own?"

I didn't say anything.

"I *could* have earned it, you know," she said. "I did graduate from Yale. Daddy may have helped me get in, but he certainly didn't earn those grades. I earned them all on my own."

"All right, easy. So you earned the money on your own, then. Fine."

"I said *could*, Myron. I didn't say *did*. I didn't ask to be born into this family. It's just my life."

"What family are we talking about here?"

She simmered silently, as if she was debating about whether to take offense to my comment, then shrugged and said, "You ever heard of Thorne Pharmaceuticals?"

"*Oh.* You're *that* Thorne family."

She nodded, kneading her handbag. Thorne Pharmaceuticals—I didn't know how big they were exactly, but judging by how often their commercials about male erectile dysfunction played just during the few hours when I watched late-night TV trying to kill my insomnia, I assumed they had to be big.

"My father is one of Morgan Thorne's seven grandsons," she explained. "The way my great-grandfather set it up, all the descendants have a certain percentage of company shares. Mine's a pretty small slice of the pie, but still, it adds up."

"I'll bet," I said.

"So there's no problem with me paying you whatever you want."

"Uh-huh. And now that you're no longer, um, able to sign checks, how do you propose to do that?"

"I figured you'd ask that. My father will pay you."

"He's a Sensitive?"

"What?"

"I mean, he can see you?" It was the second thing she'd said that made my spine straighten. I was a pretty rare breed. Extremely rare, in fact. As far as I knew, there was nobody else like me on the planet, somebody who could see *all* the ghosts *all* the time. Still, there were occasional flesh-and-blood humans who could see specific ghosts, sometimes briefly, sometimes for quite a long time. Mediums, psychics, clairvoyants, people with the second sight—there are lots of words for these folks, though in my experience, the vast majority were phonies, charlatans, and con artists. In the ghost world, the real ones were known as Sensitives, though it wasn't surprising that Karen, as a new arrival, hadn't yet heard the term.

Her eyes took on a distant cast as she contemplated my question. "I don't know," she said. "He's very distraught about my death. Sometimes, when he's very sad and not too drunk, I'll whisper to him how much I love him, and I think, maybe ..." She shook her head. "I don't know. Probably just wishful thinking on my part. But he *will* pay you. There's some things that only he and I know. If I tell you them,

9

he'll believe your story."

"Mmm," I said, trying not to show my skepticism. Billie always claimed I was too soft on the payment side of things. I'd been stiffed too many times, to use a very apt word.

"I really, really need your help," she said.

"Yes, you've said that."

"I *have* to know if he killed me, Myron—and if he did, then why. I can't rest in peace until I know."

"Well, who rests in peace anyway? That's one of the first things I learned about you folks—there isn't a whole lot of resting going on."

"It's just a figure of speech. I—I even brought his picture. So are you going to help me?"

Her voice had grown tense. I couldn't blame her. I was being pretty obtuse, even by my standards. The thing was, I knew full well the real reason she wanted to hire me, and it wasn't to find out why he'd killed her. The real reason was to find out if he'd really *loved her.* That was the burning question on her mind, and why she needed me rather than a detective from her own kind. She needed somebody to talk to him, somebody he could talk *to,* and that wasn't going to happen with my transparent counterparts.

Love is a messy business. If I've learned anything, before and after I became the freak show I am, it's that questions of the heart can never be fully answered to someone's satisfaction. I knew that better than anyone.

"I already bought the tickets," I said.

"I told you, I'll reimburse you for any—"

"I really wish I could help."

I said it with enough finality that it cut short the argument. She nodded sadly. Outside, the rain had mercifully stopped, as had my off-key singers down the hall. Thank God for small miracles. Well, thank *somebody* for small miracles. Nobody knew if the Big Guy really existed—on either side of the great divide.

That was the bitch about dying. You still didn't get all the answers.

"Well, thank you for your time," she said, rising abruptly.

I rose along with her. "I really do wish you all the best of luck."

She turned away without comment. I thought that was it, I'd never see her again, but then I did something stupid. Before she made it to the door, my curiosity got the best of me.

"You have his picture, huh?" I said.

She looked at me. "Yes," she said, a hint of her hope in her voice. "Do you want to see it?"

A thousand voices inside me screamed to say no. I'd already made my decision, so it would have been the prudent thing to do. Of course, being too prudent was one of the chief reasons my life had ended up the way it had. Sometimes, I'd learned, it was better to be impulsive and follow your instincts.

I shrugged, and she snapped open her purse. I still thought it odd that ghosts carried on as if their world were as physical and real as ours was, when I figured they could imagine just about any kind of world they wanted, but old habits probably died hard—or didn't die at all, to be more literal. She pulled out a 3-by-5, one of those glossy head shots that were more the province of actors than businesspeople, and held it out as if she wanted me to take it. But of course I couldn't take it. It may have been real to her, but it was no more substantial to me than she was. Ghosts were always forgetting this.

Instead, I merely leaned in, smiling, arms behind my back, with the kind of polite display of attentiveness that a person engages in when inspecting some new piece of jewelry a friend is particularly proud of—which may have been why the man's picture, when I finally saw it, hit me so hard.

There may have been some small part of me that knew there was at least a tiny chance I'd recognize the person in the picture, but I never in a million years expected this.

It was the man who'd shot me.

Chapter 2

A LITTLE MORE than five years before Karen Thorne walked into my office, I was riding shotgun in an unmarked police car on a cold February morning, listening to my pretty partner unleash her latest diatribe about her latest loser boyfriend, and counting the blocks until I could get my wake-the-hell-up caffeine fix. A bit of the weekend snow, a rare event in Portland, still clung to the sidewalks, but the roads were bare except for the occasional glistening patch of black ice. The Crown Victoria fishtailed rounding the corner onto Hawthorne, but Alesha, as usual, didn't slow in the least.

"Might want to take it a bit easier," I said, gripping the vinyl armrest a little tighter.

She gave me one of her looks, a look that would have been preposterous coming from someone else but always seemed to work for Alesha—a sort of Chuck Norris don't-mess-with-me attitude combined with schoolmarmy peevishness. "I'm from Chicago," she said. "I know how to drive on this stuff. And anyway, don't change the subject. As I was saying, Steve shows up at my place at two in the morning—"

While some funky all-women folk band I'd never heard of played on the radio, Alesha proceeded to unload on poor Steve, whose only

13

crime seemed to be that he didn't call to tell her his poker game was running a bit late. This apparently gave Alesha license to run down all his many flaws, from his beastly cologne, to his penchant to laugh too hard at jokes about lawyers, to his flippant attitude toward all the New Age books that Alesha devoured like other people devoured ice cream.

"Hold on," I said. "You're picking on him because he doesn't like your books?"

She glared at me, her eyes so dark that only a tiny sliver of the whites was visible. Even in the shadowy interior of the car, even in the pale light of an early winter morning, her eyes were still arresting. With her black hair cut scalp-short, a style she'd adopted lately after going with the full Afro for the better part of the year, all the focus was on her eyes. Even if her eyes had been more ordinary, she still would have been attractive—petite but athletic, nice cheekbones, skin like polished obsidian—but her eyes were what set her apart. A man had to be careful or he could lose himself in those eyes.

"I'm not picking on him," she protested. "I'm just … venting some of my frustrations. And it's not about the books. It's about whether we share a common outlook on the universe. "

"Oh, I stand corrected. That's much better. Especially since you've dated him, what, two weeks?"

"It's long enough to get a sense if you're compatible," she said huffily.

"So you're saying he has to believe in Bigfoot or you'll dump him?"

"No, he doesn't have to believe in Bigfoot. But he doesn't even believe in the stuff that everybody believes in."

"Like what?"

"I don't know. Like the stuff *everybody* knows is true."

"Death and taxes?" I offered.

She sighed.

"Elvis still alive and living somewhere in Florida?" I added.

"Will you *stop*," she said, but I saw her mouth curling into a grin.

"No, I'm talking about things like … I don't know, like ghosts."

"Ghosts?"

"That's right."

"Dead people coming back to life?"

"No," she said, "those are *zombies*. Nobody believes those are real—well, nobody sane, anyway. I'm talking about the living spirits of the deceased. Souls walking the face of the earth. Everybody knows that ghosts are real."

I said nothing.

"Oh come on," she said, "you've *got* to believe in them."

"Alesha," I said patiently, "you remember that I'm an atheist, right? You remember how I said I believe in science and rationality and what the evidence shows us?"

"That doesn't mean you can't believe in ghosts," she insisted.

I let this inane comment pass without a reply.

"So you're saying you don't believe in ghosts at all," she said.

"That's right," I replied. "That's exactly what I'm saying. It's all a bunch of hooey."

"Well, that's only because you haven't seen one."

"Maybe I haven't seen one because they're not real."

"What about all the people who *have* seen them?"

"Maybe they've seen them because they *do* think they're real."

"Oh, I see. You're saying, what, it's a self-fulfilling prophecy or something?"

"Or something," I said.

"What if I told you I'd seen one?"

I didn't say anything. Four blocks to go until Starbucks. I wondered if I could make it.

"You don't want to hear about it?" she asked.

I sighed. "Please, tell me about the ghost you think you saw."

"Did see."

"Whatever."

"Okay, now I know you're just being cranky. Is it just the lack of coffee, or did Billie kick you to the couch again?"

"Are you going to tell me about the ghost or what?"

"Ah," Alesha said, "the couch. That's, what, three times this month?"

"I don't want to talk about it."

She smiled impishly. "You don't want to talk about it. And yet you're perfectly willing to lecture *me* about my relationship problems. Must be a white-guy thing."

"Oh, here we go," I said.

"What? You *are* white. Or don't you believe in that either, honky boy?"

"Honky boy? Really? What is this, an episode of *Shaft?*"

"All I'm saying is that I'm not going to tell you about the ghost I saw unless you tell me what's up with Billie."

"Promise?" I said.

She shook her head, but I could see the smile growing. We were different in so many ways, black and white, a seven-year age gap, me into Carl Sagan and her into Deepak Chopra, but she was still the best friend I'd ever had. Even when we fought, it was a *good* kind of fighting, full of banter and mirth, not at all like my fighting with Billie. Sometimes I wondered—in fact, maybe I wondered a little too often—just what it might be like to be married to Alesha. But then, I didn't get to choose such things. *That* was something I did believe in, as irrational as it might have been: The heart was its own master.

The Starbucks was just ahead at the corner, and Alesha approached without slowing, the sides of the tires scraping the curb.

"Fine," she said, "you win. Keep your relationship troubles to yourself. But I'm still going to tell you my ghost story when you come back with your coffee, crackerjack."

"I think I liked honky boy better," I said.

Getting out of the car, I stepped over the dirty snow piled at the curb, approaching the Starbucks without really glancing at the window. A frigid wind, swirling up from the Willamette River a few blocks away, hit me full in the face, and I kept my chin tucked into my gray wool overcoat. I often wondered, looking back, if it would have made a difference had I glanced inside, if my detective training would have allowed me to spot the pending trouble before I walked into the middle of it, but I could never convince myself that it would have mattered.

As it was, I swung open the door and stepped inside just as a man started to shout.

"Nobody move! This is a robbery!"

The first thing I thought, before I even located the source of the voice, before my heart started to pound and my mouth went dry, was that it was some kind of joke. Because robbing a Starbucks? *Really?* But then I saw him, a tall, grungy, broad-shouldered man in a knitted gray hat pulled low over thick blond hair, waving a small-gauge revolver at the customers and the staff, a .38 Smith & Wesson Special, it turned out later, based on the ballistics. I knew as soon as I saw the revolver that this was no joke. After eight years on the force, I knew a real gun when I saw one.

People always say that time slows down in crisis situations, but in my experience it's not so much about time slowing down as your brain speeding up. Details I might have lingered on before—the warm air venting from the ceiling, the droplets of water on the dark tiles, the bells on the door jingling as it swung shut—were hardly noticed as all of my senses were trained on the shooter. My vision tunneled out the world, leaving just the two of us, me frozen at the door, him swinging the revolver around in my direction. Because my appearance had startled him. I could see that now. He was swinging his gun in my direction, and there was a good chance he would pull the trigger when he saw me.

I don't know why I thought this. It wasn't like I was standing there in uniform, or that he could even see my Glock strapped to my chest beneath my overcoat. I should have looked like just another late-thirties Portlander on his way to some office job, a little too frumpy to be a banker or a lawyer, maybe, with my dirty tennis shoes an odd choice to wear with my charcoal slacks, but certainly no cop. But I still knew he was going to fire. I think I knew it the first time I laid eyes on him.

The gun was coming around and I was thinking, What do I do, go for my gun? Hit the floor? Dive back outside? As he turned, I saw that he had a brown mustache so thick I wouldn't have been surprised to see it crawl off his face. Both his orange vest, as thick as a life preserver, and his dirty blue jeans had been patched multiple times with duct tape. In Portland he was just another funky dude in a city full of funky dudes.

If I'd gone for the gun immediately, maybe dived for the floor at the same time, things may have gone differently—but only maybe. I had only a second to choose, and in that second I defaulted to my standard nature: caution. I would talk to him, reason with him, try to get him out of this situation without anybody getting hurt. It was the prudent thing to do, after all.

As the gun pointed at me, I got a full look at his face. There was something distinctive about him, a certain chiseled quality to his nose and cheekbones, a certain granular quality to his olive skin, that made his features seem both the model of human attractiveness and not human at all. It was like the face of a statue, lightly powdered with makeup but fooling no one. His eyes were dull and dead; they fixed on me with all the sparkle of lead balls.

"Wait," I said.

It was the only word I managed to get out before the pop of his revolver rang out—and my whole world changed.

Chapter 3

THE RAIN-SLICKED STREETS of Portland were filled with people.

Even though it had been over five years since the shooting, long enough that I should have gotten used to the constant crowds, my first reaction whenever I stepped outside my office building was still to wonder what special event was going on in the city.

But of course there was no special event. It was just my world.

It was a Wednesday evening in the middle of November, drizzly and cold, still light enough to see but dark enough that the passing cars all had their headlights on, and any other flesh-and-blood person stepping out of my building probably would have spotted a lone person or two walking on foot. Not me. I saw dozens—three businessmen in suits and bowler hats, a stout woman in a dress that looked like it was off the set of *Little House on the Prairie,* some teenagers with long hair and bell-bottom jeans smoking pot on the corner, and two police officers in fifties-era uniforms walking down the street with a Hispanic man in handcuffs between them. Those were probably ghosts, the easy ones, though I still couldn't know for certain without a hand check. The rest of the people, more modern in appearance, could have gone either way.

It actually would have been easier if more ghosts stuck with the styles of their day, but many liked to keep up with current trends. Dying, I'd found, didn't rid people of vanity. In many cases, it only increased it.

The air had a wet, chill bite. Although it didn't appear to be raining, the yellow bubbles of light surrounding the street lamps were streaked with razor-thin lines. I buttoned up my overcoat, watching a bus slosh through the puddles, the inside packed to the hilt, people sitting, people standing, a lot of faces turned my way. I wondered how many of them had a pulse. Not many, probably.

I should have cooled my heels at the office until Billie returned—that was our usual routine—but I couldn't this time. Not after I'd seen the eyes of the killer who'd changed my life.

The first stop was Mama's Bistro around the corner, Billie's most frequent hangout, and I headed there at a fast clip. When I dodged around a woman pushing a stroller, a couple holding hands just past her gave me a funny look, which was often the only way I knew when I'd just walked by a ghost. To a real person, it always looked like I was weaving like a drunk man.

For the living, the current population of this little ball of mud we call home is around seven billion. That's no number to sneeze at, especially when you're at the DMV and it seems as if half of them are in line ahead of you. But according to the last census performed by the Department of Souls, who are charged with keeping track of such things, over a hundred billion people have lived and died on planet Earth before anyone alive today was even born.

For me, they're all still here.

The tables at Mama's, both inside and on the covered patio, were occupied, but there was no Billie. I wove through a group of cellphone-yakking yuppies decked out in REI, made the mistake of stepping in a puddle, and cursed as I slogged forward with one wet sock. No Billie at the bus depot, one of the places she liked to people-watch. No Billie at the newsstand on 26th, the one that had burned up in a fire fifty years go but was still operated by the same old codger.

I rounded the corner and stopped at our favorite neighborhood hot-dog stand. The heavyset man in the red and white sequined jumpsuit handed a little girl with pigtails a corn dog, then flashed me his famous smile. As usual, his full head of black hair was perfectly coiffed. Most mornings, he worked the street outside my window, but in the evenings he liked to rove around a bit.

"Hey Elvis," I said, "you seen Billie?"

"No, sir," Elvis said, rolling some of the franks on his grill. The way he flicked the dogs, it was like he was strumming a guitar. It was hard to believe none of it was real. I still didn't quite understand why ghosts used real-world things at all—buses, buildings, bridges—when it was obvious they could just create something out of whole cloth, just as Elvis had done with his hot-dog stand. And if they saw it, then I saw it. Just one of those weird little rules that I lived by but couldn't fully explain.

"You lost the little lady?" he said.

"Oh, she'll turn up eventually. I just need to talk to her."

"About a case?"

"Something like that."

He nodded, not pressing, which was why I liked him. It was anyone's guess whether he was the real deal, the later, heavier Elvis, or just an impersonator, but he was easy to talk to regardless. "Well, I hope you find her. Hungry?"

I looked at the glazed hot dogs, sizzling on the grill, the scent of grease in the air. Sight, sound, smell—their world was real to me in every way except touch and taste, which were unfortunately the ways it mattered most. "You know I can't do that, Elvis, as much as I'd want to."

"Oh, yeah, forgot. You're still playing live, as they say in the biz. But you know you're missing out, pal."

"That's what I hear. They say you make the best hot dogs that never were."

"Thank ya very much," he said, flashing me his winning smile.

It took a little more wandering, but I finally found Billie perched on a wrought-iron bench at the park next to the old Gothic-style church four blocks from my office. She was dressed all in black leather, her favorite style lately, her pale face nearly glowing in the hazy gloom. It was a tiny park, with a dilapidated metal play structure roughly the same color as algae, a basketball court with two backboards but only one rim, and a couple of wooden picnic tables under some leafless pin oaks. On the other side of the park, two goth girls leaned against the chain-link fence, eyeing me warily. Their cigarettes burned in the near-dark like distant jet engines.

Billie didn't look up until I was right in front of her. Even at dusk, her blue eyes were so penetrating that even now, after all these years, my heart did a little jig when she looked right at me. Her hair, which changed more often than the Oregon weather, was short and spiky, black with platinum blond highlights. She gave me the faintest smile possible, hardly more than a twitch of her cheeks. It wasn't much, but I'd come to appreciate any flicker of happiness from her when she was in one of her moods.

"Found new haunting grounds?" I said.

She rolled her eyes. My brand of gallows humor may not have been her cup of tea, but she knew it was the chief way I stayed sane.

That was true even before she'd died.

I took a seat next to her and immediately wished I'd wiped off the bench first—I felt the cool dampness seeping into my overcoat. The wide collar of Billie's black leather coat was turned up, partially blocking the henna tattoo she'd put on her neck last week. The way she was sitting, on the edge of the bench, it was as if she had somewhere to go but it wasn't quite time to leave yet.

Across the way, the goth girls were giving me a funny look. Of course they would. To them, I'd just talked to an empty park bench.

"Did you buy the airplane ticket?" Billie asked softly.

"Yep." Conscious that I was being watched, I tried not to move my lips much, a skill I'd picked up in the past few years.

"One or two?"

"Hmm?"

"You bought a ticket for me, didn't you?"

"I don't remember."

"Myron," she said, in that scolding tone of hers.

"I like it when you sit next to me on the plane," I said.

"It's a waste of money. I can sit anywhere, and there's almost always empty seats anyway. You don't need to buy a ticket for a ghost."

Instead of answering, I pointed at her leather sandals. They had thick wooden soles—Billie was always trying to be taller—and the web of black leather revealed lots of her creamy skin. "Those new? I haven't seen them before."

"Got them at Macy's," she said, with a tone of someone who'd just come from a funeral. "They were having a sale."

"Ah, so that's where you've been. They're nice. Aren't they a little cold for this time of year?"

"Is it cold? I hadn't noticed."

It was a comment that could have literally been true, but it was probably just surliness on her part.

We sat in silence. I knew that what I was about to say was not going to make her happy, so I was procrastinating. I studied her profile, the elegant cheekbones, the full lips, the ever so slight overbite that she hated so much, and wondered for the hundredth time why someone so exquisite and beautiful and artistic had agreed to marry me. If not for a chance meeting at the Portland Museum of Art nine years ago—both of us there to see the traveling Monet exhibition, her having moved to town a week earlier after fleeing a poor life in rural Maine—I probably never would have even met her.

She cleared her throat. "What hotel were you—"

"I saw him," I said.

I'd meant to sidle up to it, start with the girl in the lavender dress, talk about her story, eventually make my way to the picture. But the news was like a bad splinter, worming its way deeper into my skin, my anxiety growing with each passing second.

She looked at me, raising one neatly trimmed eyebrow. "Who?"

she said.

I started to speak, but my throat had seized up, so I had to swallow before I could try again. "The guy who shot me. I saw him."

Her eyes flashed like flares at a roadside accident, her cool detachment gone in an instant, panic and shock playing across her features.

"What?" she said.

"It was just a picture. Not the real thing."

"Myron, if this is some kind of weird joke—"

"No, no, no joke," I said, and then I went on to explain about Karen Thorne's visit to my office. Billie interrupted me several times, pressing for details I didn't have, and pursed her lips skeptically when I finished.

"Are you sure?" she said.

"I'm telling you, it was him."

"Maybe you just wanted it to be him. You only saw him for a second, after all."

"Billie, it was him. And anyway, you can see for yourself tomorrow morning. Karen's coming in at eight."

"Don't tell me you agreed to take her case?"

"I didn't agree to anything yet. I told her I wanted the night to think it over."

She shook her head. "We talked about this, Myron. We decided. Remember? Let bygones be bygones. Move on. Focus on the future."

"But that's before I knew he was still in Portland!"

"Shh!"

She flashed me a furious look, index finger pressed to her lips. I glanced at the goth girls, both of them standing there with their cigarettes half-raised to their lips, gawking at me, a silent film on freeze frame.

"Don't you remember?" Billie said, and there was a level of hysteria in her voice I hadn't anticipated. I'd expected her to be unhappy, maybe even angry, but not so panicked about the whole thing. "Don't you remember how long it took to get your life together after the shooting? Do you really want to revisit all that? Won't it just reopen all those old wounds?"

"But I've got a lead this time! A real one!"

"A lead to what?"

"The truth! Answers! Anything!" I knew I was yelling again, but I didn't care if anyone heard. "Knowing something about him will be better than always wondering!"

"Will it?"

"Yes!"

"Maybe it will just lead to more questions. Maybe—maybe those questions will just ... throw off your balance."

"Things are different now."

"Are they?"

"Damn it, Billie! Yes!"

"You can promise me?"

"Yes! Yes!"

"Because I don't want to wonder where you are at two in the morning."

"That won't—"

"I don't want to worry that you've drank yourself to death in some bar."

"I'm telling you—"

"I don't want have to pull you out of another asylum."

"You won't have—what?"

It wasn't something I had expected her to say. The bars, yes, I could understand. There were more than a few times I'd woken up in an alley to the beeping of a garbage truck, the dawn light like needles in my eyes, no idea how I'd gotten on that pile of musty cardboard, those memories permanently blotted from my brain. I knew how close I'd come to losing it all, to joining Billie on the other side, but I was better now. Or at least better enough to get through the day.

But the asylum? That was a whole other level of mental instability, a level I'd been at only once in my life. It was a low blow.

"That's what you think?" I said. "You think I'm that fragile?"

She looked at me a long time, a shadow among shadows, a ghost among ghosts. There was something there, something she wanted to say, I could feel her holding back, but I had no idea what it was. It had always been that way, both before and after death. There were worlds beyond her eyes I'd never visited and never would. She was a book written in braille, and I was a blind man who'd never been taught to read.

"I think we're all that fragile, Myron," she said.

Before I could offer a response, before I could even decipher what she'd meant, she rose and walked away. I reached for her arm, forgetting as I often did, then let my hand fall limply to my side. I watched her pass out of the bubble of lamplight, disappearing briefly into the darkness afforded by the overhanging oaks, then reappearing on the other side. I saw her footprints on the sidewalk. I saw her trailing shadow. I heard the splash of her boots in the puddles, and I wondered, as I had so many times before, how I could see and hear all these things and yet was never allowed to touch her.

At the gate into the park, she turned up the street. Going south. Headed to our home in Sellwood, most likely. It was a long walk, but long walks never seemed to bother her.

"What about the case?" I called after her.

"I think you've already decided," she replied.

"But will you help me?"

Without answering, she passed beyond the stone wall of the church adjoining the park, out of my sight. I hesitated, unsure of whether to jog after her, then decided to let her go for now. To cool off and see that this was something I had to do. There was always later. We had plenty of later.

Everyone did.

Chapter 4

THE DARKNESS COULD have lasted a second or a day or a year, it was all the same to me—an endless stretch of nothingness and no feeling and best of all, no pain. If time passed between when that bullet penetrated my brain and when I first groped toward consciousness, I didn't know it. The first things I remembered later were the voices, lots of voices. Men, women, children, they were coming and going, some whispering, some shouting, me catching only a fragment here or a few words here, fading before my rattled brain could try to make sense of it all. The voices were all mixed together anyway, like a hundred records playing at once, each set at a different volume and a different speed.

After that, there was the pain, an excruciating, blinding hot pain in the middle of my head. It felt as if a recently forged sword was embedded in the middle of my skull. It was really the pain, more than the voices, that brought me fully back. The pain pulsed and throbbed and hammered and pounded, a ceaseless drumbeat of agony that pulled me out of the depths of my darkness one ache at a time.

When I finally managed to open my eyes, blinking through the gray murk that clouded my vision, the first thing I saw was a priest standing at the edge of my bed, a lanky old man with a full head of wavy white hair that gleamed like fresh snow in the light slanting though the blinds to my right. There were no voices, the silence broken by the steady beeping of a heart monitor. My head, pulsing still, felt as if it was encased in concrete. I would have touched it, but I was so weak that even the thought of lifting my hand was exhausting.

"It'll be all right, son," the priest said.

The obscenely large gold cross hanging around his neck glinted in the sunlight. Without turning my head, sliding my gaze left and right, I scanned the room. Plain taupe walls. An IV drip. Metal sidebars on the bed. Even this little movement brought on a spell of dizziness. Nobody else was in the room but me and the priest.

"I'm not Catholic," I said.

He smiled kindly, his teeth yellowed as a smoker's would be. "It doesn't matter," he said.

"I don't even believe in God."

"Lucky for you, that doesn't seem to bother him."

His voice was Charlton Heston deep but just as warm as his smile—a *knowing* smile, as if he knew a secret about me but he wasn't saying.

Before I could ask him what that secret might be, the door burst open and a bevy of medical professionals swept into the room: a rotund doctor with more hair on his mustache than on top of his head, and that wasn't saying much; an equally rotund nurse with far too much hair, a huge mound of platinum blond that put all other bobs in the long history of bobs to shame; plus two beefy male orderlies who looked like they worked nights as strongmen at the circus.

They made quite a fuss over me, checking my vitals, tending to my head bandages, asking me if I knew who I was, the name of the President, that sort of thing, at least a full minute of breathless excitement before they seemed convinced that I was truly awake and stable.

"It's a miracle," the nurse said.

"That's what I was telling him," the priest said. He stood behind them, hands behind his back, beaming.

"Of course, there will have to be lots of tests," the doctor said. "A battery of tests. Physical, mental. A whole workup."

"Um, Doctor," I said, "how long have I been unconscious?"

The doctor and the nurse exchanged a glance.

"Doctor?" I said.

He swallowed. "Perhaps we should have the hospital psychiatrist on hand."

"Doctor, just tell me."

"It could be upsetting."

"I'm *getting* upset now!"

"Six months."

"Six months!"

He nodded glumly. I tried to process the number and couldn't. When I woke up, I figured it might have been six days. If he had said six weeks, it would have been shocking, but I probably could have dealt with it. But six months?

The pounding in my head became more pronounced, a brain-rattling thrumming as if my brain were trying to shake loose my skull. Instinctively, I tried to rub my forehead and found only bandages. The light slanting through the blinds suddenly seemed too bright, though the brightness made more sense now that I knew we were no longer in winter. It almost never shone like that in Portland in winter.

"So you're saying it's, what, August?" I asked.

"August 12, to be exact."

"Jesus!"

"It'll be all right, son," the priest said.

"We must focus on the positive," the doctor said. "This truly is a miracle. The first miracle was your survival of the shot itself. It was one in a million, the bullet traveling perfectly down the fissure between the two hemispheres without any significant damage to either one." He reached as if to point out the place, then pulled his hand back hastily as if he thought it might be in poor taste. "Although more tests will have to determine the extent of the impairment to your neurological abilities, there's a good chance there won't be much. It's not a split-brain situation, no damage to the corpus callosum. And the second miracle was you waking up from such a long coma. As much as television would have us believe otherwise, it's quite rare."

"Slow down a minute, Doc," I said. "You're saying there's a bullet still in my head?"

"I'm afraid so. However—"

"There's a *bullet* in my *head*."

"It was too risky to remove when you first came in, I'm afraid. And your body seems oddly ambivalent about it, not rejecting it as a foreign presence at all. In fact, we had far greater trouble with some of the more superficial parts of your wound, which is why you are wearing those bandages again. We did a few skin grafts two weeks ago to your forehead. That seems to have gone well, however, and you should be able to get those off within a few days."

"Well, *that's* a relief." I said it with a smile, or what at least felt like a smile, but everybody's response was to look at me with sympathy. Annoyed, I decided it was time I talked to somebody who knew me before I was a medical marvel. "Where's Billie, anyway? Somebody call her yet to tell her I'm awake?"

The nurse touched her great bob of blond hair. The doctor scratched his mustache.

"Where's Billie?" I demanded.

"Just remember, son," the priest said, from his place at the back of the room, "everything will be all right."

"Will you stop saying that!" I shouted at him.

The nurse looked perplexed. "Stop saying what?"

"Huh?" I said.

"What do you want us to stop saying?"

"I was talking to the priest."

The nurse and the doctor looked at each other with concern.

"What priest?" the doctor said.

"What do you mean, what priest? The priest standing right over there!"

I pointed at the priest. He smiled his kindly smile and tipped his head. The doctor and the nurse followed my gesture, stared for a few seconds, then exchanged that very concerned look again—which was even more annoying the second time.

"What?" I said. "Come *on*, you're really telling me you don't see him?"

"Maybe we should call that psychiatrist after all," the doctor said. "Jesus!"

The priest chuckled. "For a man who doesn't believe in God, you certainly invoke his name a great deal."

"There he goes again!" I said, pointing. "He just made a joke!"

"The priest made a joke?" the nurse said.

I would have slapped my forehead if it wouldn't have resulted in serious injury. "Will *somebody* please tell me where my wife is?"

"She's gone," the priest said, his expression turning grave.

"Gone?" I said. "What do mean she's gone?"

The nurse jumped. "I didn't—I mean, I haven't said —"

"Will you *shut up!*" I yelled at her, and then refocused on the priest, because at least he seemed to have an answer to my question, and getting the answer to that question was a lot more important than why everybody in the room was playing freeze-out to the old man. "What do you mean, she's gone? Gone where?"

"I can't say more right now," the priest said.

"When *will* she be back?" Then a sinking dread came over me. "Did something happen to her?"

"She'll explain everything in her own time, son."

"Explain what? Give me some answers here!"

The priest sighed. The doctor, saying he'd be back with some of his associates in a moment, got up and bustled past the priest without a glance in his direction. The nurse muttered something about fetching doctor so-and-so and left as well. She looked as if she wanted to cry. Even the orderlies, standing at the door like two bouncers at a bar, drifted out, closing the door quietly behind them, leaving just me and the priest. Except for the beeping and whirring of my machines and the faint hum of an air conditioner, the room was still.

"Father," I said, *"please."*

"I know you want answers," he said. "I'm sorry I can't give them to you right now. I just wanted to be here when you woke up to tell you that everything will be all right. You're going to see some very strange things now, Myron, and there's no way I can make it easy for you. I'm afraid you'll have to get through it on your own. It's the only way your mind will accept it."

"Accept what?"

Rather than answer, he bowed his snowy white head and turned to the door. I pleaded with him not to leave, but he kept on walking.

In fact, he kept on walking right through the door—passing through it instead of opening it.

Chapter 5

WITH THE HIGHER PLANE Church of Spiritual Transcendence mercifully quiet Thursday morning and no rain beating on the window, the
only sound in the office was me drumming my fingers on the desk.
The planet Saturn wall clock, a gift from Alesha when I first rented
the place, read 8:02 a.m. At 8:04 a.m., I heard creaking on the stairs,
and even now, after so many years, I still had to remind myself that it
didn't guarantee it was a living, breathing person. Even when ghosts
were out of sight, I often heard them in the same way I did the living.

At 8:05 a.m., Karen walked straight through my closed door,
looking radiant in a burnt orange suede suit jacket, a skirt of the same
color, and elaborate leather sandals with spidery straps that extended
most of the way up her elegant calves.

"What?" she said. She clutched a beaded orange handbag to her
chest. "You look disappointed."

"It's nothing," I said.

"Would you prefer I open the door? I just thought, after yesterday—"

"No, it's fine," I said. "I was just expecting ... Never mind. Please, just take a seat. I've been waiting for quite a while."

"Oh! I'm sorry. Am I late? I thought you said—"

"Five minutes is late in my book, lady. Did you bring the picture again?"

"What? Oh, yes, of course."

Flustered, she scurried into one of the office chairs across from me, sinking into the seat and clutching her bag like a teenager bucking up her courage to face the principal. She fluttered her eyes at me, her eyelids laced with just a touch of orange eye shadow. I had to admire her stylistic commitment to her appearance. Even her hoop earrings, which I glimpsed briefly inside her blond curls, were orange.

"So," she began hopefully, "did you decide to take the case?"

I was formulating my answer when I heard another pair of feet creaking up the stairwell. I waited, and sure enough, Billie materialized through the door in paint-spotted blue overalls, a tie-dyed T-shirt, and no shoes. Looking like she wanted to be anywhere else but there, she slumped into the other office chair, one leg slung over the arm. Green paint flecked her forehead, and red paint flecked her bare feet.

"Thank you for joining us," I said.

Billie shrugged. Karen clutched her purse tighter to her chest, as if she was afraid Billie had come to take it.

"Hello," she squeaked, "I'm Karen Thorne."

Billie rolled her eyes. "Who else? You got the picture or what?"

"Oh. Yes, of course. Are you his—"

"Just give me the picture."

With a gulp worthy of a cartoon, Karen fetched the photo from her purse. Billie snatched it out of the air and glanced at it idly, as if she couldn't even be bothered to turn her head, but she quickly did a double take and stared at Anthony Neuman with more intense interest. I hadn't seen her look at *anything* that way in my presence in months. Years, maybe. I'd forgotten the way her forehead, normally so supple and smooth, furrowed like the lightly raked sand in a Zen rock garden.

"What?" I said.

"Nothing," she said. "He's just … not what I expected, I guess."

"What did you expect?"

She shrugged. "Well, based on your description—"

"I've always told you that was a disguise."

"Yeah."

"It's in the eyes," I said. "I can tell by looking at the eyes."

"Excuse me," Karen piped up meekly, "but can I ask what you're talking about?"

Billie, ignoring us both, gazed at the photo in her lap. I felt the beginnings of a headache, the familiar rising pressure, like a moth fluttering in the gully between the two hemispheres of my brain. I wanted Billie to believe me. I saw, from her point of view, how improbable it must have seemed, me recognizing my shooter in the photo in front of her, but I didn't appreciate the dismissive tone.

"It's nothing," I said to Karen. "We were just … I said he looked a little like Al Pacino, that's all. A younger version."

"Oh, yes," Karen said, "I've thought the same thing myself. He's very handsome, isn't he?"

Billie harrumphed noncommittally. Apparently her harrumph hadn't been noncommittal enough, because Karen looked annoyed.

"I did some searching for him on the Internet," I said. "I couldn't really find any photos of him under that name."

"Yes," Karen said, "Tony was weird about pictures. He didn't like them. And what do you mean, under that name? "

"Well, I couldn't find *anything* of him on the Internet, period. Kind of odd in this day and age, don't you think?"

"Oh," Karen said, clearly offended, "that doesn't mean he's some sort of—"

"I don't know what it means yet. I'll have a friend at the bureau do a little more background digging, but in the meantime I want to get out and talk to people. I asked Billie if she could draw him, so I have something to show people until I come across a real photo—a photo in the *living* world, I mean. What do you think, Billie?"

With a sigh, Billie motioned with the photo to the end of my desk. I opened the third drawer and took out the drawing pad and one of the Conté compressed charcoal sticks, a brand she claimed was easiest for her to control. While Karen watched, perplexed, I opened the pad to a blank page and set it and the black stick on the end of my desk. Billie made us endure one of her painfully long stretching routines—wrists, shoulders, fingers, joint by joint, muscle by muscle— until finally, with another sigh, she stood over the pad with her legs in a wide stance and her fingers fanned over the paper.

I'd learned the hard way to be patient. Once I'd made the mistake of asking her why she needed to stretch when she didn't really have a body, and she didn't speak to me for two days.

She closed her eyes, breathed in and out deeply, then curled the fingers of her right hand as if holding an invisible pencil. Then, when the hand holding the invisible pencil began to move, the real pencil suddenly sprang to life and scratched its way across the pad in unison. Any living person who walked into the room at that moment would have seen me alone with a haunted pencil.

"Wow," Karen said, "nice trick."

Billie cracked one eye open to glare at her. "Levitating the pencil is the easy part. But you also have to have artistic ability to draw something good."

"Well, I know *I* couldn't do it," Karen said. "I'm pretty good at moving objects, but I can barely draw stick figures."

At least somewhat mollified, Billie returned to concentrating on her drawing. We watched her for a few seconds, then I turned back to Karen. Outside, a truck with a bad muffler roared down Burnside, and I waited for the sound to pass.

"Did you bring the other thing?" I asked.

"Oh, right, the list," Karen said.

She retrieved a second piece of paper from her purse, a spiral sheet folded into quarters, smoothed it out, and held it out to me. I shook my head and pointed to the table. Blushing, she set the paper in front of me. There were two columns, twenty or so names on the list, descriptions of those names on the right, including whether they were alive or dead and my best bet in finding them. I took a yellow pad out of my desk and began transcribing the information.

"Bernie Thorne," I said, reading the first name on the list. "That's your father?"

She nodded.

"And that's the one who's going to pay me?"

"Yes."

"You understand I don't work until I get paid, correct? Half the estimate up front, the other half plus expenses upon completion." It probably wasn't true in this case, but I certainly wasn't going to tell her that.

"Yes," she said, "you explained this yesterday."

"It never hurts to explain it again. So what are the magic words?"

"Excuse me?"

"What do I have to do to get him to pay?"

She started to speak, but her eyes misted and she looked away, gathering herself before trying again. "You tell him ... tell him that I finally got that diamond pony I'd always been wanting."

"Diamond pony?"

"He'll know what it means. Just be gentle with him, okay? He's been through a lot. You sure you don't want me coming along?"

"No, I work best alone."

Billie made a strange noise, and we both stared at her. She continued to draw without looking up, leaving us to wonder what she meant. I gave up and studied the list. The rest of the names included her mother, three sisters, some clients of her father's, a pair of dentists who lived in the condo next to theirs who often came over for dinner, and some other assorted folks. It was a good starting list, honestly better than I'd expected.

I finished my list at the same time Billie finished her work. I glanced at the drawing of Tony and, as usual, was impressed. It was a very good likeness.

"Good job," I said.

"It's crap," she said.

"You're always so hard on yourself."

She rolled her eyes. "We done?"

"Yeah, I guess."

I'd barely said the words and she was already out the door.

"Nice to meet you," Karen called after her.

Her voice was so earnest and hopeful, I felt bad for her when Billie passed through the door without even a backward glance. But what could I do? Like me, like all of us, she was a prisoner to Billie's changing moods, and her moods were many and always changing.

"Sorry about that," I said to Karen. "She's not one for small talk. She's not really one for any talk, actually."

"Oh, that's all right," she said, smiling furtively, and I could tell it wasn't all right at all, that Karen Thorne wasn't the sort of woman who was used to people resisting her charms. "Your assistant is ... interesting."

I laughed. In Karen Thorne's world, I knew that qualified as an insult. "Yeah, that's one word for her. And she's not my assistant. She's my wife."

"Oh," Karen said, and then, when the full implications of what I was saying dawned on her, *"Oh.* How did—"

"It's complicated."

"I see."

"Don't get your hopes up," I said.

"Oh. I wasn't—I wasn't thinking about me and Tony—"

"Sure you were. Why wouldn't you? A ghost and a living person apparently living in heavenly matrimony? Assuming he can even see you, which is a big if, it's got to make you wonder if a similar arrangement could work for you."

She was quiet a moment.

"And does it?" she said.

"What's that?"

"Work," she said.

"Ah."

Thinking this over, I glanced at the drawing Billie had left behind. She'd shown up, hadn't she? Maybe she hadn't wanted to, but she'd still come when I'd asked. She was still living in Portland with me. She hadn't left when she could have left a long time ago. She could have left a million different times and yet she hadn't. And there was no doubting how much I desperately needed her now.

But did our marriage work? I wasn't sure if Karen was asking about the whole living-with-a-ghost thing, or if she was commenting on how tense our relationship had seemed to her, but in either case the answer was the same.

"It's a work in progress," I said.

Chapter 6

THE GHOSTS CAME in all shapes and sizes, in all manner of dress, at every hour of day and night. They came when I was sleeping and when I was awake, when I was alone in my hospital room or when a crowd of doctors clucked and clamored over my chart. They came on good days and bad days and every day in between. It was impossible to say how many, because unless they made their nature obvious to me, I could not tell the living from the dead. I could not tell, not even a little, and it was the *not* knowing that was the worst part of it all.

One nurse would take my pulse, her warm fingers on my wrist. The next would come in and reach to pat my arm, only to have her hand pass right through me. Mostly the ghosts were obvious but harmless; after the priest, a little girl in a deerskin dress and moccasins wandered into my hospital room asking if I'd seen her Ma. When I told her no, she curtsied and walked through the wall. Other times they were less friendly and more strange; a week after emerging from my coma, I woke to a Civil War Confederate soldier in full uniform screaming and pointing a rifle musket in my face.

When I yelled at him to leave, he dashed to the open door of my

tiny bathroom and dove headfirst into the toilet. I heard him screaming all the way down the sewer pipe.

It wasn't long before I was screaming, too.

They gave me more Vicodin, then upgraded me to morphine, but
it didn't help. If anything, there were *more* ghosts. I woke one morning to find a truck driver with glass embedded all over his face in bed
next to me. Three young men in heavy parkas and climbing boots
rappelled out of the ceiling and straight through the floor, shouting
about an avalanche. An entire Boy Scout troop, faces blackened and
disfigured from severe burns, stood at the edge of the bed and stared
silently at me, saying nothing, their eyes full of blame.

I remembered them. My first year as a uniformed cop, their
bus plummeted off an embankment in the Cascade Mountains. But
I wasn't there. I told them that—I wasn't at the scene, not involved.
They didn't care.

Doctors bustled in and out. There was lots of poking and prod-
ding, lots of questionings, lots of tests of my mental abilities. I matched
cards to words. I played chess. I played memory games. An army of
psychiatrists—and I couldn't say how many of them were real—asked
lots of questions and nodded at all of my responses. I tried not to say
anything about the ghosts. I tried very hard, telling myself it was all in
my head, that it would pass. I was a rational man. Ghosts were just my
subconscious mind's way of dealing with the stress of the shooting.

Eventually, everything became a continual blur, a smeared watercolor of faces and sounds, day and night running on a loop, time
passing without any meaning.

Alesha. My father. Other cops, some of whom I couldn't recognize. I talked to them. I talked to the people *with* them, and often I
got strange looks when I did. Who was I talking to anyway? The hospital blurred into my house with all my books and my French music
and no Billie (where was Billie?) and my house swirled and spun and
whizzed, lots of crying and screaming to leave me alone, just leave me
be, no more doctors, no more questions, no more therapy, just leave
me be leave me be leave me be.

"Myron."

It was Billie's voice. Opening my eyes, I found myself on the floor, face pressed against vinyl padding and drenching it with my slobber, arms pinned under me. I tried to move my arms and couldn't. I rolled onto my back, squinting into the row of fluorescent lights, the room beginning to come into focus. I was in a small room indeed, not more than eight feet square, all the walls padded with the same gray vinyl as the floor, a small inset window on the similarly padded door. The reason I couldn't move my arms was that I was wearing some kind of straitjacket.

"Myron," she said again. "Over here."

It took some doing, but with a groan I managed to rock myself to a sitting position. There she was, not by the door but crouching in the corner—in gray cargo pants, heavy hiking boots, and a green wool sweatshirt with the collar turned up. Mud smeared her pants and clung to the heavy treads of her boots. Her long black hair lay matted and tangled against the sides of her face, as if she'd been caught out in the rain. She hadn't worn her hair that long in years.

"Where have you been?" I asked.

It was the only thing I could think to say, and her response was to shrug. I couldn't remember the last time I'd seen her. I remembered somebody saying something about her being gone, but when was that? Pulling any kind of memories out of my addled brain was impossible, and yet I saw both the room and her with vivid clarity. It was like being drunk and sober at the same time.

"I could have used some help," I added.

"Sorry," she said, but she didn't sound sorry. She sounded angry.

"What is this place? An asylum?"

"Kind of," Billie said.

"I didn't think we had asylums in Oregon anymore."

"It's a private facility. Shady Grove Care and Treatment Center. It's in Lake Oswego—nice place, lots of trees. Not far from where your parents live. Most people come here for drug abuse, I think."

"Is that why I came here?"

"Think, Myron. You know why you're here."

I thought. Nothing came to me. I thought some more. The edge of a memory, like the brush of a bird's wing, fluttered past my mind. I remembered the priest, the long, tortured nights in the hospital, the strange guests, the intervention led by Alesha and some of the cops to get me to this place. I remember asking for it. I remember them saying I could only go if I volunteered.

"Are you real?" I asked.

"What do you think?"

"Just answer the fucking question, Billie."

"It's not the right question."

"Well, what *is* the right question then?"

"The right question is whether I'm alive or dead."

I glared at her, biting down on my lower lip, saying nothing.

"Well?" she said. "Are you going to ask or what?"

"Why don't you just tell me?"

"I think you already know the answer, Myron. I just didn't know if you knew the right question."

"Is this a game to you? You abandoned me for ... for weeks, for weeks on end, and then you want to show up and play riddles?"

She sighed. "I didn't abandon you, Myron."

"Yes, you did. You fucking abandoned me!"

"Calm down."

"You calm down! Look at me. *Just look at me!*"

"Myron—"

"I'm in a straitjacket, Billie! I'm in the loony bin!" I flapped my one long arm and jerked and thrashed about with abandon. My cloth prison felt as if it were shrinking and tightening, squeezing the life out of me. I could barely breathe. "The loony bin!"

"If you don't calm down, the nurses will come."

"Fine! Let them come!"

She shook her head and stared at the floor. "Maybe I should go. Maybe this was a mistake."

"No," I begged. The thought of her leaving again terrified me.

"No, please don't go."

"I'm dead, Myron."

"I know, I know."

"You know I'm dead?"

"Somebody told me. I don't—maybe it was Alesha. Or maybe it was your dad. Yeah. He flew in from Maine—"

"My dad passed away eight years ago," Billie said. "We went to the funeral. Don't you remember?"

I stared at her. I did remember. I remembered it clearly, the few bits of snow remaining on the grass, the rage in Billie's eyes, how she said she was glad he'd drunk himself to death because now he couldn't hurt anyone anymore, not even himself. But I also remembered her father, ruddy-faced and smelling of scotch but perfectly healthy, sitting at my bedside in the hospital explaining that my wife was gone and he'd come out to pay his respects. He'd wanted me to come to the funeral. I'd told him that wouldn't be possible. The conversation had happened. I was sure of it.

"He was dead, too, wasn't he?" I said.

Billie regarded me the way she might regard a strange insect she'd trapped in a glass jar. "You really can't tell us apart, can you?"

"No," I said miserably.

"Amazing."

"It's a damn nightmare, that's what it is."

"You didn't even believe in any of this stuff, and now you're forced to live it every day. It's almost cruel."

I glared at her, resenting the careless way she spoke about my condition. If one of us had a cruel streak, it was her, and that wasn't a new quality at all. "Why did you kill yourself?" I shot at her.

"Ah," she said, her gaze turning distant, "you remembered that, too."

"They said you did it with pills."

She took a moment to respond, and when she did, her voice grew increasingly soft, trailing into silence. "It's a relatively painless way to go. You just ... fall asleep."

"Painless," I said.

She said nothing.

"I'm so glad it was painless," I said.

She mumbled something.

"You have to speak up," I said. "The acoustics in here aren't that great. It's all the padding."

"I said I'd explain if I could."

"So you're not going to tell me why?"

She shrugged. "What difference does it make now?"

"Are you serious? You decided to commit suicide, and you don't think it would matter to me why?"

"Myron—"

"I think I deserve a reason, Billie."

"Yeah, well, so do I."

"What is that supposed to mean?" And when she didn't answer, I pressed on. "Were you depressed because I was in a coma?"

"I was depressed for lots of reasons."

"Damn it, Billie, you're not helping here!"

"So sorry to disappoint you," she said.

Now she looked at me, and it was a hard look, full of blame and anger and who knows what else, a look I'd seen plenty of times in all the years we'd been married and still didn't quite understand. I stared right back, unflinching in my own rage. An orderly, a big black man who I remember said he'd played football at the University of Oregon, glanced through the window at me, then continued on his way. The room was so quiet, I could hear both me and Billie breathing.

I wondered about it, the breathing. Why did a ghost need to breathe, and how could I possibly hear it? There was so much about this new world I inhabited that I didn't understand.

"You could have helped me," I said, "if you'd been here in the beginning."

The smoldering fire in her eyes softened—not completely, but at least a bit. "I'm here now," she said.

"For good?"

"For as long as you want me."

"Do you still love me?"

She swallowed hard. "Yes," she said.

"You're not just saying that?"

"No."

"Because you know how much I love you."

"I know."

The skin around her eyes quivered, tiny earthquakes, quicksands of the flesh. My own throat grew tight. The dam was about to break, I could tell. We weren't the crying type, either of us, but we'd had our moments. I looked away, battening down the emotions, my face warm and tight. I heard the rustle of her cargo pants and the screech of her boots on the padded floor. I looked up to find her standing over me, not quite smiling but at least not scowling, gazing at me with those mysterious blue eyes that had gotten me to fall in love with her in the first place.

She reached for me, then let her hand fall idly to her side, shaking her head, laughing softly.

"I almost forgot for a second there."

"It's okay," I said.

"I'd help you up if I could."

"I know you would," I said.

Chapter 7

THE LAW FIRM of Heller, Kamen, and Thorne was on the top floor of one of Portland's bigger high-rises, a sleek, thirty-two-story glass tower right next to the World Trade Center and a block from the Willamette River. The gray sky, like the dull side of aluminum foil, seemed somehow more attractive in the mirrored windows than the actual thing. The guard manning the entrance to the underground parking structure checked my driver's license against his clipboard, then waved me through. Parking my lime green hybrid Prius among the Mercedes, Lexus, and other luxury cars, I consoled myself that they may have had better rides, but I was doing more for the environment.

"I thought Karen said her dad worked at a tiny little firm," I said to Billie when we were riding up the elevator. It had mahogany paneling, gold rails, and abstract paintings that looked like something Picasso would have painted but weren't by Picasso. I was never a huge fan of abstract art, though I did have a special place in my heart for Picasso.

"To her," Billie said dryly, "this probably *is* a tiny little firm."

She wore a designer jeans and a tweed jacket over a NO WAR

T-shirt, plus Birkenstocks that bared her black-painted toenails. After her attitude back at the office, I was both surprised and relieved when she volunteered to come with me to meet Bernie Thorne. Although she didn't accompany me on all of my cases, or even the majority of them these days, I really liked it when she did. Having her around, in my world, was like being in a foreign country with a translator at my side rather than trying to go it alone.

I glanced at my watch. It was a quarter to noon, so we were on the early side. I'd called Bernie Thorne as soon as Karen had left that morning, explaining to his bubbly secretary that I was a private investigator who had a few questions about Karen Thorne's death. After a two-minute wait, she returned to schedule my appointment for that Thursday afternoon.

It was almost too easy. I didn't even have to use my trump card over the phone, the diamond-pony bit, and I was glad. I really preferred to see his face when I told him who my client was.

The elevator opened into a reception area that was a peculiar mix of granite pillars, marble countertops and floors, and mahogany paneling. It was a design choice that shouldn't have worked but somehow did. Two perky blond receptionists greeted me simultaneously, I told them who I was, and after five minutes of waiting by the biggest saltwater tank I'd ever seen, one of the blondes escorted me down a hall to a smoked-glass door at the end.

"Fancy schmancy," Billie said.

Beyond the door was another reception area, only smaller, with one blonde manning the desk instead of two. Rows upon rows of leather law books filled the shelves behind her. She took me immediately into the office, and there was Bernie Thorne behind a desk that could have doubled as an aircraft carrier. He looked like the kind of man who belonged at the helm of an aircraft carrier, too.

He was big and broad in a dark blue suit, impressive even sitting, and when he rose from his swivel chair, he towered over me like a giant. At just under six feet, I was not exactly a short man, but as he approached, I felt as small as I did when I was sent to the principal's office in third grade for pulling Melanie Baker's hair. He had big bull-dog cheeks, a close buzz of rusty red hair, and a fake salesman's smile so unnaturally white it startled me. The smile lasted only a second before his face turned sober, as if he'd suddenly realized he shouldn't be smiling to a man who'd come to see him about his dead daughter.

The floor-to-ceiling windows behind him offered a panoramic view of Waterfront Park, the Willamette River, and the Morrison Bridge. The city hardly seemed big enough for this man. Yet when we shook, his big hand engulfing my own, his grip was surprisingly soft.

"Myron Vale?" he said.

"The one and only," I replied.

"Good of you to come," he said, as if he were the one who'd invited me. His breath smelled strongly of peppermint. "Please, take a seat."

He motioned to a black leather couch and two matching wing-back chairs arranged by the farthest window. On the way, passing his desk, I noticed a family portrait with three twenty-something women and a teenage son sitting with him on the deck of a yacht, everybody dressed in white and smiling. Karen was one of the women, her sailor's cap slightly askew.

Billie whistled. "Man, this guy is *riiiiiiich*."

I didn't say anything in response, but Bernie glanced at me.

"Sorry?"

"Hmm?' I said.

"Oh, I thought you said something."

"Nope."

"Well what do we have here," Billie said. "Looks like this guy is a Sensitive."

This time, Bernie didn't say anything, just shrugged and continued to the couch. As we walked, Billie waved her hand in front of his face, but he didn't react, and she made a pouty face. His ability was obviously very weak. I sat on the couch, Billie perched on the arm next to me, and Bernie sank his enormous frame into the wingback chair facing us.

"Well," he said, "I'm told you have information about Karen's death."

"Well, questions, actually."

He raised his eyebrows, eyebrows the same rusty red as his hair. "I looked you up. You're a private investigator, so somebody had to hire you. Can I ask who you're working for?"

"Well, here we go," Billie said. "Strap yourself in."

We'd reached the moment when I had to make a decision. If I told him the truth, that I was working for his daughter, it would forever change the nature of our relationship—whether he believed me or not. The trump card might not work. He might blow his top and throw me out of his office. Or he might believe me and become a sniveling wreck. If I withheld that information and lied about who my client was, it might give me an edge I wouldn't otherwise have.

But I wanted his cooperation more than I wanted an edge, and the best way to get his full cooperation was to take the biggest risk.

"I'm going to tell you who I'm working for," I said, "but first I want you to promise me that no matter how crazy it sounds, you'll hear me out."

His eyes narrowed. "This isn't some kind of prank, is it?"

"No prank, sir."

"Call me Bernie."

"Bernie. Okay. Listen, I'm just going to lay it out there for you. I'm working for your daughter, Karen."

For the longest time, he simply stared at me, his reaction so impassive that I wondered if he'd even heard me. Finally, the skin around his eyes twitched ever so slightly.

"I'm sorry," he said. "You said Karen. You must have meant one of my other—"

"I know you have other daughters, Bernie. It's Karen. Karen is my client."

A pink flush spread across his face. "Now, listen," he said sternly, "I don't know what kind of game—"

"Remember, you said you'd hear me out."

"This is insane! My daughter is dead!"

"I know that. She wanted me to tell you she finally got that diamond pony."

"If you think you're going to wring some kind of extortion …" he began, before my words registered.

The effect was immediate and profound. It was as if I'd socked him in the gut as hard as I could. He gaped at me, wide-eyed and slack-jawed, all that pink color that had been blooming in his cheeks quickly draining away, leaving his face as white as the legal documents piled on his desk. I waited for the initial shock to pass, for him to ask the inevitable and annoying questions.

"How—how did you—" he stuttered.

"She told me, of course."

"She told you."

"She said it was something only the two of you would know."

He stared at me, his pupils as dark as the buttons on his suit jacket. The lines in his face looked as hard and sharp as those on a cut diamond. In my experience, there were a couple of ways this could go, and none of them really had much to do with how good the information Karen had given me was. The outcome depended more on how much Bernie wanted to believe me. Grief was always a harsh mistress, and there was no telling how much of a hold she had over someone, or the games she was willing to play to get what she wanted.

He swallowed and licked his lower lip. When he spoke, his voice had lost all of its salesman authority, leaving only a broken and desperate man. "How—how can I believe you? How can I know you're—you're not just someone she confided in?"

"Do you really believe Karen would do that?"

"No. Not on purpose. But if she was drugged, maybe. If she—if she was not really herself—"

"Look, I'm going to be frank with you. I've done this sort of thing more than a few times. There's really nothing I can say that will convince you if you're really determined to believe I'm lying. All I can tell you is that I'm not after your money. I'm not out to blackmail you. My client—your daughter, Karen—she thinks maybe her husband is in trouble. He's missing. And she also thinks somebody killed her, that maybe those two things are connected. She hired me to get to the bottom of things."

"Nice speech," Billie said.

She said it with a snicker and I almost snapped at her, which of course would have looked insane to Bernie. As it was, he must have caught at least the sense of her comment, because he glanced around the room.

"Is she—she here now?"

"No," I said.

"Oh. Are there—are there other ghosts here?

"No. It's just us."

"Hey!" Billie protested. "Thanks a lot!"

Bernie went on staring at me with his laser eyes, but I couldn't tell if he'd picked up on her comment. I really had to fight the urge to glare at her. There was no need to complicate the situation, and telling him that my dead wife was in the room would certainly do that. We were fortunate that no other ghosts were in the room. If there had been other random ghosts, I would have lied just the same. The truth may set you free, as they say, but being free wasn't always what you wanted. Sometimes you just wanted to get things done.

"I want to believe you," Bernie said.

"It'll make things easier if you do," I said.

"Is this because of your, um, shooting?"

"You read about that, huh?"

"It was hard to miss," Bernie said. "Type your name in Google, and all those news articles come up."

"Just imagine if I'd gotten on *Oprah*," I said.

"How many ghosts are there?"

"A lot," I said. "Look, we could spend all day taking about my condition, but it's not going to get us anywhere. What will get us somewhere is if I ask the questions and you answer them."

"I'm still not sure I believe you."

"Then pretend, for Karen's sake. What's the worst that could happen? If you get the impression I'm trying to manipulate you somehow, you can always refuse to answer. But if there's even a chance that what I'm telling you is true, wouldn't you feel terrible not doing what you can to help her?"

He looked at me impassively for a moment, considering, sizing me up, then he rose and went to his window. Hands shoved in his pants pockets, he gazed out at Front Street and the river beyond. In the silence, the murmur of lunch-hour traffic far below was louder, though still barely louder than a whisper coming to us from another room.

"Fifty bucks says he's thought more than once about jumping," Billie said.

Bernie glanced over his shoulder at me. "What's that?"

"Didn't say anything," I said.

"Oh. I thought you ... Well, never mind. I have to tell you, there are times I've been sure Karen was near me. Like she was watching me. I know it sounds crazy."

"Obviously not to me, Bernie."

He chuckled. "Right. Obviously not to you. Okay, then. I'll play along."

"That's all I ask."

"So she thinks she was murdered?"

"You don't?"

He returned to his wingback chair, but instead of sitting, he stood behind it and grasped the back of the chair with both hands. With me sitting and him standing, his height and size advantage over me felt as if I was looking up at King Kong.

"I have to say it didn't even occur to me," he said. "Karen had a pretty serious drinking problem. She'd gotten into a lot of accidents. She seemed depressed all the time, but she wouldn't say why. A lot of people thought it might have been suicide, but I wasn't sure. I thought maybe she just jammed on the gas instead of the brake. The autopsy showed that her blood-alcohol level was .28. That's high enough that up can seem like down. But murder? I don't know. I guess maybe I was naive."

"She's convinced someone messed with her brakes," I said.

"And she thinks maybe Tony did it?"

"She hopes not. She thinks maybe he got himself in trouble and maybe she was killed as revenge—that maybe he's in hiding because he's afraid for his life. You wouldn't know anything about that, would you?"

"No," he said, but I saw a flicker of confusion pass over his face.

"Anything you can tell me could be helpful," I pressed.

"I have no idea where he is."

"Don't you think it's odd that he disappeared so soon after Karen's death?"

"Yes. But there are a lot of things about him that I thought were odd."

"Such as?"

"Oh, lots of things. Like how they met. It was at our firm's luxury suite at the Rose Garden, when the Lakers were in town playing the Blazers. I couldn't go and offered her my seats. I'd do that when I couldn't go—offer the seats to my kids, and it was her turn. He told her he'd gotten invited by the son of one of the partners, somebody he'd met because they were on the same racquetball league. But later, when I asked the partner, he told me his son didn't even play racquetball."

"Did you confront him about this?"

Bernie shook his head. "By the time I found this out, she was so head over heels in love with him, I thought, What was the harm? Maybe he snuck into our suite. He wouldn't have been the first. And when I met him, he was very charming. Maybe too charming. A very slick operator. There were other little things that just didn't seem to add up, but they were so happy. He was very good to her—probably the best I'd ever seen a man treat her. And you have to understand … Karen wasn't a very happy woman. She tried so hard to be happy, but it always seemed like she was paddling in a sinking boat."

"I know the feeling," Billie said.

"So you didn't want to root against her," I said.

"What father would? Maybe it blinded me. I figured he took off because he couldn't stand to be reminded of her. Money didn't seem to be an issue for him. He seemed to do quite well as a day trader."

"Day trading? Are you sure he made his money that way?"

"I never had reason to assume otherwise," he said, but there was that odd, fleeting expression of puzzlement again.

"He's hiding something," Billie said.

"Maybe," I said.

"Maybe what?" Bernie said.

"Oh, sorry, just thinking aloud," I said, embarrassed I'd responded to Billie. It was very difficult, no matter how much practice I had, to completely ignore another person in the room when they were speaking to me—even if they *were* dead. "Are you aware that your daughter changed her will just before she died?"

"My attorney—*our* attorney, did indicate that it was a recent will. But all of us update our wills frequently."

"And you didn't find it odd that Tony was cut out?"

"I didn't know that was a change. I assumed it'd always been that way—because he had his own money. They did have a prenup, after all. If they got divorced, he wouldn't benefit. That was his idea. It was another reason I was willing to overlook some of my misgivings about him."

"So she didn't confide in you her worries about him?"

"No."

"Are you surprised?"

"Am I surprised, what? That she had concerns about him or that she didn't confide in me?"

"Both," I said.

"Well, I guess I'm surprised now that she had concerns, but not that she didn't tell me about them. We weren't ... close."

"Are you close to your other children?"

His face darkened. "What does that have to do with Karen's death?"

"I guess that's a no," Billie said.

"I don't mean to offend," I said. "At this stage, I'm just grasping at straws, trying to get some idea where he might have gone. Were any of your other children close to Karen?"

"Who knows?" he snapped.

"Please. It could be helpful."

"I don't know. Maybe. I know the girls all got together for dinner and cocktails and that sort of thing. Travis—not as much. He's much younger than them. By a good ten years. He was ... something of a surprise."

"He live with you?"

"No. I get him every other weekend and three weeks in the summer. The rest of the time, he lives with his mother. Or he did, until a couple months ago. He's in his first year at Brown. Actually, I guess that means I won't get him at all, unless he comes of his own volition." His tone had turned bitter.

"I'm sorry," I said.

"Why should you be sorry? His mother just poisoned him against me, that's all. It happens. At least I'm not paying her child support anymore. That's something."

I really had no desire to take a stroll down memory land mines, but I also had no idea what bit of information might lead me in the direction of Tony. "Divorce is always painful," I said, and it came out lame enough that I wished I'd changed the subject.

"Oh?" Bernie said, his bitterness only increasing. "Have you gone through a divorce, Myron?"

"No."

"Well, then maybe you should shut the hell up about it."

"You're probably right."

"You're damn straight I'm—"

"But I do know about losing a wife. Mine committed suicide."

That stopped him dead in his tracks. He gaped at me with that big bulldog face of his, his knuckles white from gripping the back of the chair so hard.

"*Well*," Billie said huffily, "I was wondering when you'd toss that one out there."

"I didn't know," Bernie said.

"Why do you take such a perverse pleasure," Billie continued to rant, "in bringing that up at every opportunity?"

"I don't do that," I said.

"Like hell you don't," Billie shot back at me.

"You don't do what?" Bernie said.

"Sorry," I said. "Just thinking aloud again. My point is—"

"You're an asshole," Billie interjected. "You know I hate thinking about it and yet you keep bringing it up."

"—I know what it's like to lose a wife," I said, talking right on top of her. "Different ways, of course. But I'm just saying I know the pain when the woman you love abandons you. But I can only imagine—"

"Screw you!" Billie said.

"—what it's like when you feel like the love you had for her—"

"I came back, didn't I?"

"—just wasn't enough. No matter how much you loved her, it just wasn't enough."

"You're being a jerk!"

Bernie took this all in—at least, my half of it—with an expression of skeptical puzzlement. That was all right. I was puzzled, too. Sometimes I was overcome with these piques of irritation, who knew where they came from, when I felt the need to jab Billie in as many sore spots as possible. My only defense was that she did the same thing, which was a pretty poor defense in the grand scheme of things, but there it was. Billie, stewing in her anger, crossed her arms and turned toward the door.

"Well," Bernie said, "marriage is a complicated business, I'll give you that." He glanced at the clock on the wall, one that looked like it had been made from driftwood. "I'm afraid I have an appointment across town, so I'll have to wrap this is up. Is there anything else I can do for you now?"

"A couple quick questions," I said. "First, I understand your inheritance makes you quite wealthy. Can I ask why you went into law?"

"That's an easy one," Bernie said. "I'm just not the type to sit around doing nothing. Unfortunately, that's not as common a trait in the Thorne family as I would hope."

"Karen and Tony," I said, "did they live together?"

"Yes, in her condo. He moved in with her."

"But he had his own place in the beginning?"

"Yes. Well, now that you mention it, I don't know. I was never there."

"Their condo, who owns it now?"

"I do. She willed it to me. I admit, I haven't done anything with it. Just stopped in now and then to make sure everything's okay. Threw out some food, turned down the heat, that sort of thing. It's ... hard being there."

"Think I can get a key?"

"Why?"

I shrugged. "When you're looking for a needle in a haystack, first you have to find the right haystack. At this point, I have no idea what I'm looking for until I find it."

He nodded thoughtfully. "All right. I put a lockbox on the doorknob. I'll give you the combination."

"And one last thing to discuss for now," I said. "I saved the most important for last."

"Oh?"

"My fee."

"Oh."

"Karen said you would cover it."

"How much?"

I told him. He nodded and stepped to his desk, cutting me a check for the retainer and telling me to send the invoice to his attention at a post office box address he wrote on a yellow sticky note, and not to the law firm. He did it all so quickly and without any kind of fuss that I wondered if my rates were too low. He also jotted down the address of his daughter's condo and the lockbox combination. While

I was waiting, Billie muttered something under her breath and walked through the closed door to the hall.

Pocketing the check in my coat, I said, "Do you want to be kept up to date on what I find?"

"Yes, certainly," he said, "but only when you have something meaningful. And if I think of anything else, I'll certainly let you know."

He crossed around his desk and extended his hand. We shook, and it was like trying to shake hands with a bear. I suspected he was going easy on me and yet I still found my bones grinding. I told him I'd be in touch.

"I have one more minor request," he said.

"Yes?"

He fixed his gaze on his shoes, suddenly sheepish. "Could you, um, bring Karen in with you?"

"Well …"

"I really want to talk to her."

"I don't do séances, Bernie. It's not my style."

His sheepish embarrassment quickly faded, his eyes turning hard, his scowl as threatening as if he'd pointed a gun at me. "Since I'm paying your fees," he said thickly, "maybe you could make an exception just the once. What do you think?"

That scowl, coupled with the painful memory of his handshake, was as good a warning as any that it wouldn't be a good idea to get on Bernie Thorne's bad side. Still, I didn't like being bullied, no matter who was doing the bullying. I took the check out of my pocket and held it out to him.

"No hard feelings," I said, "but best to part ways now."

"What? Now hold on here—"

"I'm a private investigator, Bernie."

"I understand, but—"

"I may have some special talents that other investigators don't have, but I'm paid to investigate. Not to wash cars, clean someone's shoes, or even help them commune with the dead. I investigate. If you hire me, that's what I'll do for you."

"Okay, okay," he said, hands raised in a gesture of surrender. "Put that check back in your pocket. Let's pretend I never asked."

Pausing long enough to make sure my point had gotten across, I put the check back in my pocket and turned to the door. Then, before opening it, I glanced over my shoulder at him. Grimacing, looking appropriately chastened, he was retreating behind his battleship of a desk. As big as he was, he still cut a fairly lonely figure. Other people might not have been able to see it, but I was a man who trafficked often in loneliness.

"Maybe I can put it together," I said.

"What?"

"You and your daughter. A meeting. No promises, but I'll see what I can do."

Then, before he could thank me, I stepped into the hall and went in search of my wife.

Chapter 8

FOR MY FIRST FEW forays into the outside world, Billie took me on walks around our house, but it didn't take long for that to get old. There were certainly plenty of ghosts strolling the streets of our Sellwood neighborhood, but I was never going to get back on my feet if all I could manage were fifteen-minute jaunts to the park and back while still breaking into a cold sweat half the time. The first Saturday in July, I woke with an impulsive desire to get bolder in my efforts, and before I lost my courage, we boarded the MAX train and fifteen minutes later were stepping onto the red brick sidewalks of Pioneer Square.

I raised my hand to shield my eyes from the sun, surveying the gleeful chaos in front of me. There were people everywhere—thousands of them, more people than I'd ever seen in Pioneer Square before.

"Well, here we are," Billie said, and I could already hear the *I told you so* in her voice.

"Well here we are," I said.

Going from moving to standing still prompted a spell of dizziness, a head-swirling condition that just about anything seemed to trigger these days, but I stayed calm and waited for it to pass. It always passed, thank God, and I certainly wasn't going to tell Billie about it.

Like elsewhere, the people came in all shapes and sizes, in all manners of dress, the fashions from all periods of time. Once again, I reached for her arm, and once again, I felt stupid for doing so. How many times did I have to learn that lesson? The event taking place on that particularly sunny morning was called Sand in the City—a festive fundraiser where teams compete to design sand sculptures and donations go to needy kids. The competition was already going full throttle by the time we got there, groups of adults and kids in matching T-shirts working feverishly around massive castles, elephants, mermaids, and various other creative displays.

"You sure you want to do this?" Billie asked.

"I *have* to do this," I said.

A welcome breeze, light but warm, carried the aromas of barbecued hamburgers and teriyaki chicken. We headed for the roped-off areas, falling behind a family in matching Birkenstocks and Hawaiian shirts. Two vagrants in camo walked by with a flea-ridden dog between them. A young blond girl of ten or twelve helped an old woman with a walker. Two black guys in garish purple attire danced around an old boom box blasting out hip-hop. A juggling clown entertained a dozen clapping children. A bald, barefoot man in a toga wandered past me, muttering to himself in a language I didn't recognize.

I glanced at Billie, who for some reason was wearing an all-black sweatshirt and matching sweatpants. I figured she was in one of her nihilistic phases. "A ghost?" I said.

"Nope," she said. "He was real. Didn't you see the way everybody parted around him?"

"No. I guess just assumed, because of the way he dressed—"

"You're going to get yourself in trouble if you assume. How about the little girl with the old woman?"

"Really? She was a ghost?"

"Yep."

"But not the old woman?"

"Nope."

I felt the familiar frustration bubbling up at my inability to make any progress in this area at all. It had been eight months since the shooting, three months since Billie had returned to my life, and I didn't seem to be any further along than when the priest passed through my hospital door.

We walked through the throng, admiring the sculptures, the sun warming the top of my head. A few artist types spoke to Billie, and of course these were the easy ones, but that wasn't going to be much help most of the time—especially since they all seemed nervous in my company. When she explained what she was doing with me, most ghosts glanced at me anxiously, then quickly excused themselves. It happened three times in a row, the third being a fairly burly truck driver type with forearms thicker around than my head. He made such a hasty retreat, his face pale and his eyes bugged out, that I actually laughed.

"That's kind of rude," she said.

"Sorry," I said, "but I still don't get why they're afraid of me."

"Same reason the living get freaked out when they see a ghost, I guess."

"Doesn't really seem the same at all."

"Well, I guess you'll understand better when you're dead."

"God, you know I hate it when you say that!"

"Shh. You realize how you look right now, right?"

She pointed ahead of us. A mother with two young girls, eyeing me fearfully, was ushering the girls away from us as if I was carrying the plague. I was going to ask Billie if they were living or ghosts, but of course it didn't matter. If they were living, they were freaked out because I appeared to be talking to myself. If they were ghosts, they were freaked out because I was having a conversation with a ghost, which made me just as frightening to them. I dropped my voice to a whisper and spoke out of the side of my mouth.

"It's like I'm in a no-win situation," I said.

"It's not all that bad. You just need to ... I don't know, learn to play by certain rules."

"And what rules would those be?"

"Well, since you're one of a kind, I guess you'll have to figure out those for yourself."

One of a kind. That was me, at least as far as we knew. We walked a little farther, my heart racing, sweat breaking out on my brow, before I felt the need to sit down and take a breather. We found a spot on the red brick steps that surrounded the square, arena-style, taking a spot comfortably away from anyone else. A dark-haired man of Middle Eastern descent walked past, a bloody ax embedded in his forehead.

"Don't tell me he's real," I said.

"Don't use the word *real*," Billie said. "You know I hate that. But yes, he was a ghost."

I watched him go. Most ghosts, I found, did not appear just as they did when they died, but instead as some better version of themselves around the time of their deaths. But there were exceptions, like this man, and Billie said they were kind of like the schizophrenics among the living, mentally unhinged, not always aware of themselves or their surroundings. This man certainly fit the bill. He walked straight through both people and objects, not weaving around them as ghosts usually did. A few of the people—living ones, I assumed—flinched when he passed through them.

"Had enough?" Billie asked.

"A few more minutes," I said, and then, because I knew what she was really asking: "I think I'm going to call the bureau on Monday."

She sighed. "Myron—"

"I've got to get back to work, Billie."

"Do you really think you're ready?"

"No, probably not."

"Well, then."

"But I don't think I'll ever really be ready. Looking at kids playing with sand castles certainly won't do it. I just have to jump in with both feet."

"Myron, this is your first real big outing. You could barely go ten minutes without needing to sit down. You've got to learn to adapt better. To everyone else here, you look like a crazy person mumbling to yourself. How do you think that will look to the other detectives?"

I chuckled. "Half of them talk to themselves anyway. "

"Be serious," she said tartly.

"What do you want me to do? Sit around collecting disability checks? I can't just do nothing, Billie. *I can't.*"

"I'm not telling you to do nothing. I'm just suggesting—"

"Well, it certainly sounds like it."

"I'm *suggesting,*" she said, glaring at me, "that you just be a little more patient. I don't want you getting in over your head. You've got to be pragmatic here—"

"Screw being pragmatic," I said. "This is my life we're talking about. And being pragmatic never got me anywhere before."

"What's that supposed to mean?"

"It doesn't mean anything. And anyway, this isn't about me. It's about you."

"What are you talking about?"

"You don't want me back on the force. You never liked me being a cop."

"Oh, Jesus," she said, rolling her eyes.

"It's true."

"Myron, you're being completely unfair."

"You told me yourself. You said you hated that I might get shot."

She sighed. "That was before. Things are different now."

"Oh, so now that you're dead, you don't care if I end up dead, too?"

"You know that's not true!"

I was about to shoot back with another retort when a little voice said, "Mister, who are you talking to?"

The little boy who belonged to the voice was probably five years old, six tops, a blond cherub of a kid in a blue swimsuit and a Spider-Man T-shirt, a bright red plastic pail in one hand, a yellow miniature shovel in the other. He stood barefoot at the bottom of the arena steps, his tan toes pebbled with sand. His expression was not fearful but curious. When I used to imagine how our son might look—back when I spent a lot of time imagining sons and daughters—he pretty much was a spitting image of this kid.

I was going to say something to him when Billie stood. "He's alive, just in case you were wondering," she said.

With that, she descended into the crowd and disappeared—leaving me to find my own way home.

Chapter 9

AFTER LEAVING Bernie Thorne's office, I wandered Portland's downtown streets for a little while in the brisk November morning, hoping Billie might show herself, but it was not to be this time. It was not to be *most* times, truth be told, when Billie felt wronged or slighted or provoked in even the smallest of ways. Where she went, I didn't know, but the one thing I could always count on, whether she was gone for an hour, an afternoon, or even, as it had been lately, a day or two, was that she would always find her way home eventually. She might make me sweat it out a bit, but she always came back to me.

I didn't know what I would do if she didn't.

As I climbed into my Prius, my mind was buzzing with dozens of different things I could do next, people to speak to, leads to follow, but for the first time since Karen had shown me the picture of her husband, I was feeling a creeping anxiety about the whole thing. *This was the man who'd shot me.* Since seeing the picture, I'd been so focused on just doing the next thing that I hadn't given myself a chance to process what this was all about. Now, alone in the cool and dank garage, I was really feeling it—a pressure on my chest, a tension in my neck and back, a dryness in my mouth.

I needed time to think.

Instead of heading back to my office on Burnside, my house in Sellwood, or to any of the other addresses I had written on the little spiral notebook of people who might help me find Tony Neuman, I drove aimlessly through the downtown streets. I figured I'd just clear my head, but a few minutes later I found myself heading west on US-26. When I passed out of Portland into the tree-lined hillsides that bordered the highway, I realized I wasn't driving aimlessly at all.

By the time I reached the Forest Grove exit a half-hour later, at least some of the anxiety was gone.

The Mistwood Senior Living Center was a sprawling series of tan brick buildings on a side street lined with rust red dogwood trees, close enough to Pacific Avenue that it was easy to reach while still comfortably nestled in a vibrant residential neighborhood. With its huge sweeping grass lawns and dozens of duplexes surrounding the larger complex all connected by a web of sidewalks, the place had the feel of a small college campus. It was the main reason I'd chosen it. Looking at pictures of it online, it hadn't seemed like a nursing home at all.

I parked in the lot nearest the main buildings. An old man dressed in a black tuxedo and red bow tie was sitting on a wooden bench next to a lion fountain. When I got out, he pointed a white cane at me.

"What in tarnation is that thing you driving, boy," he said.

"Hi, Bill," I said.

"Eh?"

"I said hello!"

"We met?"

"More than once." I patted the hood of the Prius. "It's a hybrid," I told him, probably for the tenth time.

"A hy-what?"

"Newfangled technology. It can run on electricity or gas."

"Really! What will they think of next? You going to the ball?"

"Not this time, Bill."

"Well, that's too bad. I'll tell Agnes you said hello."

I smiled and headed for the building. A wet wind whipped across the lawn and shook the dogwood trees, knocking a few leaves loose. One of them drifted right through good old Bill, settling on the bench, but he didn't even notice. I wondered where Agnes was, and whether she'd ever come back for the ball. After our first encounter, I'd looked them both up and found out he'd died ten years ago, his wife two years after him, but I'd never seen her around. Then again, I'd discovered quickly that not everyone was willing to stick it out in marriage when they had all eternity in front of them. A lot of couples took the whole "Until death do us part" vow quite literally.

Inside, a teenage girl was playing Beethoven on the grand piano, while a crowd of seniors gathered around to listen. The hall, with its wide, dark green carpet and soothing tan walls, was just as crowded as always, far too crowded for the number of rooms the Mistwood had. At night, though, I'd noticed that many of the seniors just slept wherever they found themselves—on couches, recliners, or even in their wheelchairs. Many of these people weren't even ghosts.

The air had the faint whiff of mothballs and the pine air freshener I know they used. When I reached Dad's room, the door was open, and I heard Mom haranguing one of the caretakers.

"Don't give him the green Jell-O," Mom was saying, her smoker's voice as rough and grating as always. "He doesn't like it. Give him the red stuff."

I entered the room to find the aide, a pert young blonde wearing glasses that could have doubled as a windshield on an airplane, setting the lime green Jello-O on Dad's food tray, next to a tuna-fish sandwich and a glass of milk. He was seated in his favorite recliner, a well-loved brown leather La-Z-Boy he'd had forever and insisted on bringing with him when he moved into the facility, and staring transfixed at the TV in the corner. It was some kind of financial show. The sound was off, but a ticker of stock numbers whizzed past on the bottom of the screen.

Dad was dressed in tan slacks and a brown polo shirt, his belt cinched so tight that the extra could have looped around his waist a second time. The clothes appeared clean and wrinkle-free. What was left of his hair, a fringe of brown-gray in a typical arc of male-pattern baldness, was neatly trimmed and combed. Other than one red nick on his chin, his face looked good: a close shave, a bit of color in his cheeks, the bags under his eyes not quite as dark as last time. I was always startled by how gaunt he was—it didn't matter how many times I saw him, I would always have the image of the stout, thick-in-the-chest man of my youth fixed in my mind—but at least it was a healthy gauntness.

The way Mom was perched behind his chair, bony fingers clutching the leather like claws, dark hair slicked back like wet feathers, the black shawl over her shoulders covering all but a hint of the gray shirt underneath, made me think of a raven perched on a branch. Her ruby red lipstick appeared all the brighter because of the blinding paleness of her cheeks. She was a tiny woman, short as well as petite, but the harshness of her cheekbones and searing intensity of her dark eyes, the irises almost as black as the pupils, made her far more intimidating than her size warranted.

Mom saw me first. "Well, it's about time."

"Hello everybody," I said.

Dad went on staring at the screen, which was no surprise. The blonde, however, jumped a little.

"Oh!" she said.

"Sorry," I said, "didn't mean to scare you there."

"Don't apologize to her," Mom said. "She's nothing but a little tart."

"No, it's okay," the blonde said. "Are you Myron?"

"That's right." I peered at her name tag. "And you're Holly, I take it. Are you new here?"

"Two weeks," she said, smiling furtively. It was a hell of a smile, even if it was tentative. "That's one week less than how long it's been since your last visit, by the way."

"Ouch," I said, covering my heart in mock wounding.

Holly wagged a finger at me in admonishment and we both

chuckled. We locked eyes for a beat longer than necessary, the kind of gaze, though brief, that was rich with possibilities. There was something about those glasses that made her even more attractive. The green uniform, boxy and ill-fitting, didn't do much for her figure, but I could still tell there was a great figure underneath. Maybe the glasses made me think of librarians. I always had a thing for librarians.

"Your father tells me you're a cop just like him," she said.

"Private investigator, actually," I said. "I was a cop, though. Before."

"Really? That sounds interesting." And the way she said the words, it did sound interesting—at least to her. "I'd love to hear more about it sometime. He's always telling me stories of his time on the force." And there was a flash of that smile of hers, a weapon of male destruction.

"You stay away from my son," Mom scolded her, wagging a finger of her own. "He's too good for you. And I know what you do with the vibrator of yours, you little tart. It's revolting."

I winced. "Sorry," I said.

Holly raised her eyebrows. "Sorry for what?"

"Hmm? Oh, nothing. I mean—sorry, if Dad talks your ear off with his stories."

"Oh, that's no problem. He's really proud of you. Isn't that right, Hank?"

Dad stared at the screen.

"Hank?" Holly said, stepping closer. "Hank, I was just telling Myron here how proud you are of him."

"Leave him alone," Mom said. "You'll probably give him herpes if you get too close."

With Holly looming right in front of him, Dad finally looked at her, his face brightening as if it was the first he'd realized that someone else was in the room with him.

"Oh!" he said. That deep baritone of his was one thing that hadn't changed. "Hello."

"Myron's here, sweetie," she said.

"Myron? Oh, yes! I see him! Hello, Myron!"

As always, whenever he looked at me these days I felt both the joy of him seeing me and the sadness of knowing that the person doing the seeing wasn't the man he once was. "Hi, Dad," I said. "Good to see you. You're looking great."

Holly patted Dad's shoulder. At the touch, Mom glared at her as if she was imagining plucking out Holly's eyes, which she probably was.

"How dare you!" Mom spat. "He's much too old for you!"

"I was just telling Myron," Holly whispered, leaning in close, "how proud you are of him. You really should tell him yourself."

"Of course I'm proud of him!" Dad said. "Everybody is! My brother here played football at Notre Dame! They beat Duke for the championship and he scored the final touchdown!"

"Oh," Holly said, "no, Myron is your—"

"It's okay," I said.

"But—"

"No, it's okay, Holly."

"Isn't that so, Jack?" Dad said to me. "Tell this sweet little thing here what kind of player you were."

"You would know," I said to Dad, and I had to fight a bit to keep my voice even. I was standing in front of him, alive and well, his only son, and his brother Jack had died two years after that game in a mountain-climbing accident, dead long before I was born, and yet it was the ghost who wasn't even present that he saw and not his only son. "You would know because I used to give it to you good when we were growing up in Klamath Falls."

"Damn straight!" Dad said, slapping his knee and letting loose with one of his blow-the-house-down laughs.

"You're upsetting him," Mom said, her eyes welling up with tears. "You're all upsetting him."

Dad's laughter was like nitroglycerine—a huge burst, but then it was spent. His attention quickly returned to the television. Holly regarded me with concern. I shrugged.

"Well," she said, her own voice cracking a little, "it really is good to see you here. I hope—I hope you'll come more often."

"You can count on it," I said.

With another smile, this one more sad than suggestive, she took her tray and left. I felt vaguely guilty flirting with her. When she'd departed, I shook my head at my mom.

"You know she can't hear you," I said.

"Of course she can," Mom said. "She's just ignoring me. The whole staff at this place is rude beyond belief. It's terrible."

"I'm sorry you feel that way."

"It's not just me. Half the people here, they completely ignore."

"Half the people here they can't even see. They're ghosts."

"Don't be profane!" she snapped.

"Sorry."

"You know how I hate it when you use that language."

"And what language would that be, Mom?"

"Don't mouth off to me, Vincent. I may be old, but I can still put you over my knee."

"I have no doubt of that, Mom."

"But anyway, you're here now, I guess that's what matters. It won't take us long to pack our things. Is that woman you married in the car, or is she back at your place? Maybe she could make us a nice dinner for once. I've never met a woman who was a worse cook. It's no wonder that you're so thin. The suitcases are under the bed."

I sighed. I knew this conversation was going to happen, it always did, but that didn't make it any less unpleasant. Through our entire exchange, Dad stared at his television. In the early days of his time at Mistwood, I felt bad talking as if he wasn't in the room, and consciously tried to avoid it, but I eventually gave up on the idea. Mom would seldom, if ever, leave his side, so if I wanted to talk to her about him, I had to do so in his presence.

"I just came for a visit," I said.

"What do you mean?"

"You know the two of you can't come live with me."

Her shocked expression seemed so authentic, I could almost believe she wasn't acting. She flapped her mouth open and closed a few times, those twig fingers of hers fluttering to her mouth, her eyes even darker than usual.

"Well!" she said. "And after you promised us and everything."

"I never promised."

"Your father is going to be very disappointed. He's been looking forward to coming to live with you for a very long time."

"Mom—"

"Some way to show gratitude to the parents who raised you. Dump them off in a Siberian prison and let them rot."

"This is hardly Siberia. They even have indoor plumbing. And if you're very good, you can watch *Wheel of Fortune* on the big-screen TV."

"Don't make jokes with me, young man! Your father always took that attitude with me, too, and I could never stand it."

"It was probably in self-defense."

"What? What is that supposed to mean? This isn't like you, all this coldness. Where's my nice little Vincent?" Her voice changed instantly from shrill to a soothing purr. She circled around her chair and brought her hand to my face as if to pat it, lowering it only at the last moment. "My little boy. That woman has corrupted you, hasn't she?"

"Mom—"

"You'd never act like this on your own. I know she hates us."

"Billie doesn't hate you."

"Oh, yes she does. She's told me so before. She's said it right to my face."

"She's done no such thing."

"Are you calling your mother a liar? And who names their child Billie, anyway? It's a white-trash name, what somebody names a tramp."

"Careful, Mom."

"I'm sorry. I shouldn't have said it. Sometimes I just speak the truth without thinking about people's feelings. It's my flaw. I know. But don't worry about her right now. Worry about your parents, that's all I'm asking." Her tone turned pleading, desperate. We were right on schedule. "We're your flesh and blood. We belong with you. Don't leave us in this prison any longer. Oh, Myron, if you could only—"

"Oh, it's Myron now, is it?"

"I just—I just want what's best for your father."

"Me too," I said.

"Can't we talk about this?"

"No."

"All the other people here make fun of him behind his back. If you could only see it."

"I have a hard time believing that, Mom."

"It's true! One time, I even—"

"Mom, Dad has to stay here."

"But—"

"He has to. I can't take care of him around the clock. And much as you'd like to think you can, you know you can't either."

Pink blossomed in her cheeks. "Well! I've been taking care of him all my life. Why would you think—"

"Because you're dead, Mom."

"How dare—"

"You're a ghost."

"I'm no such—"

"You are," I said sternly. "You know you are. And as much as he leans on you, he still needs the help of flesh and blood people. I've got to make a living, so who do you propose stays with him all day?"

She glared at me with enough intensity to melt what was left of the polar ice cap. Behind those flaring eyes of hers, I could see her mind racing, trying to come up with some new line of attack that would wear me down. Instead of waiting, I bent down in front of Dad so I was directly in his line of sight.

It took a few seconds, but he blinked a couple times and focused on me.

"Oh, hello!" he said.

"It's me Myron, Dad."

"Myron ... I, uh ... Well, I know that!"

"I know you do, Dad. I'm just reminding you. I just wanted to say hello and make sure you're doing well. You doing okay?"

"Like a can of peaches, son," he said, and grinned.

It was one of his oldies, an expression I hadn't heard from him in a long time, and him saying it along with my name, his eyes as alive and full of intelligence as I'd seen them in a long time, was enough to get me to choke up. I patted him on the shoulder, then, impulsively, leaned in and kissed him on the forehead. That wasn't something he would have permitted in the old days, not being a man comfortable in the realm of physical affection, and he probably wouldn't have allowed it if he'd been his full self now, but what the hell. These weren't the old days.

When I turned to Mom, I saw a new visitor had entered the room—a black cat with a white starburst over his left eye. He sat primly by the door, staring at me.

"Well, hello little friend," I said to him. "What's your name?"

Mom wrinkled her nose. Since the skin on her face didn't generally move much, this wrinkling must have taken enormous effort. "Oh, that horrible beast is back. I keep telling them it's carrying germs all over the facility, but no one listens. It just showed up one day like a rat out of the rain and people let it stay. Terrible. Some people even feed it scraps while they're eating!"

While she spoke, the cat turned its attention from me to her—or at least it certainly seemed to.

"Well, that's funny," I said.

"What's that?"

"That cat ... There, it's doing it again. It's looking from me to you. It's almost like it sees you."

"Well, why wouldn't the little vermin see me? I'm standing here, aren't I?"

I didn't have the heart to explain to Mom what I'm sure she already knew: Animals didn't see ghosts. Despite all the folklore, that included cats. In the past five years, I'd had plenty of opportunities to witness animals around ghosts, even on zoos and farms, and not once did they seem to react to anything ghosts did—even when ghosts walked right through them.

Animals also didn't seem to have ghosts of their own, a troubling fact that I couldn't quite understand. Being a big believer in evolution, I couldn't see why humans deserved to exist beyond death when primates, cats, or even earthworms didn't, but that was the world I lived in. But I'd been told that perhaps there *were* animal ghosts. We just couldn't see them.

Of course, I didn't know for a fact that this cat was real. Maybe I *was* witnessing a cat ghost.

"Does it have a name?" I asked.

"Heavens," Mom said, "I don't know what they call that thing. Oh, wait, yes I do. They call it Patch."

"Well, that's fitting," I said. I squatted on the floor on front of it, extending my hand. "Come here, Patch. Here, kitty. Come on, kitty."

Patch eyed me curiously for a moment, then strutted forward. He was slender but muscular, body rippling under his fine coat of fur, a little panther. His patch made me think of a mask someone might wear to a masquerade ball. Before reaching me, however, he veered around Mom's legs, his black tail appearing to curl around her calf. Mom yelped and danced away, a little jig that got me to laugh.

When Patch pushed up against my palm, he was as warm and real as any cat could be. I let out the breath I didn't know I'd been holding.

"Good kitty," I said.

He started purring immediately.

Chapter 10

IT WAS SUPPOSED to be a routine stop, the questioning of a distant relative of one Larry Elton, our beer-for-brains murder suspect. Larry was wanted in a two a.m. fight at a dive bar on MLK Boulevard, a fight that had left Larry's co-worker and fellow Blazers fan, Mario Balamo, unconscious and bleeding from the ear in the alley behind the bar. Three witnesses pegged Larry as the assailant, apparently in a dustup over who was the best player to ever suit up for the Blazers. Larry insisted it was Bill Walton, Mario went with Clyde Drexler, and the next thing everybody knew the two were arguing it out with their fists.

Unfortunately for Larry, Mario died on the way to the hospital from internal bleeding in his brain. Rather than turn himself over to the police, Larry had also chosen to run, which was why Alesha and I were involved. It wasn't exactly an exciting case, but that also meant it was a good one for my first day back on the force after a seven-month absence.

It was nearly noon and my stomach was grumbling. The apartment complex where the cousin lived was an ugly house of cards a half a mile from PDX, chipping brown paint on walls that looked like they might crumble at any moment. A mini-mart was on one side, an abandoned auto shop on the other. A big jumbo jet on a landing approach screeched overhead. The only pretty things in the neighborhood were the oaks lining the street, their leaves showing the first signs of yellow and crimson.

Alesha parked the cruiser at the curb and killed the engine, mercifully also putting her music out of its misery. The street was filled with people, some sitting outside the apartments, some wandering the cracked sidewalks, so many people for this part of town and this time of day on a Tuesday that I knew most of them had to be ghosts. But which ones? Two heavily tattooed white skinheads were playing catch with what I thought was an odd-shaped ball, until I realized that the reason the ball was odd-shaped was that it wasn't a ball at all.

It was a baby.

"You okay?" Alesha asked.

I stared, transfixed, at the baby—pink and healthy, dressed only in a cloth diaper. The arms and legs were moving, which meant it wasn't a doll. That meant the baby was a ghost, too. Or at least I hoped so. Since Alesha wasn't jumping out of the car to do something about it, I was probably right.

The hunger pains in my stomach were replaced with a queasy nausea. Why were all the weird ones out today? Most of the time, I'd learned, ghosts were just as boring as the living, but every now and then the freaky ones showed up to really mess with me.

"Myron?" Alesha pressed.

"What? Yeah, I'm fine."

"You don't look fine."

"I'm fine, I'm fine!" I insisted.

"You can wait in the car," she said. "It's no big deal. It'll just take two seconds, then we can get some lunch."

"I'm not going to wait in the fucking car. Let's go."

I got out of the car before she could protest. The air was crisp but warm, a staple of fall days in the Willamette Valley, usually my favorite time of year. If there weren't so many damn ghosts everywhere,

I might have been able to even enjoy it. Making matters worse, the blood rushed to my head, and I had to steady myself with a hand on the warm hood.

"You sure you're okay?" Alesha asked. "Don't play tough guy with me, Myron. I'm your partner. Be honest. I'm not going to tattle on you to the shrink or anything."

A woman with a big red perm and wearing seventies bell-bottoms was pushing a boy on a tricycle right toward me, no intention of swerving. I managed to avoid her at the last second, giving her a long hard stare as she passed. She noticed my stare and shrieked, pushing the boy so fast down the weedy sidewalk that the pedals thudded repeatedly against his calves, prompting him to cry. The lady glanced back at me repeatedly, her face panic-stricken. Most ghosts didn't like to walk right through the living, but some either didn't care or actually liked doing it for kicks. Try as I might, I just couldn't let them pass through me if I had a choice in the matter.

"Myron?" Billie said.

"I'm fine," I said.

Many of the other ghosts, including the two playing catch with the baby, were now looking at me. Dozens of ghosts. It did make it more obvious which of the people were living and which weren't, since the living were still mostly ignoring me, and there were only a handful of them at that. But I shouldn't have made eye contact. It was one of the first things I'd learned, that if I didn't make contact, most of them would go on ignoring me. Show them that I could see them and anything could happen. Sometimes very bad things.

"Myron—"

"Let's go," I said.

Studiously avoiding eye contact with anyone living or dead, my head still spinning, I led the way up the sidewalk to the driveway that led to the inner parking lot. The two skinheads followed, one of them with the baby under his arm as if it were a football. I picked up my pace.

"Hey," Alesha said, "what's the rush?"

The unit I was looking for was on the second floor, toward the back. In one of the empty parking spaces, a naked and bloated old man was sprawled on his back, not moving. I waited to see if Alesha would notice him, but she didn't. Another airplane, much louder, rumbled toward the runway somewhere past the moss-covered roof and the oaks behind it.

"Hey, you," one of the skinheads called to me.

He was on my heels, closing fast. I reached the concrete steps that led to the unit and started up, Alesha behind me. The skinheads followed, and even worse, the baby started crying. It was a real doozy, too, a full-throated roar bordering on a scream. I needed to make a choice. Since it was obvious they weren't going to leave me alone, I could continue to try to ignore them while we talked to the suspect's cousin, or I could let Alesha go up ahead without me. With my head already swirling, I wasn't sure how well I could function with the two skinheads badgering me. Especially with the baby going nuts.

I stopped halfway up, grabbing onto the iron rail, feigning sickness—or half-feigning it, anyway.

"What is it?" Alesha asked, touching me on the elbow, leaning in close.

The skinheads stopped two stairs below. I glanced in their direction, letting my gaze sweep past without stopping on them, and saw the baby squirming, its little pink face contorting in its unhappiness.

"Maybe I will sit this one out," I said. "As long as you think you got it?"

She rolled her eyes. "I think I can handle it. I was working with Jaffe while you were out. It was pretty much like working by myself anyway. Never seen a guy eat so much. Head back to the car and I'll be there in a minute."

"No, I'll—I'll be waiting here, at the bottom of the stairs."

"You sure? I think you'd be—"

"I'll be here."

Alesha grimaced, then patted me on the back and headed up. I heard her mutter something about stupid white guys, obviously just loud enough for me to hear. She wore a gray trench coat and black pants, similar to what I was wearing, but somehow she made the outfit look great. Maybe it was the form-fitting cut of the clothing, but it probably had more to do with the figure underneath. I caught myself admiring the swing of her hips. I would have forced myself to look away if not for the skinheads breathing down my neck, and wouldn't you know it, Alesha happened to glance back and *saw* me admiring her.

She raised an eyebrow. I smiled, then looked away, embarrassed. The weird thing between us had only gotten weirder lately.

"Hey, man," the skinhead with the baby said. "Hey, we're talking to you, man. Look at us."

Instead of looking at Alesha, who was proceeding down the balcony to the unit at the end, I fixated my attention on a wheelless Corolla, up on wooden blocks under one of the carports, half chipping blue paint, half dull gray metal, the back window not glass but duct tape and semi-clear plastic. An oil spot under the back fender reflected the warped smear of a rainbow.

"Hey, man, what's your deal?" the other skinhead said. "You can see me, right?"

I kept staring at the beat-up Corolla. Alesha had reached the door and was knocking on it.

"Yeah," the other one said, "he can see us. He's trying to pretend he can't."

"You're the dude we've heard about," the first skinhead said.

This got my attention, and I couldn't help but look at them. Seeing them up close, I saw that their faces were sunken, their skin pockmarked and pale, their hair thin. The tapestry of tattoos on their arms and necks distracted a little from their haggard appearance, but only a little. Meth heads, most likely. The one holding the baby was a little taller, but otherwise they could have been twins.

"I *knew* it," the skinhead holding the baby said. There wasn't much left of his teeth but a few blackened nubs. "You the one, right?"

"I guess," I said in a whisper.

"Well, shit," the other guy said. A tattoo of a swastika covered most of his neck. "Dude's like a celebrity."

"Who's been talking about me?" I asked.

"Like everybody, man," the skinhead with the baby said. The baby was starting to work itself up again, squirming all over the place. "They're calling you the ghost detective."

I shook my head, glancing up at Alesha. She was knocking on the door and didn't appear to have noticed my whispered remarks. The apartment door opened. Because of the angle, I couldn't see who answered. Alesha, relaxed and at ease, showed her badge. She was talking, but I couldn't make out what she was saying—especially now that the baby was sputtering into another cry.

"So," the swastika skinhead said, "you joined any gangs yet?"

"Gangs?" I said.

"You gotta have friends."

"What, like you?"

The skinhead with the baby smiled his toothless smile. "You could do a lot worse than us, man. We could protect you from, um, certain elements."

"I think I'll be all right," I said.

Their glassy stares turned more hostile. Instinctively, I shifted a little, moving my hand so it could easily slip into my coat and get to my Glock, but then I realized how fruitless that would be. While we all stared at each other, another airplane roared overhead. When the whine of the jet engines passed, the baby's cry was louder than ever—a real ear-splitting shriek. Neither of the skinheads paid it much mind.

"You really should reconsider," the swastika skinhead said in a low, menacing tone.

"Nah. Where'd you get the baby?"

"What?"

"You deaf? I asked where you got the baby?"

They stared at me blankly for a few seconds, exchanged a confused glance, then stared at me again with even more defiance.

"Found it," the one carrying the baby said.

"Uh huh. Where?"

"Some slut left it. She just put it on the grass out front."

"Or you took it from her. Where does she live?"

"I don't like all these questions, man."

"Too bad. Where does she live?"

"Fuck you, asshole. Let's go, Jake."

"Wait a minute," I said.

They were turning to go, their tough-guy gangbanger act suddenly revealed for the false bravado it was, their scowls quickly melting into a jittery panic, and I reached for the guy with the baby. I did it without thinking, forgetting again who I was dealing with, trying to grab his arm before he could descend the staircase. My hand passed right through him, of course, and because I wasn't expecting it, I stumbled in his direction. I fell two steps and only saved myself from rolling all the way down by throwing my arm between the rails, catching myself in a painful jolt.

My surprise was nothing compared to the reaction of the skinheads. The one holding the baby screamed like a topless woman in a horror movie and scrambled down the rest of the stairs. Swastika guy's response was even better, staring in horror at me and pissing a dark spot in his jeans for a second or two, before snapping out of his paralysis and barreling after his friend—who dropped the baby at the bottom of the stairs and ran full tilt for the other end of the parking lot.

The baby hit the pavement first with a sickening thud as its bare back banged against the concrete, then a wet fleshy smack as its head hit next. They were the kind of sounds that would stick with me for years, revisited in both quiet moments of reflection and in heart-pounding nightmares, one of those fringe benefits of the job that was part of the day-to-day life of every cop—and was only worse now. Images burned into the brain. Sounds seared into the psyche.

The baby didn't move for a second, and I thought, ridiculously, that it was dead, then it spasmed with all its limbs at once, letting loose with another wail. If I'd thought the baby was loud before, it was nothing like this. It was a baby scream that put all other baby screams to shame, a wailing wall of sound filled with blame and anguish and a dozen other primal emotions all mixed into one.

I was there next to the baby without even realizing I'd moved. There was blood behind its head, pooling on the cracked white sidewalk, and I thought there was blood on its face too until I realized that the redness was from all the screaming.

I reached to scoop up the baby and despaired when my hands passed right through it.

The screaming went on endlessly. I'd never felt so helpless. I caught movement to my right, under one of the carports, and saw a woman in a white bonnet and long blue dress, the kind of dress a woman wore in the frontier days. She dashed toward me and scooped up the crying baby. Up close, I saw that the woman wasn't really a woman at all but a girl, sixteen tops, her face tearstained and free of even the slightest bit of makeup. Cradling the baby against her chest, she glanced down at me with her watery eyes. When she spoke, I could barely hear the sound over the baby's screams.

"Thank you, kind sir!" she said. "I been lost without my Anna since the Injuns took her."

"Myron, look out!"

This time it was Alesha, shouting at me from the balcony above, her voice barely penetrating the screaming. I turned and just barely had time to see our suspect, Larry Elton, shirtless, barefoot, dressed only in a pair of dirty jeans, as if he'd read a casting call for an episode of *Cops*, looming over me like a great white hairy whale, before he plowed into me.

It was like being hit by a refrigerator, one that reeked of beer and chips. He was one big sweaty mess of a man. I went down like a bowling pin, his fleshy foot smashed into my shoulder, then he was pounding across the parking lot.

The amount of time that elapsed since he hit me and I staggered back to my feet felt like only a split second, but he was already rounding the corner. For a big man, he could really move. The woman with the baby, still wailing, rose and started to flee, blocking my path momentarily, and the delay cost me another second.

Worse, when I took a few steps in his direction, my head started to spin, forcing me to stop and steady myself. By then, he was surely long gone, but I started after him anyway.

"Myron, don't bother," Alesha said.

I turned. She was coming down the steps, one hand pressed to her forehead over her right eye. Blood was trickling around her hand, dark rivulets on dark skin.

"Jesus!" I said, reaching for her.

"It's okay," she said. She flashed me a smile and there was blood on her teeth, too. "Looks worse than it is. Sucker got me with a bottle to the head, can you believe it? But it didn't knock me out—just hurt like hell. Another thing the movies got wrong."

"We've got to get you to the hospital," I said, taking her by the elbow and guiding her toward the car.

"Not before you call this in," she said.

"You're bleeding like crazy."

"Call it in, Myron."

"All right, all right."

As we hustled back to the car, I took out my cell phone and called dispatch. Fortunately, a beat cop was only a few blocks away, responding to a domestic disturbance, and by the time I put the phone back in my jacket, I already heard the sirens—a sound that got us both shaking our heads, because the sirens would only alert the suspect to the cop's presence. A rookie mistake.

"Never a good idea to let them know you're coming," I said.

I opened the car door and helped her inside, then fetched the first-aid kit from the back. When I handed her some gauze, she was glaring. I knew what it was about and I already felt terrible.

"Speaking of that," she said.

"I know, I'm sorry."

"Why didn't you hear me? Why didn't you hear *him?*"

"I don't know."

"You were bent on the ground weird. Hunched over. Moving your hands and stuff. What was that about?"

It was hard to reckon with the guilt I was already feeling, failing my partner when she needed me most, and looking Alesha in the eyes made it even worse. I looked over the top of the car, my gaze settling on the stretch of threadbare lawn in front of the complex. The skinheads were gone, but the pioneer woman was there, cradling her baby against her blue dress. I couldn't tell if the baby was cooing or making any other sounds, but at least it wasn't crying. At least it was back with its mother.

"Myron?" Alesha said. "It's okay, you can tell me. Were you going to throw up or something?"

I looked at her. I knew then that things were going to have to change for me. I didn't know how, but I knew I couldn't go back to my life the way it was. That life was gone forever.

"Or something," I said.

Chapter 11

On my way back from the always-fulfilling visit with my parents, I got a text from Alesha asking if I wanted to grab some lunch. She had information for me. I messaged her back that I'd pick up a couple of sandwiches from Subway and meet her at my office. The November weather, always fickle, showed a brief glimpse of sunshine before dissolving into a dreary drizzle all in the span of twenty minutes. When I got to the office, Alesha was waiting for me, lounging with her iPhone in one of my chairs. There was also a copy of the Bible on my desk.

"You've got to be joking," I said to her.

"You'll find all the answers you're looking for inside," she said.

She was smirking. Her sleek black hair glistened from the rain, and her leather jacket and her boots were pebbled with water droplets. I set the bag of sandwiches on the desk and took a good look at the Bible. It was faux brown leather, badly worn, frayed at the edges. Someone had gotten a lot of use out of it. I doubted it was Alesha.

"You remember I'm an atheist, right?" I said.

"Just open it," she said, with barely suppressed zeal.

I opened the cover. It was no ordinary Bible. Inside, placed in a cut-out rectangle where the paper had been removed, was a police badge. My badge, no doubt. Now it was me who was smirking.

"I can't believe you defaced the good book," I said.

"Well, if it makes you feel any better, I didn't. I found it in the evidence room. Some druggie used to hide his stuff in it."

"You lifted it from evidence?"

"Long, long dead case. Like ten years back."

"Still," I said.

"Well, see the kind of trouble I get into when you're not around? Now you have to come back, Myron. Without you, nobody keeps me in line."

This was a little game we played. She'd probably tried to give me my badge twenty times over the past five years, getting increasingly more creative. The last time it had popped out of a jack-in-the-box. The time before that she'd put it in the smallest doll in an oversized nesting doll. The bottom of a box of Lucky Charms. In a bag of what appeared to be never-opened men's underwear. I figured one of these days she'd run out of ideas, but so far it hadn't happened.

"What about Jarret?" I asked. "Hasn't he been a good partner for you?"

She snorted. "That little jack-off? He couldn't find his own navel with Google Maps and a guide dog."

"He's young. He'll learn."

"I doubt it. He's pretty much useless."

"Careful. You were young once, too."

"I was never that young. I need somebody smart, somebody I can count on. I've been asking the chief to give me a new partner, but she hasn't listened."

"Maybe it has something to do with the number of partners you've gone through in the past five years. What is it, six?"

"Yeah, well, I couldn't count on any of them. I need you, Myron."

She'd said the last part so emphatically that it caught us both off guard. The words hung in the air, the double meaning obvious, our gazes locked in one of those intense stares that seemed unavoidable when we were together. Finally, she looked away.

"I guess that's a no again, huh?"

"Alesha—"

"I just don't get it," she said, turning to me again. "I know you had a bit of trouble when you came back before, but you seem to be okay now. Why would you rather spend your days in this little rat hole than hanging out with me?"

"Hey now," I protested, "I decorated this place myself. Try not to hurt my feelings."

"You can barely keep the lights on. You spend your days peeping on cheaters and chasing down phony worker's comp claims. How is that any fun? You gave up a good salary, a pension, and everything else—*for this?*"

"Had to be done," I said.

"Why? Did I do something wrong?"

"Alesha, I've told you a million times—"

"I know, I know, it wasn't me. So you say. Then what was it? And don't give me any of that shrink crap about post-traumatic stress. I talked to my astrologer about you and she said it's none of those things. She said everything you're doing is your own choice."

I clenched my jaw. Here was Alesha with the crystals and the palm readers and the meaning in the stars. I wanted to snap back at her that the words of wisdom she'd gotten from her so-called astrologer was the kind of generalized nonsense that could apply to anyone. Of course I was making my own choices. In the end, we all made our own choices and lived with the consequences. We couldn't always dictate the hand the universe dealt us, but we had at least some control over how we played our cards.

What answer could I give her? After the shooting, I debated long and hard about telling her about my condition. If anyone would most likely believe me, it would be Alesha, but for some reason I just couldn't do it. I didn't know why. Maybe it's because I just didn't want to be that person to her. I wanted to be the old me, the guy who'd been her partner, the Myron who'd never believed in ghosts or any of that nonsense. I didn't tell many living people about the way I saw the world, and only when circumstances dictated that I must, but the number was growing. I'd just told Bernie Thorne, hadn't I? One of these days Alesha was bound to find out, I knew it, and she'd be pissed when she did.

But for now, I wasn't ready. The truth was, I didn't think I'd ever be able to come back to the bureau. I didn't think I'd ever trust myself to be in a situation again where she was counting on me. I could afford to let myself down, but not her. Not Alesha.

I took her sandwich out of the bag and handed it to her. "Hungry?" I asked.

"You're trying to change the subject."

"It's Philly cheesesteak, your favorite."

She took the sandwich, trying to keep the glare in her eyes, but I saw the smile creeping into her face.

"Fine," she said, "you win this time. But I'm not giving up."

"I'd expect no less. So you said you had information?"

"I do."

"I assume it's about Tony Neuman?"

"Yep."

She unwrapped the sandwich, a full footlong because she always complained if I bought her anything smaller, and bit into the end. For someone so lean, she really could wolf down the food. She made me wait while she took three more bites before she finally spoke.

"Funny thing," she said, the words garbled by her mouthful of food. "Tony Neuman is dead."

"What?"

"Got a napkin?"

Impatiently, I handed her a paper napkin from the bag, and she took her time dabbing her face with it.

"This is great sandwich," she said.

"Alesha—"

"So anyway, I don't mean your guy is dead. I mean your guy lifted the name and Social Security number and all that. The real Anthony

Neuman died in the first Gulf War. Kid was an orphan, bounced around foster care, joined the Army right out of high school. Nobody around to care when he died. The strange thing is, I really had to dig to get this info. Your guy, he paid the right people to scrub the records … So what's that look for?"

"Huh?"

"You look kind of relieved."

"Oh, I don't know. My client really doesn't want him to be dead."

"Well, you don't know that he's not dead. You just know that he's not the real Anthony Neuman."

"Fair point."

"So who's your client anyway?"

I debated about what to tell her. I hadn't told her anything so far, not that my client was dead, and certainly not that I thought this was the guy who'd shot me. I'd only told her it was a missing-person case. The problem was, if I didn't have at least a somewhat plausible answer to her question, she would see through me, and if she saw through me, she'd start nosing around a lot on her own. While I was thinking, a lone baritone down the hall in the Church of Spiritual Transcendence started up with a Gregorian chant.

Alesha, between mouthfuls of what was left of her sandwich, mumbled, "Nice voice."

"One of the many fringe benefits of this place. But at least they don't discriminate in their choice of hymns. They're willing to use just about any religion's music."

"Hmm. Don't change the subject. I asked about your client."

"And I was debating what I can tell you. He's a bit squeamish about confidentiality. Let's just say it's a relative who has a vested interest in finding him."

"The father?"

"I can neither confirm nor deny …"

"Because he thinks Neuman killed his daughter?"

"Alesha, don't you have your own detecting to do?"

"I'll take that as a yes." She devoured the last third of her sandwich in a single bite, wrinkled her wrapper and napkins into a tight ball, and shot it into the trash can in the corner. "She shoots, she scores, she lands a shoe contract. Another black athlete gets out of the ghetto."

"You know, if I made that last comment, you'd call me a racist pig."

"That's because you *would* be a racist pig. I gotta get back to work. We still on for pool Sunday night?"

"Sure. And Mike can come, too."

"Ah," she said. "Alas, I must admit that me and Mikey are no longer an item. Was a little too, I don't know, black for my taste ... Why are you smiling?"

"Perhaps because you fail to see the irony contained in your past couple of statements."

She flipped me the bird. For Alesha, it was just as good as a hug. When she turned to go, I cleared my throat.

"What?" she said.

I held the badge out to her.

"Ah," she said, a lot of disappointment wrapped up in that one little word. She forced out a smile, but she didn't do anything to hide that it was forced. She took it from me, our fingers brushing a little, and slipped it into the pocket of her trench coat. "You know I'm not giving up on this?"

"Heaven forbid," I said, and it wasn't until she left that I realized I'd made my own little play of irony.

For heaven to forbid anything, it would have to be real first.

AFTER ALESHA LEFT, I leaned back in the chair and debated a bit about my next move. On my way into the office after coming back from Forest Grove, I'd checked in with Elvis, who told me he hadn't seen Billie. That meant she was either at home in her studio, hanging out at one of her favorite sulking places, or out wandering wherever she went when she needed to wander. Really, it didn't matter. When she was pissed at something I'd done, I'd learned a cooling-off period of at least five hours was the absolute minimum.

I decided a visit to Karen Thorne's place might yield some interesting information. I knew it would have been polite to ask her permission first, but she wasn't due back at my office until Monday to see what kind of progress I'd made, and I had no way to contact her before then except by what ghosts called the SRS—the Spiritual Relay System. That was a fancy acronym that meant I would tell a ghost I was looking for her, who would tell a ghost, who would tell another ghost, and so on. Ghosts really had no way to communicate except by word of mouth. That system obviously left a lot to be desired when privacy was at a premium.

Besides, there was a good chance she was still living there, and if that was the case, I'd do her the courtesy of knocking first.

By the time I stepped outside, the rain had stopped and the sun was again flirting with making an appearance. Little rivers flitted along the edges of the streets to the drainage grates. Burnside was mostly deserted, both of the living and the ghosts, which I always found odd. There was no reason ghosts should have felt stymied by the rain, but it was rare to find one who didn't go on pretending that was the case. I waved to Elvis and walked two blocks the other way, where my Prius was parked in a lot I paid for by the month.

Karen's condo was in the Pearl District, an industrial blight of ramshackle warehouses and railroad yards until the late nineties, when the area underwent a significant urban renewal that turned it into a trendy area known for its art galleries and upscale residences. Her building, the Paragon, was a glass and white brick tower with a concave exterior that gave almost everyone a good view of the Willamette River and the distinctive steel tied arches of the Fremont Bridge.

When I parked the Prius on the street, it was going on three o'clock and the cloudy afternoon light was already slanting into the long fade of evening. Some of the street lamps had already brightened, soft, gauzy yellow bubbles on the thick air. Two clowns juggling a half-dozen bowling pins passed a group of black-clad goth teenagers on the wide sidewalk, neither group even glancing at the other. Some or all of them could have been ghosts. A MAX train rumbled past a block away, and traffic from the bridges was a constant background murmur, but the street was otherwise quiet. I navigated a maze of giant concrete planters with baby spruces in them to the double glass doors leading into the Paragon.

The doors were unlocked. Inside was a lobby with floor-to-ceiling windows, the dark-stained hardwood floor filled with Swedish Art Deco furniture, everything in muted earth tones. The air smelled faintly of whatever lemony cleaner they'd used to polish the floor. A bespectacled old man in a Mr. Rogers blue sweater sat hunched behind the counter, and a stocky woman in a gray pantsuit lounged in one of the chairs by the unlit fireplace. She was paging through *Cosmo*. Safely ensconced in his fortress of opaque black glass, Mr. Rogers didn't look up even when I stopped at his desk.

I took out my wallet and opened it to my private investigator license. When he still refused to acknowledge me, I cleared my throat. It finally dawned on him that someone was standing there and he looked up.

"Hi, thanks for engaging," I said. "I'm Myron Vale, a private investigator. I've been hired to take a look at Karen Thorne's place, so if you could tell me … What's wrong?"

The longer I spoke, the more his face paled. I'd thought his face was pale before, but it was nothing like the stark whiteness his skin became. His eyes, already large behind his glasses, bloomed even larger.

"Please don't hurt me," he whined softly.

"What?"

"I—I've heard of you. I haven't done anything wrong. I mind—I mind my own business."

"Oh, geez."

Embarrassed at my mistake, I fled for the elevator. What kind of ghost hangs out at an empty reception desk? When I glanced back, I saw that he was crying and the woman reading *Cosmo* was staring at me just the way you'd expect someone to stare at you when you appeared to be flashing your license to an empty desk and talking to no one.

Karen's condo was 2021, and there were twenty floors, so I used my amazing detective powers to deduce that she lived on the twentieth floor—the penthouse suites. The wait for the elevator took an eternity, and though I intently focused on the closed doors for the entire time, I still had to listen to the old man's quiet sobbing.

I rode up in an empty elevator, Beethoven's *Ninth Symphony* playing faintly from the overhead speakers. The green carpet felt as plush as the green on a top-of-the-line golf course. It deposited me in an empty hall with beige carpet and ferns in wicker pots. The hall was long and the doors were spaced very far apart. Karen's was on the end, next to a window that looked out on the river far below. As Bernie had said, there was a lockbox on the door. It seemed out of place in such a nice building.

I knocked. There was no answer. I knocked again.

"Karen?" I said.

After giving her a good thirty seconds, I entered the combination and took out the key. The door opened easily. Inside was a short hall with oak floors that led to a living room at the end, where a white couch and loveseat were situated in front of the spacious windows. The air smelled slightly musty. Heading to the living room, I called her name again. No answer. The living room, dining area, and kitchen all blended together into one big room, giving it a spacious feel, everything done in white and black. It was as spotless as a high-end hotel, fake flowers on the kitchen counter, architectural magazines spread neatly on the coffee table.

Not a speck of dirt anywhere. I had a hard time believing anyone lived like this. I also had a hard time believing that Bernie, or someone, hadn't given the place a thorough cleaning.

There wasn't much to find in the kitchen or living room. The refrigerator did have a couple of photos of Karen and Tony, at least, the same kind of glossy head shots as the one she'd shown me back at the office. Two were of them together, two of them separate, both of them wearing jeans and black turtlenecks. Very chic. The one of Tony by himself was similar to the one Karen had shown me, except in the one she'd shown me, he'd been wearing a leather jacket over the turtleneck.

I studied his picture for a long time. Even though there was little apparent similarity between this rakishly good-looking man, with the clean-cut face and the square jaw, to the bearded crazy person who'd shot me, I was even more sure that he was the same person. It was the eyes. I never forgot a pair of eyes.

"I'm going to find you, buddy," I said.

Now I really *was* talking to nobody. I took the photo and put it in my inside pocket, right next to Billie's drawing. The drawing was plenty good, but a photo was better.

After admiring the view—even though it was too overcast to see Mount Hood, the sweep of the river and the city was still plenty impressive—I proceeded to the master bedroom. *Bed* was the operative word, because there wasn't much to the room *but* the bed; it was one of those low riders that was all mattress and plushy bedspread, no headboard, only inches from the ground. I'd expected black and white decor, and I wasn't disappointed. Even the fake roses on the dresser were white.

A thorough search turned up nothing, except the clothes were more neatly packed in the drawers than seemed humanly possible. I kept expecting a perky blond saleswoman to step into the room and say, "All suites at the Paragon are of similar quality to this impeccable showroom." Of course, then she'd take one look at the frumpy private investigator stinking up the place and call security.

Nothing in the end tables—not nothing of value, but *nothing*. The closet and the master bath were the same. Frustrated, I moved on to the second bedroom, which turned out to be an office. Here, at last, I was surprised by a change in style. Instead of black and white, the room was done in shades of gray. A bold choice! There was a light gray glass desk, a dark gray leather chair, and a rug checkered in every gray imaginable.

I stepped through the open door a few feet into the room, contemplating the desk and wondering if I should even bother searching the drawers. I was standing there, rubbing my chin, when I heard the floor creak behind me.

I started to turn, going for my Glock at the same time, but it was too late.

Someone knocked me on the back of the head with something heavy, and I dropped into darkness.

Chapter 12

THE CALL FROM DAD came in when I was doing my best to drink myself into oblivion at Oliver's, a trendy little bar a few blocks from my house that was always packed with the type of people who liked trendy bars—more important, the living kind. Generally, I hated crowds. Generally, I also hated trendy bars, so this was a toxic combination. But a bar crowded with living people was a good place to be if you wanted to avoid the nonliving kind of people. If there were no tables or bar stools available, most ghosts went elsewhere.

The place smelled of sweaty bodies, salty peanuts, and microbrews. If Oliver's had an air conditioner, it wasn't doing any good against the merciless August heat. The steady beat of some horrible techno music coming from the jukebox was like someone tapping their fingers on my temples. The girls next to me, and they were so young they couldn't be called anything but girls, were shouting to be heard over the music—something about some guy on Twitter who tweeted something nasty to some girl about something she snarked about on Facebook over a lewd photo her friend posted to Instagram. Or something.

It took me a moment to hear my cell phone's chime over the wall of noise. When I did, I took the phone out of my leather jacket and set it on the counter, blinking with my bleary eyes at my parents' number.

The time was just after midnight. Suddenly, a rope jerked me out of my long slow slide into the abyss of nothingness I'd been venturing into with such abandon and with such frequency. My parents never called so late.

Plugging my left ear, I held the phone to my right and answered it.

"Hello?" I said.

"Son?"

It was Dad, not Mom, which was almost as big a surprise as the time he was calling. Dad never called. Worse, there was something off about his voice, something strained.

"Dad, what's wrong?"

"Is that you Myron? I can't hear with all the—"

"It's me, it's me! What's wrong?"

It took him a few seconds to respond. I looked up into the mirror behind the bar and saw a black woman in a frilly white wedding dress sitting at a table along the wall. She had a noose around her neck and her eyes bulged in an unnatural way. Even here, I wasn't safe from them. There really was no place on earth I was safe. I would know. I'd spent the last year looking.

I got up and headed for the door. It was already obvious there was an emergency. I just didn't know what kind.

"Hello?" Dad said.

"I'm still here," I said.

"Is this the hospital?"

I felt a sinking feeling in the pit of my stomach, and it was the first inkling I had that my problem was going to be much worse than I'd even imagined. "Dad, it's me, Myron. What happened?"

"Please," he begged, "send an ambulance. Something's wrong. Eleanor—she's fallen. I keep asking her to get up, but she won't."

"Dad, what do you mean?" I asked, pushing through the door

into a wall of heat that was still punishing, even as the sky had melted into lavender. "What happened to Mom?"

"Please," he begged.

"Dad, have you called—"

But he'd already hung up.

I CALLED 911 and hopped in the Prius, pushing my little hybrid so hard I thought the doors might fly off. The gasoline engine, which usually took a backseat to the electric one at low speeds, roared the whole way. Even with fairly deserted streets and an even more deserted I-5, it still took twenty minutes before I pulled into their white Cape Cod–style house on the lake. The paramedics beat me there, of course, probably by a good while, and when I saw that the ambulance's lights were not flashing, an icy blanket wrapped itself around my heart.

A police cruiser, lights also off, was parked next to it. A couple of gladiators, in full Roman garb, were sparring in the front lawn, metal swords clanging against metal shields.

The front door was open, and the first confirmation I received that what I'd feared had indeed come to pass was the sound of my father sobbing. I'd only heard Dad cry twice in my life, once when Mom had her miscarriage and the other time when he retired from the force, and neither had sounded like this—an outright, no-holds-barred, bellowing wail. They were in the living room, all of them, the paramedics lifting Mom onto the gurney, Dad on the couch with his head in his hands, the big, cathedral-like window that looked out on the lake as black as a shroud.

As I came into the room, me in the kind of fog I hadn't been in since I'd been in the hospital drugged up on morphine, a burly police officer with an outlandish handlebar mustache approached me. In the cavernous room, Dad's nonstop crying echoed off the high walls, creating a surround sound of sorrow. The house, in all its air-conditioned glory, was as cool as an icebox, just the way Mom liked it.

"Sir," he said, "are you Myron?"

"What happened? Why aren't you doing something?"

"I'm sorry, sir. She was gone when they got here. Apparently, she ... Well, she'd been gone for a long time."

"What?"

"Sir—"

I pushed past him. Dad, face still buried in his hands, hadn't even looked up. What little of his face I could see was flushed red. He was dressed in a white T-shirt and red plaid pajamas, his hair disheveled. The paramedics, two young guys with buzz cuts and the kind of build that you could only get from spending long hours in the weight room, were starting to roll the gurney toward the door. They hadn't looked at me either. Seized with rage at their obliviousness, I grabbed the gurney.

"Just hold on!" I cried. *"Just hold the fuck on!"*

The paramedics gaped at me as if I'd suddenly materialized out of thin air. The police officer, gripping me firmly by the arm, said something in a soothing voice, something to placate me, but it was a jumble of words. I just wanted to look at her. She lay motionless, her eyes closed, her face more peaceful than it had ever looked in life. Dressed in a flowing white nightgown, an exquisite combination of silk and lace, there was an almost angelic quality to her. It was the kind of nightgown that was indistinguishable from an evening dress, but she still would have been mortified to be seen this way by anyone other than her husband.

Dad's sobbing had finally subsided into something like a soft keening, a sound even more pitiful and disturbing, especially the way it was muffled by his hands.

"How—how long ..." I began.

"Probably eighteen hours," one of the paramedics said.

"Why didn't—why didn't Dad ..."

The cop, dropping his voice to a whisper, leaned in close. "Your father seems very confused."

"What?"

"Does he have someone else who can watch him?"

"What are you talking about?"

The cop regarded me with sympathy, which only enraged me further. Yet some part of me knew, even then, what he was talking about. Some part of me knew, even as I'd denied it to myself, that Dad's ever-increasing forgetfulness and absentmindedness the past few years wasn't just the usual minor age-related mental deterioration that any man might suffer as he approached his seventieth birthday.

My rage dissolved into a kind of impotent sorrow. I felt myself sinking away from them all, down the rabbit hole into my own grief, the world receding tunnel-like until it was happening far away. One of the paramedics said something about getting my mother to the morgue. There was a conversation. I heard my own voice, but it wasn't me. The cop said something. They rolled my mother toward the open door, where I saw that the two gladiators, faces dripping with sweat, were peering curiously into my house.

"Get out!" I screamed at them. "Get the hell out!"

Alarmed, the gladiators fled. The paramedics, ashen-faced, re-treated almost as fast as the gladiators. The cop said something about them just doing their jobs. Through it all, Dad went on moaning and rocking like a small child. The cop was still talking, explaining where I needed to go, the people I needed to talk to about my mother, words that broke apart into meaningless bits as soon as they hit my brain.

As soon as the gurney rounded the corner out of sight, the wheels still rattling along the paved stone walkway, I heard another sound, a distinctive one I knew all too well—the forceful click of heels on the hardwood floor.

I turned toward the hall, the one that led to the bedroom, and there she was, my mother, dressed in charcoal gray slacks and a beige cardigan over a white shirt buttoned all the way to the top, her black heels giving her another couple of inches of height. It was the kind of outfit most women would wear to an office or to church, but it was too casual for Mom to wear anywhere but around the house.

"*Well,*" she said, with all the indignity only she could muster in a single word, "I hope you're not expecting any dinner, Vinnie, because we ate hours ago."

I felt sweat break out on my brow. A cold chill rippled down my spine. She looked just as alive now as she'd looked dead on the gurney. I'd been seeing ghosts for nearly a year, but never like this, never someone I loved so soon after dying. "Mom," I said, and the word came out a gasp.

"Sir?" the cop said.

"What's this?" Mom said, striding into the room like a CEO into a boardroom. "Why is that policeman here? What's wrong with your father?"

I started to answer, then caught myself. Somehow I had the presence of mind to face the cop and carry on, if only for a moment, as if Mom wasn't in the room.

"If you don't mind," I said to him, "I'd like to be alone with my father."

"Of course, of course," the cop said.

"What do you mean, alone?" Mom said. "What's going on? Somebody better explain to me what's happened right now. Hank, stop this nonsense!"

"If you need anything—" the cop said.

"I'll call," I said.

"I don't appreciate being ignored!" Mom said.

While she glared at us, I showed the cop to the door. He gave me his card. I told him I'd be along to the hospital shortly. Shutting the door, I heard the clink of swords somewhere down our drive, but I didn't look. When I came back to the room, Mom was sitting next to Dad on the couch, who finally, mercifully, had stopped crying. Now he was staring blankly ahead, his eyes red, his face pink and swollen. In the stillness, I heard the faint whisper of cool air blowing through the vents.

"Now will you *please* tell me what's going on," Mom said. She sat with her legs pressed tightly together and her hands clasped on her lap. "Your father is in one of his moods and has decided to ignore me.

Why was that police officer here? Did one of the neighbor boys throw another egg at the house? Terrible little scads. No manners."

Dad didn't react to her voice. I waited for his eyes to focus on me. When they didn't, I knelt in front of him on the faux bearskin rug. Dad had wanted a real bearskin rug, but Mom refused to have, in her words, anything so vile in her house, and this had been the compromise—nice and soft, but fooling no one. He'd made a fair amount of money as a broker since he'd retired from the force, mostly catering to his fellow police officers, but to my knowledge he'd never once bought anything unless Mom approved.

It took a long time, but finally he blinked and registered my presence, brow furrowing.

"Myron?" he said.

"Dad," I said, "do you know what's happened?"

"Where's Eleanor?" he asked. He scratched at the stubble on his face, his long fingernails leaving red streaks. "Where's your mother?"

"What?" Mom said. "What do you mean? I'm right here!"

I sighed. "He can't hear you."

"Who can't hear me?" Dad asked.

"Well of *course* he can hear me," Mom said indignantly. "I'm sitting right here, aren't I? He's just being stubborn. Just like your father. He wasn't happy with the soufflé I made tonight and he's decided to punish me. He wanted steak and eggs and he knows what the doctor said about that."

"Where's Eleanor?" Dad asked again, the panic rising in his voice "Where is she? She was here just a minute ago."

"How *dare* you be so rude!" Mom shot at him. "You may be unhappy with me, Henry, but I don't appreciate this sort of behavior!"

"Dad—"

"Eleanor!" he shouted suddenly, and both Mom and I jumped. "Eleanor! Eleanor!"

As unresponsive as he'd been before, he was just as agitated now, a coiled spring of tension, his body alive with spasms and twitches. He made a move to rise, and I clamped a hand on his knee. The cotton pajamas collapsed around a joint so bony and small it frightened me. I'd known he had been losing weight, that he'd become a bit more gaunt over the years, but this person was hardly more than a skeleton.

He tried to overpower me, rising against my will, but there was so little strength in him that he didn't manage more than to jerk his leg a little. His eyes flared with animal-like rage. He leaned forward and I pushed him back toward the couch. I'd meant it to be only a gentle push, but he was so light he crumpled like a sheet of paper.

"Henry!" Mom cried.

"Where—where—where—" he stuttered.

"Please, Dad," I said.

"Where—where—where—"

"Dad, she's gone," I said.

"Where—where—where—"

"Gone?" Mom said.

"Where—where … What?"

He stopped fighting me, his body stilling, a bit of sanity returning to his eyes. I squeezed his hand. It was cold and leathery, like a baseball glove left out in the snow. Outside of being a cop, that had been his big love, baseball, and he'd drag me outside to play catch all year round. I'd never liked it as much as him, never liked it at all, really, but it hadn't occurred to me until that moment how much I missed tossing the ball around with him. When was the last time? Even as an adult, every time I'd be over he would ask me to play catch—until recently. A year? Two?

The signs were all there and I'd missed them. Or if I hadn't missed them, then I'd surely ignored them, which was a far worse crime.

"Dad," I said, keeping my voice as calm and measured as I could, "I want you to listen carefully to me. This is going to be hard, but I need you to hear it. Are you listening?"

"Why are you talking to him like he's a child?" Mom said curtly. "Don't talk to your father that way. Henry, tell your son. Tell him he can't talk to you like that."

Dad nodded to me. It was a barely perceptible nod, a slight tilt of his head, but there was something about the deliberate nature of it that told me he was fully present. My throat was tightening on me and my face was burning hot. I didn't know how to do this, so I just went ahead and blurted it out.

"Mom is dead," I said.

If the news reached Dad in any measurable way, he didn't show it, but Mom gaped at me as if I'd slapped her.

"What?" she said. "What kind of nonsense is this?"

"Mom is dead," I said again, keeping my attention on Dad. If anything, he seemed to be receding from me, his eyes turning as flat and unresponsive as the eyes in a painting.

"That's *quite* enough, Vinnie," Mom said. "I don't know what kind of silly game this is, but—"

"Mom is dead," I said, a bit more forcefully.

"How *dare* you talk about me in such a—"

"Mom is dead!"

"I am *not!* I'm right here! Why are you both ignoring me?"

"Mom is dead!"

Fueled by all of my own pent-up grief and petty resentments, all my years of failing to live up to her expectations, I bellowed it at the top of my lungs. I hadn't meant to lose control. It wasn't an intentional ploy to break through Dad's mental fog. Yet my emotional outburst did get him to flinch.

His eyes focused on me, his pupils wide and dark enough that I saw the vague outlines of my own reflection kneeling before him. His face was still pink and raw from the crying. The lines on his face were etched deep. This was an old man, somebody who'd been through the meat grinder of life and was trying to hold on, but there was no question that this was my father. He was here. He was here and he saw me.

Then he did something I didn't expect. He reached forward and cupped that rough hand of his around my neck.

"It's going to be okay, son," he said.

Mom was crying in her usual way, a silent trickle down a stone cold face, her body as stiff as a mannequin's. Even in this, as in almost everything with her, there was an undercurrent of passive aggressiveness. It was a way of crying that said, *You did this to me, look at what you did.* As for me, it took everything I had to bottle up my own tears. That Dad would try to comfort *me,* after losing the only woman he'd ever professed to love, was so unexpected that it very nearly blew apart the carefully constructed tough-guy persona I'd spent years building and fortifying.

I would never be as tough as Dad. He was as tough as knotted wood. He didn't have to try. He just *was.* The hybrid-driving, love-song-listening, sensitive, needy, artsy-fartsy Myron that was the real me, despite my best efforts to change it—that guy could never be as genuinely tough no matter how hard he worked at it. But I wasn't about to lose it now. Not now, for God's sake.

Mom took a long, shuddering breath. "I just don't understand why you're being so needlessly cruel," she said, sniffling. "Why would you say such a thing? Hank, tell him how cruel he's being. Hank, listen to me. Why aren't you listening to me?"

Dad, of course, said nothing. He didn't see her. Unlike me, he would never see his beloved wife again. I rose shakily to my feet, feeling like a burnt-out husk of a man, ashes held together by static that a strong wind might scatter. When I looked at Mom, all prim and proper and entirely contained, despite her tears, I felt neither anger nor resentment. I felt a sympathy for her I hadn't felt in years—maybe never. I realized now how much she'd been compensating for Dad's weaknesses, how she'd managed to fill in the ever-growing gaps in his mind with the force of her own will. The very stubbornness about her that I'd so long hated was probably the one thing that had helped him the most.

Outside, a dog explained his loneliness to the night in one long, mournful howl. I tried to think of a way to explain to Mom what had happened to her. I tried to think of a way to soften the blow, to make it easy for her just this once, but my mind froze. I just couldn't do it.

"Hello, Eleanor."

It was Billie, approaching from the front door. I'd never been more grateful for her and all her many contradictions than in that moment. She'd died her hair bright orange, crayon orange, and cut it short and spiky. She was dressed in a black leather jacket and leather chaps over blue jeans, a black motorcycle helmet under her arm. When she stepped up next to me, I could smell the gasoline on her. So real. So real I always had to remind myself that if I reached for her, nothing would be there.

Mom eyed her the way she might eye a dog that had just crapped on her driveway. "What's *she* doing here?" she said.

"I've come to help you," Billie said.

"Well, isn't that *big* of you. Vinnie, please kindly tell your wife that I don't need anyone's help. I especially don't need the help of someone who can barely help herself."

"Mom, please," I said.

Dad glanced at me, his attention lingering between me and somewhere beyond, though he didn't say anything. I realized I was going to have to be careful. Dad was confused enough. I didn't want to add to his burdens.

"Eleanor, listen," Billie said, "I'm just going to tell you how it's going to be. I don't care if you don't want to hear it. You'll figure it out eventually, we all do, but if you go on denying the truth you'll just make it tough for Myron. And he's had it tough enough already. You're dead. That's it, plain and simple. You died and you're not among the living anymore."

The whole time she spoke, Mom pointedly kept her gaze fixed on me. "Vinnie, I'm afraid I'm going to have to ask your wife to leave. I don't understand why you all keep saying this foolish thing about me dying. It's cruel. I can understand *her* being cruel, she's always been cruel, but you, Vinnie … I'm so disappointed."

"Nobody's being cruel, Eleanor," Billie said. "We're just trying to tell you the truth."

"Vinnie—"

"Myron, he goes by Myron."

"*Vinnie*, as I was saying—"

"Haven't you wondered why you can see me?" Billie asked.

"—I really must ask both of you … both of you …"

This last question finally got to Mom. I could see the realization blooming in her eyes, that the woman she was talking to was currently dead. There was no way for her to deny it. She'd been at Billie's funeral! And if Mom was talking to a dead person, what did that mean about her? She swallowed hard, and her fingers, clasped in her lap, twitched a few times.

"But *Vinnie* can see me," she protested.

Billie glanced at me, her eyes asking permission. I gave it to her with a nod.

"Myron can see you because he's different," she said.

"I don't know what you mean."

"Myron can see ghosts."

"What? Don't be absurd."

"He can see both of us because we're ghosts. It started to happen after he got shot. You remember he got shot, don't you?"

"Well, of course I do! That doesn't mean I believe all this nonsense."

Billie folded her arms, coolly staring down at Mom the way a teacher might stare down a misbehaving pupil. "Touch your husband," she said.

"What?"

"Touch him. On the leg. The shoulder. Something."

"I will do no such thing!"

"I'm not asking you give him a hand job—just to make some physical contact, for God's sake."

"How *dare* you!"

"Touch him."

"Stop saying that!"

Mom's face blushed bright red and she glared at Billie with rabid intensity. With a frustrated groan, Billie looked at me, raising her eyebrows. I knew what she wanted me to do. I also knew that what she wanted me to do would undoubtedly work. It would sever the last cord Mom had with the world of the living. It would be painful and cruel and Mom would resent me forever for it.

I took a few timid steps in her direction, slowly raising my arms. I had to swallow a few times before I could speak. It felt as if I had a tennis ball lodged in my throat. "Mom," I said.

"What?" she said.

"I want to give you a hug."

She hardly moved, but still it seemed as if she sank into the couch, deflating, becoming as small as she could.

"No," she whispered.

"Just one hug."

"We don't—we don't do that. We don't hug."

"Just this once."

"Vinnie … Myron … *please* …"

She started to move, a feeble attempt to turn away from me, and I bent over her and swept my arms through her.

I expected to feel nothing more than a slight tingle, what I often but not always felt when I passed through a ghost or a ghost passed through me. Yet this time I felt something more, a lot more, not just a tingle but a painful jolt that was like an electrified needle jabbed straight into my heart. It was an injection of fear and giddiness and remorse and a lifetime of other emotions all packed into one wallop, everything my mother had ever felt, good and bad, everything she'd never shared with me, or probably anyone, laid bare to me for one fateful second.

She knew it, too, based on her startled expression. I knew her better in that moment than I'd ever known her. If she would have been embarrassed to be seen in her nightgown, this was far worse, an exposing of her soul that was a total violation. I knew, despite the brave front she'd put on all this years, how small and scared she really was. She was such a scared little person.

I stood. The moment lasted a few seconds, the two of us staring at one another. I heard Billie exhale slowly. Dad started crying again, but they were silent tears. Mom's face, naked in its fragility, suddenly hardened, the walls coming down, the eyes turning to steel. She brushed off her pants and stood, glaring at me, the two of us nose to nose.

"How could you," she snapped.

Then she swiveled on her heels and marched out of the room, walking even more stiffly than usual, a marionette without the strings. I watched her go. For the first time in as long as I could remember, I wanted to tell her I loved her.

I wanted to, but I couldn't make myself say the words.

Chapter 13

WHEN I FINALLY crawled back to consciousness, I was greeted by the mother of all headaches.

EvI told youer since the shooting, I'd become intimately familiar with every variety and breed of head-related pain, but this one tested even my own elevated tolerance level for the stuff. There were almost as many words to describe headaches as the Eskimos had to describe snow. Throbbing. Earsplitting. Head-pounding. Piercing. Pulsing. Crippling. The always excruciating migraine, which stepped up the sufferer to the expert level. All those words and more couldn't have described the eyeball-stabbing, skull-vise-squeezing, ice-pick-penetrating utter agony that paralyzed me for a few minutes on the hardwood floor of Karen Thorne's condo before I finally gathered up enough strength and courage to rise, groaning, to my knees.

The room was dark and quiet. Only the faintest moonlight rimmed the curtained windows. How long had I been out? My eyelids felt as if they were coated with sand. I touched the back of my head and winced at the pain, but at least I didn't feel blood. I heard the hum of the fridge in the other room, and there was faint glow from down the hall, probably the oven light. The left side of my face, which had been pressed against the floor, was numb.

Taking the Glock out of my coat, I crawled to the desk and used it for support to climb to my feet. A digital clock in the corner read 8:05 p.m. I released the safety and took my time searching the condo, the rooms, the closets, even under the bed, always keeping my Glock at the ready. There was nobody there.

By the time I finished, my headache had subsided to a dull ache behind the eyes. I was in the kitchen, massaging my pulsing temples and trying to understand what somebody thought they might find in such a sterile place, when I heard the distinctive click of heels from down the hall. I stepped back, deeper into the kitchen, and pointed the Glock where I knew the person would be in seconds.

It was Karen, dressed in a long black overcoat, dark nylons, and black sequined shoes that matched her sequined handbag. Her blond hair had been brushed into luxurious, gleaming curls. She set her handbag on the counter, and when she finally saw me, her eyes flew wide and her hands fluttered to her throat.

"Oh," she said.

"Surprise," I said.

"What—what are you doing—"

"Detecting," I said.

"Detecting?"

"Sleuthing. Looking for clues. You know, my job. Hope you don't mind. I would have asked first, but, well, I didn't." I holstered the Glock. Pointing a gun at somebody had the undesirable effect of making them jumpy—even with ghosts. "So where were you? You look dressed for a night on the town."

She blinked at me a few times, her eyelashes long and dark, the kind of eyelashes that took a woman a lot of effort to produce. "I was … I was just out with some friends. Some old friends. People I hadn't seen in a while."

Her voice was a little slurred—not a lot, but enough that it was obvious she'd been drinking. It was another one of those things that continued to amaze me. A ghost had no reason to show any signs of inebriation, or any physical effects of alcohol or drugs, but they still usually carried on as if it was so.

"Did any of those old friends die of liver failure?" I asked, having a hard time hiding my irritation.

"What?"

I motioned to the living room. "You want to sit down for a minute? I've got some questions."

I turned on a side lamp and the two of us took our seats, her on the couch, me on the loveseat. She brought her handbag with her, clutching it against her chest as if she was afraid I might snatch it from her. Her eyes were wide and shiny, like saucers full of water, and she continued to blink rapidly.

"So when were you going to tell me about your drinking problem?" I asked.

"What?"

"I spoke with your father. He said you were basically an alcoholic."

She blushed. "I'm no such thing. I like—I like a drink now and then, it's true, but I never … I mean I haven't …"

"He said that when you died, your blood-alcohol level was through the roof. He said that's why nobody even suspected foul play."

"I *told* you, that's not why I died. It was the brakes. It doesn't matter how much I … It was the brakes. They just didn't work."

"I'm not saying I don't believe you. I'm just saying that when a client starts lying to me about little things, then I start wondering if they're lying to me about bigger things."

"I wasn't lying! I just didn't … I didn't think it was relevant."

"Well, why don't you let me decide that from now on, okay? Another question. Is there any reason somebody would hide in your apartment, then hit me over the head before I could see them?"

The blinking came back in full force. She really had to be careful, or she was going to blink those eyelashes of hers right off her face. "I don't—I don't understand—"

"It's not a hypothetical. It just happened."

"Oh! Are you—"

"I'm fine. There's nobody staying here but you, right?"

"No! I mean, I don't think so."

"What do you mean, you don't think so?"

"I mean ... I mean I haven't been staying here all the time. Just some of the time. Now and then. I don't really—I mean, I don't like being alone all that much. I stay with my sisters. My dad. They can't see me, but it's ... It's easier with them around. Not so lonely."

"But you're here tonight," I said.

"Yes."

"Why?"

"I just—I just wanted —"

"Who did you see tonight?"

She stared at me coldly. "I don't see how it's any of your business."

"It probably isn't. But if you want me to find Tony, you really should just answer my questions."

She held my gaze for a moment longer, her jaw set and her body as stiff as a plaster mold, then sighed. "Fine. I met my sisters. We meet once a month or so. A regular thing, at a bar downtown. You know, just to catch up and chat. Kind of like a book club."

"Except with booze instead of books."

"I guess."

"But they didn't know you were there?"

"Of course not."

"They don't have your dad's, you know ..."

"No. As far as I know, they've never sensed I was near them."

"They talk about you?"

She studied the cuticle of her thumb. Judging by the general pall hanging over her, I assumed they had. I also assumed that something they'd said had upset her, which was why she was back here at her condo. Getting that information out of her might prove tricky, so I decided to take a more roundabout approach.

"They both live downtown?" I asked.

"No, but they're close. Janice lives in Vancouver, just over the river. Her husband is the vice president of a local bank. Beth lives in Lake Oswego. Well, when she's not at her cabin near Mount Hood. That's where she goes when she needs to think. She's a *writer.*" She spat out this word as if it explained everything.

"A writer? Of what?"

"Of whatever strikes her fancy. Novels. Poems. She's been working on a memoir for the past five years. I don't think she's ever been published or anything. But boy, she really makes it sound like she's doing the most important thing in the world."

"She's not married?"

"No. Wouldn't want a man to get in the way of her art." She said the word with the same distaste as she'd said the word *writer.*

I pulled out my trusted spiral notebook and a pen. "I'd like to verify their contact info," I said. "You may have given it to me already, but let's make sure it's up to date."

"Why?"

"So I can do my detecting thing."

"But they're not going to know anything."

"Humor me."

"I'm telling you, they *hated* Tony. They thought he was terrible. They never—they never said so around me, of course, but now that I'm gone ..."

Her eyes clouding, she looked down at her black sequined shoes. Now I had a pretty good idea what her sisters had talked about tonight. I moved to the couch and sat next to her. I would have put my arm around her, because she looked like she wanted to lean into someone and have a good cry, but sitting there was going to have to do.

"I'm sorry," I said.

She sniffled. "I love them, but they can be so ... cruel."

"Everybody has their opinions."

"They said he was just using me. For sex. For money. But I never gave him any money! Not really. A few dollars here and there, maybe. Sometimes he was between big deals and I covered the bills for a while. But he wasn't using me."

She went on like that for a while. I didn't say much. My own history with Tony would never let me see him in any sort of objective light, but mostly she just wanted someone to hear her out, to let her vent, and even though I was feeling the itch to get out of the condo, I felt obligated to give her a sympathetic ear. I knew she was struggling with her own contradictory feelings about Tony, about what he was and what he wasn't, and she didn't need me to make those feelings any more complicated. There might be a time to press her, but it wasn't now.

Finally, I begged my leave, telling her I'd see her on Saturday, hopefully with news. She gave me her sister's contact information, then followed me to the door. She had such a sad-puppy way about her, hanging her head, shuffling her feet, that I felt the need to offer her at least a little more encouragement.

"It's going to be all right," I said.

"Is it?"

"Sure. Just don't give up hope, okay?"

"I'll try," she said, but there wasn't a whole lot of try in her voice. "I just … I didn't know dying would be like this."

"Nobody does. That's the bitch of it all."

"You do. You know how it is."

"Well, besides me."

"Does it make it easier? I mean, knowing what's coming. For you. For everyone."

"I don't know. Not really. Most of the time, I feel like I'm already dead."

"What do you mean?"

I sighed. "Who knows. Probably the bump on my head talking. I've got to get going."

I reached for the door handle.

"You know," she said, her voice and demeanor suddenly turning demure, "you don't have to go."

"Karen—"

"You could stay here. With me."

She batted those enormous eyelashes at me. She hadn't really cried, but there had been enough moisture to darken her mascara, deepen the lines around her eyes. It made her seem both more vulnerable and more alluring. All that luxurious blond hair, the way it flowed down her black overcoat. That knockout figure, every curve and slope to her somehow accentuated by that same overcoat, as loose as it was. It was hard not to look. She saw me looking and tilted her head slyly to the side.

"You're a very handsome man," she said. "Has anyone ever told you that?"

"Karen, I really should go."

"Silly me," she said. "Of course women have told you that. I'm sure you hear it all the time."

"I think I'm double parked," I said.

"I think you're nervous. You shouldn't be."

"I'm a married man."

"And I'm a married woman. It doesn't seem to be working out too well for either of us."

"Karen—"

"I'm lonely, Myron. Stay with me."

"Karen, you've had a little too much to drink. In the morning, when—when your head is clear—"

Before I could finish, she reached out with her hand and touched me on the chest. *Touched.* It was only a tap, hardly stronger than a puff of air, but I'd felt it all the way through my jacket. More than that, this had not been any ordinary touch. It might have been weak in the physical sense, but it sent an electric shiver through my entire body. The feeling was so unexpected that I gaped at her, speechless. She smiled.

"Can your wife do that?" she asked.

I said nothing.

"Didn't think so," Karen said. "Just the drawing thing, right? I haven't been a ghost for long, but I've already realized that not many of us can, and those that do usually have an attachment to a certain kind of thing, like your wife. So just think of that, Myron. Think if you were lying on my bed in the other room—naked—what I could do for you. The way I could make you feel."

I swallowed away the lump in my throat. My face felt warm and my collar felt damp with sweat. It had been a long time since any woman, dead or alive, had propositioned me in such a way.

"I'll see you Saturday," I said.

"Don't go," she said.

"Saturday."

"Myron—"

I opened the door and went out without looking at her again, closing the door immediately behind me. Besides me and the plants in their wicker pots, the hall was empty.

I didn't linger long before heading to the elevator, just a few seconds to learn to breathe again, but it was long enough that I caught the unmistakable sound of crying from the other side of the door.

Chapter 14

HE WAS TALL and black, impressively tall and deeply black, the kind of height and skin color that would have made heads turn on any street corner in Portland. There were more African Americans in the city than in the rest of the state, but they still didn't amount to more than five percent of the city's population. He had to be nearly seven feet tall. He wore a sharp gray business suit, which, as he strolled down the sidewalk toward my house, made him stand out even more. People in my mostly residential neighborhood didn't generally wear suits except for the brief walk from their cars to their front doors.

So it went without saying that people should have noticed him. The old man sticking his envelope in his mailbox, the mother loading her baby into the car seat of her minivan, the fit young woman jogging in time to the music piping through her headphones—they all should have at least glanced his way.

But they didn't.

I watched him approach, feeling the familiar clench in my stomach. Would he be one of the normals or one of the weirdos?

It was a Tuesday morning in March, more than a year and a half since the shooting. After almost two solid weeks of near-ceaseless drizzle, the sun had made a return appearance. Though it was still cool, it was warm enough that I could feel the sun's rays through my cotton sweatshirt. I was on my hands and knees in the wet grass, a plastic bucket half-full of weeds next to me, and I was adding to the collection with a hand shovel. After working on the yard long enough that my fingers were cramping, it was a toss-up whether I'd even made much of a dent. Still, the smell of wet grass and fertile earth was a welcome change from the smell of booze.

The black man stopped in front of me, hands behind his back. Based on his lean build, I'd judged him to be a younger man from farther away. Now I saw that he was at least in his early fifties. His face was lined with age, and his curly stubble was more gray than black. Since my front yard was elevated almost three feet, boxed in by a moss-coated concrete retaining wall, we were about at eye level with me on my knees. His eyes were as black as his skin, a deep, brooding black that seemed neither menacing nor kind. The suit fit him very well for his build, which meant it was tailored, which also meant he had money. Or would have, if he were still alive.

"Myron Vale?" he asked. He had a voice deep enough that it would have given James Earl Jones a run for his money.

I wiped the sweat off my forehead with the sleeve of my sweatshirt and glanced at him briefly. I'd been doing my best to avoid making eye contact with ghosts, figuring maybe they'd go away if I ignored them long enough, but it was very difficult when they were talking to you.

I looked left and right to see if anyone was watching. No one was.

"Who wants to know?" I asked.

"My name is Frank Brown," he said. "I'm from the NAANCP."

He extended his hand, which, with his enormous wingspan, reached me without forcing him to lean precariously over the muddy border where I'd planted rose bushes the previous weekend. I studied his hand, then looked at him with raised eyebrows. It took him a few seconds to realize his mistake, and when he did, he chuckled softly and dropped his hand to his side. There was something familiar about him, though I couldn't say what.

"Sorry," he said. "Just habit. I've never really dealt with somebody … Well, like you."

"Lucky me," I said.

"Do you have a few minutes to talk?"

"I don't know. I got a lot of weeding to do."

He nodded at my grass. "It looks like a big job."

"Somebody's got to do it," I said. "Did you say you're from the NAANCP?"

"That's right."

"Don't you mean the NAACP?" I recited the letters very slowly to emphasize the missing *N*.

He smiled thinly, as if he'd had this particular exchange before and it was his burden to bear. "A common mistake, I'm afraid. That's the National Association for the Advancement of Colored Persons. No, I'm representing a very different organization. The National Association for the Advancement of *Non-Corporeal* Persons."

"You've got to be kidding," I said.

"Do I look like the sort of person who kids?"

"And the fact that you're black is just a coincidence?"

"It's an annoyance, is what it is. People often make the same mistake you did. Be easier if I was a short white dude like you."

"Hey, I'm almost six feet tall."

"Like I said. *Short.*"

"Play basketball?"

He sighed. "Yes."

"Any good?"

"I was all right. Not a basketball fan, huh?"

I realized I'd heard a slight variation of his name before. "Wait a minute. Are you telling me you were *Frankie* Brown? The Hall of Famer?"

"I'm *still* Frankie Brown, the Hall of Famer. I just decided to go by Frank in my new life."

"Three championships with the Sixers? Two MVP awards?"

"So you *do* watch some basketball."

"More as a kid than now," I said, grinning, "though you were a bit before my time. You were definitely one of my dad's heroes. He told me stories about your matchups with Wilt Chamberlain—two titans going head to head. Dad always said the only way Wilt could beat you is if he cheated."

He was grinning a little now. "Just think how I would have handled him if I'd been in my prime. I was already in my late thirties by the time he came along. My back was like solid wood by that point, and I still held my own against him."

"Real shame about your heart attack," I said. "You weren't even sixty, were you?"

"Fifty-eight," he said.

"Way too young."

"Yeah, well, that's one bus ticket we don't get to buy on our own, do we? Anyway, I'm doing more good now than I was in those later years. When I wasn't screwing women half my age, I was trying to single-handedly keep the liquor business profitable. If it hadn't been my heart that killed me, it would have been my liver. Now at least I got some kind of purpose to my life. Without purpose, what's a man got?"

He looked at me knowingly, and I felt my defensive walls rise. As much as I knew about him, at least the old him, it was obvious he knew plenty about me. Lately, the fights with Billie had been brutal, mostly about the booze, sometimes about other things too, but in the end, those other things were usually tied up with the booze, too.

I put down the hand shovel and stood. Now, elevated by my yard, I was looking down at him.

"What do you want?" I asked, and I heard the brittleness in my own voice.

"Hey now, no need to be rude. I just want you to know … Well, I know what you're going through."

"You have no idea what I'm going through."

Frank raised his hands in a defensive gesture. His hands were so big he could have shoveled dirt with them. "All right, all right, fair enough. I can't say much about the other thing, about your ... specialness. But I know what it's like to be searching for some kind of answer to my troubles in the bottom of a bottle."

"I think you better leave," I said.

"Hold on, now. Mr. Vale—Myron, can I call you Myron? You can call me Frank. Even Frankie if you want. Let's be friends."

"We're not friends. Did Billie send you?"

"Myron, that's not why I'm here."

"So Billie did send you?"

A twenty-something young man on a mountain bike whizzed by at just that moment, and he eyed me warily. Frank waited until he passed, then lowered his voice to a whisper.

"Can we speak inside?" he asked.

"Why are you whispering? They can't hear *you*."

"Please, just for a few minutes. I have a proposition."

"Whatever you got to say, just say it. I've got a lot of weeding to do."

Frank regarded me silently, shaking his head. Even now, I could see fierce competitiveness in those deep dark eyes of his. "Man, you ain't gonna make this easy for me, are you? Fine. I'll lay it out straight for you. If you want to drink yourself to death and play gardener while you do, that's your call. But if you want to man up and get back to work doing something similar to what you used to do, the NAANCP could use someone with your talents."

"Nice speech," I said.

"Thank you," he said.

"Too bad you didn't try your hand at coaching after you blew out your ACL. You probably wouldn't have been half bad."

"Yeah, well, there's a lot of things I might have been good at if I hadn't been so busy drinking all the time." He raised his hand quickly. "I'm not saying it as a message to you. I'm just saying it 'cause it's a fact."

A goth teenager on a skateboard rolled past. He didn't look at either Frank or me, his expression flat and his eyes dull, but I still waited until he was gone to speak.

"I see," I said. "And what is it, exactly, that you think I might find I'm good at if I stop hanging out in bars and come work for you?"

"Oh, well, we think you're going to be good at lots of things—"

"Specifically."

"We don't have an official job description yet, but—"

"Just a general sense is fine."

"Well ... There's a number of responsibilities you'll have in your new role. One of them will be acting as a translator to people on either side of the divide. There's a long list of non-corporeal people who have important information to convey to their flesh-and-blood loved ones, but conveying that information has always proven difficult. It would be nice to have an official process we could use."

"Uh-huh."

"But that's not all," he continued quickly. "We also think you'd be great at transporting sensitive documents or important items that we find challenging to move on our own."

"I see."

"And there are other—there are other duties that we—"

"So let me get this straight," I said. "Basically what you're looking for is someone to perform séances and also act as some sort of glorified messenger boy?"

He frowned. "Now hold on, Myron, I don't think that's a fair way to describe—"

"Oh you don't, do you? How would you describe it?"

"Now look," he said sternly, "I don't know why you're being so hostile. I'm trying to help you here."

"No, you're trying to *use* me here."

"Jesus Christ!"

"As you well know," I said, "that fellow doesn't seem to be any-where around—if he ever was."

"You're impossible," he said.

"Now I'm *convinced* you talked to my wife."

"You know, money would not be a problem if you came to work

for us. It would not be a paycheck in the usual sense, but trust me, you would be well compensated. We have ways of making money flow when we so desire."

"That's nice. We done?"

"Myron—"

"It was an honor to meet you, really. I'll have to tell Dad. He'll get a real kick out of it. But like I said, I got a lot of weeding to do. Better get back to it."

"Myron, if you'll just hear me out."

But I was done hearing him out. Without looking at him again, I returned to my knees. I returned to the weeds and the dirt and everything I knew was real, because I could feel it. I could feel the hand shovel digging into my palm. I could feel the soft push of the grass on my other hand, the moistness of it seeping into my skin. The tickle of the breeze on my face, the warmth of the sun on my neck, the call of the blue jay in the oak overhanging my house—this was all real. This was all the world I needed and would ever need.

He stood there another minute, as tall and silent as a mountain, then turned with a grunt and walked away.

Chapter 15

Stepping out of the elevator in Karen Thorne's building and still feeling the heat of her amorous gaze on my body, I was eager to hightail it back to my Prius before I could change my mind about her offer. My brain may have been fully faithful to Billie, but my body didn't always show the same level of commitment, and I wasn't all that confident my brain would win a boxing match between the two—especially when a temptation so gorgeous was waiting on one side of the ring.

Still, the whole ride down, I couldn't help but fantasize what sex with Karen would have been like, the same kind of fantasies I'd had about Billie lots of times. The difference with Billie was that she didn't have the ability to interact with the physical world that Karen had.

Or did she? She'd said her ability to move objects was limited to her art—pencils, paintbrushes, and the like—but there was always some part of me that wondered, fair or not, if she was just holding out on me.

All this was on my mind when I stepped out of the elevator and saw the same bespectacled desk clerk still at the counter. The lobby was otherwise empty, a morgue-like stillness pervading the place.

When he saw me, his face shriveled.

"You again," he whined.

"Me again," I said. "I'm not going to hurt you, okay? I just have a few questions."

"Questions?"

He rasped out the word as if someone was strangling him. His eyes, magnified by his glasses, bulged. I would have worried that talking to me was going to kill him if he weren't already dead.

"Who did you see come through here since I went upstairs?" I asked.

"Come through here?" he squeaked.

"Are you going to answer my question or just repeat what I say?"

"Repeat what you—" the old man began, then caught himself. He tugged at the collar of his sweater. His forehead, already sweating, gleamed under the fluorescent lights. "I'm—I'm not sure. There's been a few. People, that is. A few people."

"Dead or alive?"

"Um. I don't know."

"You don't know? I thought all ghosts could tell the difference."

He swallowed, and in the quiet of the room, the sound was comically loud. "I'm sorry, Mr. Vale. What you say is true. It's just that I—I have difficulty. It's a problem. I just can't, um, seem to do anything to fix it."

Him knowing my name was only a small surprise. That had been happening more and more over the past few years, as my reputation grew. But him not being able to tell the living from the dead, that was a first, and I felt an immediate and powerful sympathy for the guy.

"Well, I know the feeling," I said. "What's your name?"

"My name?"

"Careful, you're doing the repeating thing again."

"Sorry. It's Perry, sir."

"Don't call me sir. Just Myron. It's good to meet you, Perry. Sorry if I scared you."

"It's quite all right, sir. Myron, I mean. It's not your fault."

"It's not my fault I scared you or not my fault that I'm scary?"

When he only stared at me, perplexed, I laughed. After a momentary pause when he seemed a bit surprised by my laughter, he even joined in a little. I pulled out the picture of Tony Neuman, the one I'd gotten upstairs, and put it on the counter.

"How about this guy? You know him?"

"Oh, yes. That's Mr. Neuman, sir."

"You're doing the sir thing again."

"Sorry, sir. Myron. Perhaps I could call you Mr. Vale? It would be easier for me."

"Well, if you insist," I said, with obviously fake irritation, but poor Perry didn't seem to catch the joke, reacting with alarm. "Relax, I'm just kidding you. Have you seen him today?"

"Today? Oh no, Mr. Vale. I have not seen Mr. Neuman today. I have not seen him in at least … Well, let me think. I suppose it's been about three weeks or so."

"Really? Three weeks? Are you sure?"

Perry opened his mouth to reply, then shut it, wincing as if he'd swallowed something sour. He glanced around nervously, and when he spoke to me again, dropped his voice to a whisper. "I'm sorry, Mr. Vale. I forgot myself for a moment. I'm really supposed to show more discretion about our residents. They would not appreciate it if they knew I was so forthcoming about their comings and goings."

I wanted to slap him. Instead I forced a bright smile and drummed my fingers on the counter.

"Discretion, huh?"

"That's right, sir. Mr. Vale."

"Did you know his wife was murdered?"

He gaped at me. "Murdered! But I—I just saw her come through her a while ago."

"She's a ghost now."

"Oh."

"Really is tough not being able to tell them apart, isn't it?" When he nodded glumly, I went on: "See, that's how it is for me, Perry. I'm investigating her murder. I'm trying to figure out who killed her, and it's tough. It's especially tough for me, not being able to tell the living apart from the ghosts. And it's even tougher when somebody who can help me decides to get in the way of a murder investigation for something as silly as discretion."

"Oh, well, I—"

"But that's fine," I said, talking right over him. "I understand that you have to do what you feel is right. I'll just call up Frank Warren of the NAANCP and tell him *exactly* how helpful you've been in the investigation."

He swallowed hard. The fear was back in full bloom, but this time I could see it wasn't about me. "You mean ... You mean the NAANCP is involved?"

"In a manner of speaking," I replied.

"I didn't—I didn't realize—"

"Well, now you do. You think you might want to be a little more helpful now?"

"Of course, sir. Mr. Vale, sir. I'll do—I'll do whatever I can to help."

"That's great. Frank will be glad to hear that. Let's get back to Neuman. You said you saw him three weeks ago. Was he with anyone or by himself?"

"I believe he was alone," Perry said.

"Has he been in a lot in the past three months?"

"No ... No, actually, I believe that's the only time I've seen him."

"Did he leave with anything?"

"I don't—I don't think so. He did seem upset when he left."

"Can you tell me for certain whether he was alive or dead?"

"Well ..."

"Did he open the front door? Did he use the elevator? Did other people look at him who you're pretty sure are alive? Did he ignore you?"

Perry's brow furrowed as he attempted to unwind my questions, and I thought I saw the faintest glimmer of a lightbulb going on behind his eyes. "Um, yes. Yes, to all of them. I guess now that you say that, it seems fairly likely he was alive and not, um, like me. I never really thought to piece it together like that. That's—that's helpful."

"Believe me," I said, "when you can't tell ghosts from the living, you start using every trick in the book to make it through the day. So let's talk about Tony and Karen's marriage. How was it? Did they have ups and downs?"

Clearly uncomfortable, Perry was hesitant to say anything that might be considered improper, but with lots of coaxing, I managed to pry a fair bit of information out of him. I learned that while Tony and Karen began their marriage seeming very much in love and inseparable at the hip, the last year or so saw them spending more time apart than together. Tony was often coming and going at odd hours. He would often be gone days at a time. When they did go out together toward the end, they did not look happy. In the last few weeks before she died, Karen often came home drunk and alone.

Perry said he couldn't be sure if anyone else had been into their condo, because since Perry's passing, nobody checked in at the desk. Though when I described Bernie, he agreed he'd seen him a few times, but not in the past month or so. I asked him about Karen's mother, sisters, friends, anyone else that seemed to belong with them, and he said he honestly didn't know.

I asked him to describe the people who'd left the building in the past few hours. He remembered three women and one man. One of them, a Mrs. Janet Habershaw, was an elderly woman who'd lived in the building for many years. The other two he didn't know, and his descriptions of them were fairly generic: a young woman with red hair, maybe in her twenties, and a chic-looking Hispanic man in jeans and a black turtleneck. There were no security cameras in the lobby.

When I thought I'd squeezed as much out of poor Perry as I possibly could without turning him into a sweaty mess, I asked him if there was anything else he could tell me that might help. He chewed at it his bottom lip.

"I suppose I should add one more thing," he said.

"Yes?"

"Well, this is awkward, really not my place at all—"

"Just spit it out, Perry."

"Um, well, I think there's a good chance Mr. Neuman was having an affair."

"What makes you say that?"

Perry adjusted his collar again. His face was so slick it looked as if he'd just come from a dip in the hot tub. "I can't say for certain, of course, but he took a call in the lobby on his cell phone. No one else was here. He stopped right next to my desk, leaning on it, so it was very hard not to hear. I wasn't trying to eavesdrop, you understand. But he was talking to a woman. He was making plans to meet. He said—he said he loved her, and some other, well, fairly explicit things. Things he would, um, do to her."

Now Perry had really piqued my interest. Since Perry was a ghost, and the lobby had been otherwise empty, Tony had felt comfortable talking as if he were alone. "What makes you so sure it wasn't Karen on the other end of the line?"

"Well, I thought so at first, but then he talked about her. He said Karen would be home soon, so they couldn't meet at the condo."

"I see."

A middle-age woman carrying grocery bags from Whole Foods, two kids in tow, entered the building. I waited until she'd gone up the elevator. Poor Perry, all twitchy and pale, resembled someone suffering from dysentery. It really was time to make my leave. "Thanks for all your help," I said. "If I have other questions, will I find you here?"

"Of course, Mr. Vale. It's my job."

"Uh-huh. Can I ask you something personal?"

He blinked a few times. "All right."

"Why are you here?"

"Why am I ..."

"Here, behind this desk. You could be doing anything. A lot of ghosts go on cruises. Take up a new hobby. But you, you're working as a clerk at a condo building. And the people living here, they can't even see you."

His face turned thoughtful. For the first time since I'd met him, he no longer seemed afraid. "Well, I ... I worked here before. Before I ... you know. And since the condo hasn't replaced me, I thought, well." He shrugged. "I guess I just liked doing something I was good at, you know. Something that gave me purpose. I'm—I'm not sure how to explain it."

His answer made me smile. I thought how long I'd struggled with those very issues and how easily Perry had summed up what probably should have been obvious to me in the beginning. I would have liked to believe that my current job was a little more meaningful than Perry's, but in the end, that was probably all in the eye of the beholder.

"Believe me," I said, "I understand perfectly."

IT WAS JUST after ten o'clock when I reached my house in Sellwood—a two-bedroom, turn-of-the century bungalow that Billie and I had bought shortly after I'd made detective. It had a den in addition to the bedrooms, on the back side of the house near the detached garage, and the light from the room formed yellow squares on our cracked driveway. The den was Billie's art studio, but the light didn't mean she was home. I left the light on in her studio all the time, as I did the porch light, since she couldn't turn it on.

The house hadn't looked like much when we'd first bought it, but we (or actually, mostly I) had dolled it up nicely: new slatted fencing surrounding the small porch, repairs to all the broken wooden siding and cracked concrete foundation, and a fresh coat of gray-blue paint with white trim. The house was deeper than it looked from the front and offered more than eighteen-hundred square feet of living space, more than enough for two people.

On the way over, the throbbing where I'd been knocked over the head had grown worse. I was exhausted but in too much pain to sleep. I was hungry but too nauseated to keep anything down. As I got out of the Prius, a sudden breeze shook loose the rain clinging to the oak above my head and splattered me in the face, making me even more cranky.

So I certainly wasn't in the mood for unexpected guests when I stepped into my dark living room.

"Billie?" I said, flicking on the light.

There was no Billie, but there was someone else. There on our futon by the wood stove, his black robes nearly touching our bamboo floor, was the same old priest who'd shown up in my life only one other time so far—at my bedside when I'd woken from my post-shooting coma five years earlier.

"She's not home," he said.

His hands were folded neatly in his lap. He looked just the same as the last time I'd seen him. Same wavy white hair. Same kindly smile. Same ridiculously big gold cross hanging around his neck. The house was still except for the steady tinkling of the faucet in the kitchen, just off to my right, a drip I'd been meaning to fix for months.

"What are you doing here?" I said.

"Waiting for you," he said.

"I didn't realize that trespassing was part of the Catholic faith."

He chuckled softly. "Oh, come now, Myron. I hardly think this qualifies as—"

"Just because you can sneak into the homes of other living people doesn't mean you should do it to me. I don't care how big your cross is, you should give me the same courtesy as you would have when you were alive."

"Myron—"

"Who are you, anyway?"

He leaned back in the futon and steepled his fingers, looking at me over the tops of them.

"A friend," he said.

"Funny way of showing it. You got a name?"

"Certainly."

I waited for him to tell me. He didn't.

"Am I supposed to guess?" I asked.

"My name's not relevant. What *is* relevant is why I'm here."

"Is that some kind of riddle?"

"I'm not even supposed to be talking to you, Myron. But I can tell you this much. I'm with the Department of Souls—one of the more, um, shadowy divisions. You have to understand. There are those who think of you as a threat. I'm your friend on the inside."

From everything I knew about the Department of Souls, they were the equivalent of the Department of Administrative Services— big, bureaucratic, and benign, charged with running everything from the Non-Corporeal Tourism Board to the Immortal Living Adjustment Bureau. "I didn't know the Department of Souls had any shadowy divisions."

"Well, that's because they're shadowy."

"Who thinks I'm a threat?"

"Let's just say there are certain people who don't like random elements they can't control."

"Come on, you've got do better than that."

He smoothed out his robe and stood. I felt a queasy trepidation. The last time he'd appeared, it was to tell me how hard my life was going to be. He stepped up to me, his robes swishing over the bamboo floor, and regarded me with his deep and soulful eyes. There was a musty smell to him that reminded me of old books. Then he did something unexpected. He reached out with his hands and squeezed my shoulders.

This wasn't a touch like the one I'd experienced not long ago with Karen Thorne. This was a genuine squeeze, indistinguishable from the real thing, ten fingers pressing into my flesh in ten different spots, no electric charge to go with it.

"You need to trust me," he said.

"How—how did you—" I stammered.

"Just like you do."

"You're alive."

"No. Like you, I have some gifts. This is one of them." He lowered his hands. "I'm here for one reason, Myron. I want you to drop this case."

"What?"

"You've done very well the past few years. The transition was difficult, as I warned you it would be, but you're in a good place now."

I snorted. "You call this a good place?"

"What I call it doesn't matter. But the truth remains that you've done good work. You've helped lots of people who couldn't have been helped without you. You've saved many lives."

"I think that's a bit of an exaggeration."

"Whoever saves a life," the priest said, raising his index finger to emphasize his point, "it is considered as if he saved an entire world."

"Uh-huh. Isn't that from the Talmud?"

He smiled. "Caught that, did you? Catholics have no monopoly on wisdom, as you well know."

"I wasn't sure Catholics had *any* wisdom."

The priest placed his hand over his heart. "Ouch. But a criticism that is somewhat justifiable, I'm afraid. I'll concede as much. But I don't have much time, so I best get back to the point. Drop this case, Myron. Let it go."

"Why?"

"Because it's not good for you. Because it could unravel everything you've built. Because if you become unraveled now, those people who see you as a threat may decide that you're just too much of a loose cannon."

"What does that mean? You're saying they'd kill me?"

"The only reason they *haven't* killed you is because they're more afraid of what you might become on the other side."

"And you know this because ... ?"

"It's not really relevant."

"Not relevant? We're talking about the guy who shot me in the face!"

"Things are not as straightforward as they seem."

"Oh, so you're saying he's *not* the one who shot me?"

He said nothing, nor did his eyes betray his thoughts. Obviously if I'd hoped to squeeze some information out of him, I was going to be disappointed. Standing so close to him was a bit unnerving, especially after his shoulder squeeze, so I moved away, toward our country-style kitchen with its white cabinets and shiny oak countertops. The bungalow had an open floor plan except for the narrow hall that led to the three bedrooms and the bathroom, so there was plenty of space for the both of us, but somehow I was still nagged with the feeling that I was locked in a prison cell with him.

"I think you should go," I said.

"You really should trust me on this," he insisted.

"You've given me no reason to trust you on anything."

"I guess you'll just have to take it on faith."

"That's a joke, right?"

He smiled a prim little smile. "There are more things in heaven and earth, Myron, than are dreamt of in your philosophy."

"Oh, now you're quoting Shakespeare?"

He nodded. "Wisdom wherever I can find it. You *are* a literate man, Myron, which I quite like. And it's also why I know you're smart enough not to let yourself become like poor Hamlet. The need for revenge is an inferno that consumes all, leaving nothing and no one unburned."

"Who said anything about revenge?" I shot back. "I just want to find the guy. Bring him to justice."

The priest raised his eyebrows.

"Really!" I said.

He bowed his head slightly. "I've said all I can, and now I must go. You would do well to heed my advice, Myron. Drop the case."

Having absorbed all I could of this nonsense, I pointed to the door. My head was pounding, I was feeling dizzy, and the wariness I'd felt toward the priest was quickly being subsumed by a growing anger. "I'm tired of your games and your riddles," I said. "If you're not going to be more forthcoming, I want you out of my house."

"I've been as forthcoming as I can be."

"Get out."

"Of course, of course," he said. With another slight bow of the head, he headed for the door, then stopped suddenly. "One thing, just out of curiosity. I noticed that your third bedroom is completely empty. Why is that?"

"None of your business," I said.

"It seems like it might be nice for a better studio, the windows being bigger. I was just wondering—"

"Get out," I said.

"Myron, please."

"Get out!"

I was screaming, and I felt the veins in my neck bulging. My heart was a booming beat in my ears. The priest nodded sadly, then, with steepled fingers, he turned to the door and walked straight through it.

Chapter 16

AFTER SENDING Frank Warren packing, I worked my weedy lawn furiously until the bright light of morning faded into a cloudy afternoon. A bank of menacing storm clouds gathered in the distance, blocking where I knew Mount Hood would show its craggy face on a clearer day. The temperature, already cool, dropped precipitously. When my anger had reached its peak, I tossed the hand shovel in the bucket and went in the house searching for Billie. Mrs. Halverson, the old woman who'd died the previous winter, was out in her white terrycloth robe and pink slippers at the mailbox, waiting for the postman. Unlike the old days, she couldn't get the mail anymore, but she was still there every day, rain or shine.

Even if she *could* get the mail, it wasn't her house. Her niece, who'd inherited the place, had sold it to the young man who worked for Intel. He often didn't collect his mail until the box was overflowing, a point of pride for him and a fact that I knew drove Mrs. Halverson crazy.

As soon as I entered, I heard the slap of paint hitting canvas coming from Billie's studio. I washed my hands in the kitchen, downed a cold drink of water, and gobbled up the rest of the ham sandwich I had left from yesterday, the whole while making as much noise as possible—banging cabinets, slamming the glass down, thunking the drawers closed with unnecessary force.

Billie didn't come out. I wandered to her doorway and found her intently painting a still life of a cow skull in the middle of a fruit basket. A pair of tangerines filled the eye sockets of the skull. She was barefoot and dressed in paint-spattered overalls and a red plaid shirt rolled up at the sleeves, her jet-black hair tied into a tight ponytail with a rubber band. She had a bit of black paint on the end of her nose.

Leaning against the doorframe, arms crossed, I watched her silently. I liked to watch her work, though I didn't take any pleasure in it now. The walls were filled with her recent paintings, mostly different kinds of animal skulls in slight variations of the same still life. When Alesha stopped by shortly after Billie and I returned to the house, she saw nothing but blank canvases hanging on the walls—I put a new sheet on Billie's easel when she said she was done—and a matching still life that consisted of a small white table covered with a white tablecloth and nothing else.

"Good weeding?" Billie said finally.

"Just swell," I said.

She looked at me, paintbrush paused mid-stroke. "Something wrong?" she asked.

"No. Why?"

"You just sound … on edge."

I shrugged.

"You're scowling," she added.

"No, I'm not."

"You're most definitely scowling."

I shrugged again. She studied me with the same intense focus she applied to her paintings, then turned back to her work. I watched a while longer, the knot in my stomach growing, then left her alone. I banged around the kitchen some more, not sure what I was looking for, then settled on a bottle of Rolling Rock beer I'd hidden in the refrigerator among the salad dressing. I plopped myself on the futon and turned on the television with the remote. I drank a few sips, channel surfing, not really registering what I was seeing, waiting for Billie to show up and see me with the beer. She didn't. Growing ever restless, I took my beer and headed for the bedroom—and stopped at the spare bedroom door, the one we always kept closed. I touched the handle, hesitating, my pulse quickening.

What the hell. I opened the door. Stale, musty air wafted out to greet me. The room was empty except for the bamboo flooring and the white walls, motes of dust floating in the shafts of pale afternoon light slanting through the curtainless windows. The light, gray and colorless, matched my mood.

I stood in the doorway, listening. The house was silent. I no longer heard Billie's paintbrush. Good.

Beer in hand, I went to the window. Mrs. Halverson was still at the mailbox, waiting. A couple of young men in deerskin hats and moccasins, rifle muskets slung over their shoulders, were walking down the far street. Ghosts or simply a costume party? Who knew. I sat along the far wall, knees bent in front of me, my free hand flat on the floor. The bamboo felt gritty with dust. The room had no overhead light, nor did any of the rooms in the old house, but I wouldn't have turned it on even if I could. I wanted to sit there until the darkness came—or until Billie did. It was a toss-up which would come first.

Billie did, and it didn't take long. I heard the creak of her footsteps, a sound that never ceased to amaze me because I knew it was all in my own mind, and yet there was no discernable difference to me between the creak of her footsteps now and the creak of her footsteps when she'd been alive. None. Not one bit of difference, and it was a sound I knew well.

She appeared in the doorway half in silhouette, lit by the light in the hall behind her. Now it was she who had her arms crossed over her chest, the paintbrush nowhere to be found. Shadows masked her face, but I could still pick out the dark deep curve of her frown.

"I thought we agreed," she said tersely, "that we weren't going to go in here."

I took a sip of my beer and balanced it on my stomach, feeling the coldness of the bottle through my thin cotton T-shirt.

"Drinking too?" she said.

"It's just a beer," I said.

"You want to tell me what this is about?"

I took another drink, made her wait. I'd had enough alcohol now that I felt the warmth of it spreading into my neck and face.

"Your friend came by," I said.

"What?"

"Frank Warren."

"Oh."

I glared at her. "Oh."

"So that's what you're mad about?"

"I'm not mad."

"You sound mad."

"I'm not mad, *damn it.*"

She stared at me. I couldn't see her face well enough to know if she was wearing that smug expression of hers, the one she got when she knew perfectly well what I was doing and why, the eyes narrowing, the jaw tight, the lips a small firm line, but I *imagined* she was wearing it. I imagined all the self-righteousness and condescension and irritation, and imagining it somehow made her expression all the more intolerable.

"I just don't appreciate you meddling," I said.

"Oh, I'm meddling?"

"You know exactly what you were doing. You were telling me to get off my ass and get a job."

She sighed. "Myron, I just bumped into Frank the other day at a meeting. He was the one who brought up the idea of you working for them. He asked how receptive I thought you would be to the idea. I told him I didn't know but it wouldn't hurt to try. That's all I did."

"Right," I said.

"I'm serious. Sorry if even that was too much. I'm just trying to help you."

"I don't need your help."

"Myron, if you're not going to be a detective, then you should at least be *something*."

"Oh, thank you for those words of wisdom. You get that from Dr. Phil?"

"Myron—"

"Why can't you just let me be?"

"Because I don't want to watch you destroy yourself."

I couldn't think of a retort to this, so I took another drink. She tapped her foot, waiting me out, and I responded by waiting *her* out.

"I see you're not interested in having an adult conversation right now," she said. "That's fine. That's your right. When you really want to talk, come find me."

She started to leave, all smug and holier-than-though, but I wasn't going to let her go like that.

"Have you ever wondered?" I said idly.

"What?"

"About, you know, the baby."

She became absolutely still. This was akin to throwing a hand grenade into a weapons locker. I knew exactly what I was doing and I didn't care.

"Don't," she said softly.

"You ever wonder if it's out there, somewhere? I keep wondering if I'll see it someday."

"Why are you doing this?"

"How many weeks was it?" I continued, undaunted by the sound of her sniffling. "Ten? Something like that, right. That's about when you lost it."

"Myron, please."

"I mean, the question is whether a fetus gets to become a ghost, right? I don't know. I can't say I've ever seen one. But I've wondered. When does a human being develop enough in the womb that it gets a soul? That's what we're talking about, right? I mean, I've never liked the term, but I don't know what else to use. Something survives beyond death. But what if you're never born?"

She was crying. I could barely see her in the poor light, but the sniffling was unmistakable. Since Billie almost never cried, the tears were all the more shocking, but I wasn't about to show sympathy. I took another swig of my beer. She made no move to wipe away the tears. I heard the squeak of bus brakes one street over.

"Satisfied?" she asked.

I shrugged.

"Because I assume this is what you wanted," she said. "You wanted me to cry. Congratulations. You win."

"Oh, Jesus," I said.

"First place, Myron Vale."

"Stop."

"You know how much I wanted a baby," she said, her voice growing louder and more shrill. "I wanted one just as much as you. I'm sorry I couldn't give you one. I'm sorry my body was broken."

"Now you're just being melodramatic," I said.

"Oh, *I'm* being melodramatic? You're the one who's so pissed at me for trying to do something to help you that you've staged this little drunken sit-in in the nursery!"

"I'm not drunk," I said.

"And now I *can't* conceive, Myron. Do you understand how hard that is? I can never have a child. *Never.*"

"What about when you could?" I shot back.

"What?"

We engaged in a staring contest, the seconds pounding away like our beating hearts. All that resentment and anger mixed with the alcohol to form a strange cocktail, one that was pushing me to cross lines I'd so far been unwilling to cross. I should have let it go, but I couldn't stop myself. These feelings had been brewing between us since she'd returned, and it was time to let them out. It was *time.*

"After the miscarriage," I said. "That next year. We could have tried again."

"I don't believe this," she said.

"You barely even touched me. When I got into bed, you—you rolled the other way."

"That's not true."

"It is true. It is!"

"I was in a bad place," she insisted. "I wasn't ready yet. I wasn't ready."

"For a whole year?"

She shifted a little, more into the light, and now I could see her face. She was no longer crying, but the earlier tears still clung to her face like frozen dewdrops. "I don't understand why you have to punish me like this."

"I'm not punishing you," I said. "I'm just trying to understand why we didn't try again."

"I was afraid," she said. "I was afraid of losing the baby again. I was—"

"But at least we would have tried!"

"I was afraid of losing you, too."

"What?"

"I wouldn't be able to take care of the baby. I wouldn't be able to provide for it." She was digging her hands into her overalls, her fingers curling and pinching like claws. When she spoke, there was a strange halting brittleness in her voice. "You were a cop. You could have died. You—you almost did. What would I do? I've—I've never been very good at making money. I was afraid."

"You know I never asked you to," I said, and I felt my anger slipping away. In the end, no matter how mad I was at Billie, my empathy for her always got the upper hand. "And I always had a good life-insurance policy, you know that. You wouldn't have had to work a day in your life. Both you and the baby would have been fine."

She shook her head violently. "It's not just the money. I just didn't … didn't know if I was capable."

"Capable of what?"

"It doesn't matter. It doesn't matter anymore."

"Damn it, Billie! It matters to me. Capable of what? Of being a good mother?"

"No," she said.

"Then what? Capable of bringing the child to term? Capable of surviving another miscarriage? Capable of being a good Scrabble player? Give me something! Anything!"

"Capable of being the kind of woman you wanted me to be!" she shouted.

In the empty room, her words resounded off the walls like the shot of a cannon. She was breathing hard, and so was I. The most shocking thing about what she'd said was that she hadn't said *mother,* but *woman.* I didn't know what to say.

"Billie," I said.

"I'm done with this," she said, and marched away.

I stayed there on the floor in the empty room. I stayed there a long time, and I didn't drink another drop of my beer. When I came out, to find her, to talk to her, to do something, anything, to make amends, she was gone.

I didn't see her again for nearly three months.

Chapter 17

EARLY FRIDAY MORNING, two things hadn't changed from the previous night. When I woke to the squeal of the garbage-truck brakes, having fallen asleep on the futon watching Charlie Rose, the back of my head still felt as if it had been the target of a drone missile. And my lovely wife, who'd taken off in a huff at Bernie Thorne's office, was still missing.

I hadn't closed the curtains, and the early-morning light, as weak as it was, stabbed at my eyes. The crick in my neck hurt almost as much as the throbbing in my head. It was going to be a glorious day. The only good thing about it so far was that no smug priest was standing in the room, waiting to deliver some smug, cryptic warning.

A cup of instant coffee, a hot shower, and a couple of Aleve later, I was starting to feel almost human. I was also pissed as hell. After five years, I'd finally gotten a lead on the man who'd shot me in the head, and everybody wanted me to let it go. I wasn't about to let it go. I was going to get some answers.

The problem was, I still didn't have much to go on. Somebody didn't like me nosing around Karen's condo, even though the place was so sterile it made hotel rooms seem cluttered. Why?

I needed to know more about Tony, but so far I hadn't turned up much. Somebody had to know something about him, and I decided the two sisters might be a good place to start, since Karen said they really didn't care for the guy. Maybe they knew something about him that Karen didn't. There was also the younger brother. He was out of town, but he might have had a perspective his sisters didn't.

I called Travis, the son, first, just because it was still a bit early and Travis was at Brown in Rhode Island, on East Coast time. He answered on the first ring, croaking out a hello, still sounding like I'd woken him even though it was closing in on noon there. When I asked him about Tony, he said he'd never met the dude and hadn't even been back to Portland since Karen's funeral, three months earlier, and that was the first time he'd seen his sisters or his dad in a year. When I asked him if he had any reason to think someone might want to kill his sister, he told me maybe it was because she was a total bitch and hung up. Nice kid.

Beth, the oldest child, had three numbers, a landline at her house in Lake Oswego, another landline at her cabin near Mount Hood, and a cell phone. She didn't answer any of them. I left messages, explaining that I was a private investigator looking into Karen's death and that I wanted to talk to her.

Janice, the second youngest daughter, answered her house's landline on the first ring.

"Hello?" she said.

Her voice sounded much like Karen's, but wearier. I heard children shouting gleefully in the background.

"Is this Janice Charlton?" I asked.

"Yes," she said, now sounding both weary and suspicious.

"Janice, my name is Myron Vale—"

"Hold on," she said.

She cupped her hand over the receiver, and I heard her yell at her kids. When she came back, there were no more shouting kids.

"Sorry about that," she said. "Who are you now?"

"Myron Vale, ma'am. I'm a private investigator, and I'm looking into your sister's death."

There was a pause. The line had a faint background hum. When she spoke again, there was a nervousness that wasn't there before.

"Why?" she asked.

"There are certain suspicious details that raise questions."

"Who hired you?"

"Your father."

"My *father*? I don't believe this."

"I was wondering if you might have a few minutes to answer some—"

"Can't he just leave the whole thing alone?" Janice snapped. "Karen had a drinking problem. We're all sad she's gone, but ... Wait a minute, what kind of suspicious details? What did my father tell you? He thinks somebody *killed* her?"

"Well—"

"Who?"

"It's a bit early to—"

"Tony? He probably thinks it was Tony, right?"

"Right now, I'm just trying to narrow down the—"

"Forget it," she said. "I don't want to know. I don't want to know about any of it. Look, I've got to go. I've got to get my kids to school. I really don't want to dredge this whole thing up. I'm still trying to heal, okay? I don't have anything to offer anyway. Just leave me out of this."

"Janice—"

She hung up. There was a frantic edge to her voice that raised all sorts of alarm bells in my mind. I called her again, but she didn't answer. Vancouver was a good thirty minutes away from my house, on the other side of the Columbia River, and there was no guarantee she would return to her house after dropping off her kids. But I didn't have any better leads, so I grabbed a bagel and hopped in the Prius. After digging through the various maps I kept in my glove compartment, I found the one for Vancouver and located Janice's house. Billie was always pestering me to get a smart phone with GPS, but I didn't want a phone smarter than me.

The sky was gunmetal gray, and the moisture was thick enough in the air that I had to turn on the windshield wipers a few times. With the early-morning traffic, it took almost twenty minutes just to get downtown. I was going north over the Interstate Bridge, entering Vancouver, when I become suspicious of an all-black Ford Explorer two cars back. Didn't I see that one behind me near my house?

There was a Chevron station a few minutes over the bridge, and I stopped there to refuel, even though my Prius's tiny tank was nearly full. I got out to wash the windshield, and sure enough, the black Ford Explorer pulled into the Denny's parking lot across the street, easing into a spot facing me.

I glanced at it without making it obvious I was looking. It was a late-nineties model, no hubcaps, the sideboards caked with months of dirt. The Explorer also had slightly tinted windshield, so I couldn't see who was inside, but the driver's hairy arm was sticking out of the open driver's-side window. I asked the gas-station attendant, a girl with three nose studs and painted-on eyebrows, if the bathroom was in the back.

With practiced boredom, she handed me a key attached to piece of driftwood. Just in case the obscenely large wood wasn't enough to keep someone from walking off with the key, the driftwood had also been painted pink.

Making sure to hold the key on the side facing the Explorer, so it was obvious what I was doing, I took my time sauntering behind the building. There was a Honda car lot right next door. Leaving the key on the curb near the bathroom, I crouched low and ran behind a row of Honda Pilots. I was so intent on not being seen by whoever was in the Explorer across the street that I nearly ran headlong into a young Asian couple who were peering into the driver's-side windows of one of the Pilots, hands cupped around their eyes to block the sun's glare.

"Excuse me, sorry," I said, twisting to avoid them.

Both the man and the woman gaped at me with alarm, then dove into the Pilot—straight through the glass and metal. Nice. I'd managed to scare another couple of friendly neighborhood ghosts. I kept running, to the far end of the lot, far beyond where the occupants of the Explorer should have been looking, then timed my dash across the street to their side when a semi was blocking their line of sight.

Winded, shirt sticking to my sweaty back, I approached the Ford Explorer from behind and at an angle, hopefully out of view of their mirrors. My jacket was unzipped, my Glock within easy reach. I smelled frying bacon on the cool breeze. A large family was heading into the restaurant. An old man in red suspenders was trying to hand out Gideon Bibles at the door, but neither the adults nor the children even glanced at him. It was hard to say whether he was a ghost or not, though in a sense, he was invisible either way.

The Explorer was burning oil, the exhaust filling the air with the stench of it. The driver, whose arm was hanging out the window, was holding a smoldering cigarette. It was a big, muscular arm, light brown skin, a gaudy gold watch on the wrist, a tattoo of intertwined snakes on his forearm. They were listening to Latin music with a good beat, which helped cover the sound of my footsteps.

I took out my phone and turned on the camera. My other hand was perched on the zipper of my jacket, ready to go for the Glock. When I stepped in front of the driver's-side window, I held the phone aloft.

It took a second before the two men in the car, both Hispanic, turned to look at me.

"Say cheese," I said, and snapped the picture.

They stared, dumbfounded, so I went ahead and snapped another one, making sure the guy in the passenger seat was fully in view. I was nothing if not thorough. They were both young and lean, with their short black hair slicked straight back, though the driver was dressed in a sleeveless white T-shirt with a low-cut neck that showed off all his gold chains and his many tattoos, whereas the guy in the passenger seat was decked out business casual, a stylish blue golf shirt and tan slacks, no tattoos or chains but instead a small diamond in his left ear.

"Shit," the driver said, fumbling for the gearshift. His Mexican accent was pretty clear, even in that one word.

"Why are you following me?" I asked. I sounded remarkably calm for how hard my heart was beating.

"Go, go!" the passenger cried, and that was two for two with the Mexican accents. "Get out of here!"

"Shit, shit," the driver said, finally managing to get the car in gear.

"Did you guys jump me at the condo last night?" I said.

The Explorer squealed out of the parking spot in reverse, a cloud of exhaust choking the air and stinging my eyes. When he was shifting gears, I snapped a picture of the license plate. He roared out of the parking lot, banging onto the street without stopping, forcing a red Volvo to swerve, horn blaring, into the far lane. The Explorer raced down the road and screeched around the corner, out of my sight, the whole incident lasting less than a minute from when I'd taken their first picture.

I texted the license plate to Alesha, asking if she could ID it for me, then waited a minute to see if the Explorer would return. When it didn't, I started for my Prius, then stopped when I saw how the old man with the Gideon Bibles was sitting cross-legged on the ground, head bowed in defeat, a stack of pint-size green Bibles next to him on the ground.

There was nobody coming or going from the restaurant. I put my phone in my jacket and walked over to him. He looked up at me, his face a minefield of moles and scars, one of his eyes whitened by cataracts. I reached for the top Bible, and sure, enough, my hand passed right through it.

"Can I ask you something?" I said.

His mouth fell open. He didn't have any teeth.

"Don't freak out," I said.

"You—you can see me."

"I told you not to freak out. I just have to know. Do you still believe?" And when he blinked his wizened eyes, I added, "You know, do you believe in God? Now that you've crossed over. You're trying to hand out these Bibles to people who couldn't care less, who can't even see you. Do you still believe?"

"More than ever," he said, a warble in his hoarse voice.

"Have you met him? God, I mean?"

"Nobody—nobody has. This is just purgatory, is all. Heaven is still real."

"How can it be purgatory if nobody leaves?"

"Heaven is real," he insisted.

"Okay."

"Can you see all ghosts?"

"Something like that. But you still think God's real, huh? Even after dying and waking up to this?"

He nodded. Two men in business suits, one carrying a briefcase, exited the restaurant. Both looked at me, but not the old man. I waited until they'd gone a good ways toward their car before speaking to the old man again.

"Why?" I asked. "Why do you believe in him if you've never met him?"

He thought about it a moment. "Well, I hadn't met him when I was alive either. I believed then. It just took a little faith. Why should I stop now? What if—what if this is just one more test?"

The old man had me there. I may not have seen a lot of logic in it, but using logic with him wouldn't do me any good. If people wanted to turn the crappy things that happened to them into heroic challenges to their beliefs, rather than as evidence that maybe their beliefs were just as crappy, there was nothing anyone could do to dissuade them. Especially if even death couldn't do the trick.

"Good luck with the Bibles," I said.

IT WAS PRETTY obvious that Janice Charlton was not happy to see me. I deduced this fact by the scowl on her face when I said who I was.

"I told you on the phone I didn't have anything more to say," she said.

We were standing on the arched portico of her stately brick house, the kind of residence with its perky white shutters and neatly trimmed boxwood bushes lining the drive that just shouted that a banker lived inside. Her face was flushed pink and coated with a sheen of sweat, her brown hair tied into a ponytail with a pink band that matched her leotard and her wristbands. The earbuds in her hand, attached to the iPod fastened to her arm, were still playing the steady beat of some rock song.

Other than the hair color, she looked remarkably like Karen, except that she was probably twenty or thirty pounds heavier. It wasn't a lot of weight, a tad more in the hips, a fair amount in the breasts, a stomach that bulged a bit, and might have been barely noticeable if she hadn't been wearing a leotard a size too small. There was also a certain sexuality that oozed from her, straining to get out just as her body was straining to get out of that leotard.

"I just want a few minutes of your time," I said.

She shook her head. "I'm sorry, but this whole thing has just been so—"

"How well did you know Tony?"

She looked, for just a second, like a woman who'd been caught eating Ben and Jerry's ice cream in the car outside a Weight Watcher's meeting. One of the things I'd learned as a detective early on was that if you asked questions quickly, when people weren't expecting them, you could often see reactions in their faces that would tell you more than their words ever would. When she'd suggested on the phone that her father might think Tony was behind Karen's death, there was a certain dismissiveness to her tone that didn't match up with the low opinion Karen said both her sisters had of him.

"Not—not well," she said. "Why?"

I'd gotten far more out of her than I'd even been expecting, but I didn't yet know what it meant. Rather than admit my ignorance, I decided to see if I could bluff her into telling me more than she wanted.

"Come on, Janice," I said, dropping my voice to a conspiratorial whisper, "you know what was going on."

"I don't know what you're talking about," she said, her voice even more of a whisper than mine.

"You don't? That's not what I heard."

"You—you better leave."

"Okay," I said, with a shrug. "I'm just doing this to help Karen. I hope you feel good about doing your part."

I started to turn away. It was all vague innuendo at this point, but Janice started to cry before I'd even taken a step. They were big rolling tears, and like thunder following lightning, she followed them with a childlike sob. She didn't even build up to it, just let it all out at full force.

"Whoa," I said, "it's all right."

"I didn't—I didn't mean for it to happen," she blubbered.

"I know you didn't."

"It was just one night."

"I know."

"I wanted—I wanted to tell her. I just … I just couldn't …"

"It's okay," I said.

She looked like she desperately wanted to be comforted, a pat on the shoulder, a gentle hug, but since we were strangers, all I could offer her was a sympathetic face. When she'd calmed down just a bit, I asked if I could come in and she nodded, leading me into a cozy entryway with gray stone flooring. Still sniffling but no longer sobbing, she directed me through open French doors to a den lined with teak bookshelves and a baby grand piano in the far corner. The room smelled of leather and old books. It was dim but cozy, lit by a Tiffany lamp between the suede couch and loveseat. A blue plastic dinosaur lay on its side in the middle of the Oriental rug, and Janice picked it up on her way.

I didn't see her until I was fully in the room, but an old Hispanic housekeeper in a white uniform was cleaning a bookcase with a white feather duster. She was working the same spot, a corner of the trim, so slowly that for a moment I didn't even think she was moving.

"Your housekeeper over there is certainly thorough," I whispered to Janice, nodding in the old woman's direction. My thought was that she wouldn't want to talk around the housekeeper and would suggest we move to another room.

Janice glanced where I was looking, then back at me with raised eyebrows. "What housekeeper?"

"Ah," I said, realizing that, once again, my curse had foiled me.

"Is that some kind of joke?"

"Nope, just meant that whoever does your dusting of that bookcase is very thorough. It looks nice. Figured it has to be a housekeeper."

She stared blankly at me. This was going swimmingly. I was kind of hoping she'd offer me something to drink, but instead she just stood there.

"I don't understand," she said.

"It's okay, I don't either. Can we sit down?"

"Does my father know?"

"About the affair? No."

"Oh, please don't call it that," she said, tearing up again. "It wasn't an affair. It was … It was stupid, was what it was. God, Michael doesn't know, does he? It would destroy him if found out. Absolutely *destroy* him."

"No, no," I said, figuring Michael was her husband. I went ahead and took a seat on the loveseat, figuring she'd take the hint and sit on the couch. She didn't, opting to stand there clutching that toy dinosaur against her chest. "Nobody knows but me."

"How did you find out?"

"I'd rather not say."

"I don't understand! I didn't tell *anyone*, and it's been killing me."

"I don't think anyone else knows," I reassured her. "Remember, I'm a detective. Sometimes I detect things."

"Please don't tell anyone! I feel so terrible as it is, and I'm never going to do anything like it again!"

"Why would I tell anyone? People make mistakes. All I want is your help finding out who killed your sister. I know you want to be helpful, right?"

I motioned to the couch. This time, she took the hint, moving with all the haste of a chastened toddler, still clinging to the dinosaur. I caught the smell of her sweat, and something else, an apricot-scented perfume or deodorant. The old Mexican housekeeper still hadn't finished dusting the same spot. I wondered how many years she'd been working at it.

"I'll do anything," she said.

"Great," I said, "tell me what you know about Tony. Anything at this point could be helpful. Do you know much about how he made his money?"

"I really didn't plan it, you know," she said, dropping her gaze to the floor. "He stopped by to drop off a Crock-Pot my sister had borrowed for a dinner. I invited him in. We—we had a drink. Kids were at school. Michael was at work. I was complaining about how hectic my life was. I think—I think I started crying. He gave me a hug. One thing led to another."

"Yes," I said, "I know you didn't—"

"I just get so lonely sometimes. I love Michael! I do. It's just, he works a lot of hours. And the kids—they're so hard. I love them, I do, I love them so much."

"Janice—"

"I think I was just feeling a little sorry for myself, that's all. Tony has such a way about him. The way he looks at you. He really makes you feel like you're the only one in the room."

"We all do things we—"

"I just wanted to feel like a woman again, you know? Not a mother or a wife, but a *woman*. One who was sexy and confident and could really turn the heads of any man in the room. I just wanted to be that Janice again. Just for a little while."

It didn't seem to matter that I was in the room at all, since most of her confession was directed at the floor. It was interesting in an Ann Landers sort of way, but I wasn't learning a whole lot about Tony except that a lonely, rich housewife had found him sexy and available at exactly the right time. The problem was, I didn't want to seem insensitive either.

"Don't beat yourself up too much," I said. "So you succumbed to temptation once. It's not the end of the world. And you're definitely an attractive woman. You have nothing to worry about there."

Her face brightened a little. "Really?"

"Really. And if it really bothers you, maybe you should tell your husband."

"Oh no, I couldn't."

"He might surprise you."

"No, no. Michael is ... no. Just no."

"Sometimes a little honesty can bring two people closer. And if you don't ever tell him what happened, how can he ever forgive you? You're not even giving him a chance."

"I don't know," she said, shaking her head.

"Well, it's something to think about, anyway. Listen, can you tell me anything about Tony that I might not know? I have reason to think he might have killed her for her inheritance, because he didn't know Karen had changed her will. She made sure he didn't get much."

She looked at me with surprise, the self-pity gone. "Who told you that Karen changed her will? My father?"

"Something like that."

"He wouldn't know anything," she said bitterly. "He hardly knew her. He hardly knows any of us."

"Let's just say it's true. Is there anything Tony did that would make you think he was capable of murder?"

"No! He was very suave and gentle. I've never even seen him raise his voice. Kill somebody? No way."

I thought about the crazed madman who'd shot me. That guy had yelled plenty, though it now seemed pretty clear that it was all an act. *Why* he'd been acting that way in a Starbucks coffee shop, and for what purpose, was more inexplicable than ever to me. He must have really been in dire straits to stoop to armed robbery. Janice was watching me expectantly, turning over the dinosaur in her hands. The Mexican housekeeper had now shifted her dusting three inches to the left.

"But he did disappear after her death," I said. "Didn't that make you suspicious?"

"Well ... I figured, you know, he just needed to grieve on his own. It wasn't like he disappeared because the police were asking a bunch of questions or anything. And after our ... Well, I guess I was kind of relieved he left town. I thought that might be part of it, too, honestly. That maybe he was kind of ashamed like I was and it was better not to be around temptation again."

"Did he ever seem like he was in trouble? Like he needed money real quick?"

She responded with a dismissive snort. "Tony always had plenty of money. He was always picking up the check when we went out to eat. Buying everybody little gifts. He never went to someone's house without giving them a fifty-dollar bottle of wine."

"You sure it wasn't just an act?"

"No!"

"He never asked you for money?"

"Never! I always got the feeling that if *I* needed money, he'd be there for me. He was really generous. He was always telling me about ..." She trailed off, her face troubled.

"About what?" I pressed.

"I don't know. I mean, he never asked for money, not like a loan or anything like that. But he was always telling me about different investment opportunities, different stocks that could make Michael and me rich. I offered to invest a thousand dollars, but he said we would need at least a hundred thousand for these kinds of trades. He said it was the only way to make money."

"I see," I said.

"So you think he was just going to take the money for himself? Not invest it or anything?"

"I don't know. But let me ask you something else that might seem a little out of the blue. Did he ever talk about dealing with any Mexicans around Portland? Especially street-gang types?"

"Mexicans? No, not that I can think of. Why?"

"Not sure yet. Did he—"

"Oh, wait," Janice said, "wait a minute. There was one time when he was over when he got a call on the cell. I couldn't make out the other person, but it did sound like they had an accent. Could have been a Mexican accent. The guy seemed pretty upset. When Tony got off the phone, I asked him what that was all about, and he just frowned and said it was just a business associate who was unhappy. I asked him why, but he told me it was nothing." She looked at me. "It was probably nothing, right?"

"Hard to say. Was this just before Karen died?"

"I guess. A month or so before."

"And he was over here at the house?"

"Yeah."

"Just the two of you?"

She started to answer, then realized what I was really getting at and blushed.

"So it was more than once, wasn't it?" I prodded her.

"It might have been a few times," she said in a quiet voice.

"Two or three times a week?"

Her blush deepened to a nice shade of scarlet. "Not that much. More than once, but not that much."

"It's okay," I said. "I'm not here to judge."

"I'm a terrible person."

I smiled. "Well, so am I. Join the club."

"I did break it off. I really did."

"I know," I said, though I really didn't. "Look, is there anything else you can tell me that can help?"

"I don't know. I can't think of anything."

"Did you get along well with Karen?"

"Pretty well. Why?"

"Just asking. You haven't visited her condo since she died, have you?"

She shook her head. "No. Dad took care of that stuff. I didn't want ... Wait a minute. You don't think *I* had anything to do with her death, do you?"

"I'm just asking questions, Janice."

"Well, I don't! That's ridiculous. I don't know why anybody would want to kill Karen. She was kind of a lush, but she was a sweet person. A little naive, maybe, but very sweet. I still can't believe Tony would ever do such a thing. Are you really sure it was murder?"

"I'm not sure of anything right now," I said. "That's why I'm just fishing around with all these questions. Speaking of that, I better get going. I've taken enough of your time."

I stood. She stood, too, looking even more anxious than ever. The sweat and tears on her face had dried, leaving track marks in their wake. Since I'd entered, the Mexican housekeeper had moved approximately six inches to the left. Janice followed me to the door right on my elbow, repeatedly glancing at my face, still clutching that dinosaur. When we reached the door, she grabbed the handle and started to open it, then paused, looking at me. We were only inches apart, close enough that I once again caught a whiff of her apricot-scented perfume.

"You're not going to tell anyone, are you?" she asked.

"No."

"Because, you know, if you wanted money ..."

"That's not necessary."

"Or—or something else ..."

Her eyes flitted from my face to my crotch and back again. I couldn't believe it. After just telling me how she would never do anything like what she did with Tony again, here she was offering to bribe me with sexual favors to keep me quiet. There was also a subtle change to the way she carried herself. The way she moved, the tiny shifts of her hips and breasts, there was a lot of sexuality bundled behind all that spandex. I thought about telling her to go take a cold shower, but there was a fragility to her that made me think this kind of rejection might make her crumble. She might crumble anyway as soon as I was out the door, but I wasn't going to deliberately contribute to it.

At least not until I found out for sure whether she had anything to do with Karen's death.

"Your secret is completely safe with me," I said. I took out one of my cards and handed it to her. "Call me if you think of anything else that could help."

Chapter 18

IT HAD SEEMED like a good idea when Alesha invited me, but I'd only taken a few steps through the door into the little ranch house in Tigard when I realized it was a mistake. The living room was packed elbow to elbow, filled with the hubbub of conversation and laughter, way too much noise and stimulation for my shaky state of mind. With Billie gone a little over month, the loneliness had finally gotten to me. I'd thought, stupidly, that a brief jaunt to a cop's retirement party might cure me of some of my blues.

"Wow, a bit crowded," I said.

Alesha, shaking the water off her umbrella on the little concrete porch outside the door, gave me one of her patented you're-stupider-than-I-thought expressions. "Crowded? What are you talking about? We're one of the first ones here."

That's when I knew the party wasn't just a mistake, but a big mistake. Surveying the sunken living room and the adjoining dining-room area, I counted at least twenty people—mostly men, half in police uniform, most of them gray-haired and wrinkled but a fair range of other ages as well. Based on the noise coming from the kitchen and down the hall, there were probably that many and more spread throughout the rest of the house. There was so much raucous noise that I could barely make out the rain pelting the roof, and it was a hell of a downpour, even by Oregon standards.

It was also hot and stuffy, the air laced with plenty of sweat, perfume, and cologne, and that was always the hardest part of my condition for me to grasp. I could understand seeing ghosts, but *smelling* them? It may have made sense on some weird logical level—there was no reason ghosts could be detected merely by one sense, the eyes, and not by others—but it was still jarring.

Alesha placed the umbrella in the large clay pot next to the door, along with three other umbrellas. Three umbrellas? Did that mean that the vast majority of the people in the room were ghosts?

Still waiting for my reply, Alesha blinked her eyelashes at me—long and dark and luxurious eyelashes. The eyelashes thing was something new for Alesha the past few weeks, along with a touch of silver eyeliner and lavender lipstick, and it was amazing what just a little bit of makeup did for her face. She was already an attractive woman, with those lean features and arresting eyes, but there were times when it seemed like she was trying hard *not* to be feminine, like she wanted to be seen as just another one of the boys, and when she actually played up her feminine side rather than hiding it, she really was stunningly beautiful.

The designer jeans, calf-high black boots, and low-cut purple cashmere sweater also helped her cause.

"Oh," I said, "I just, well—"

"Alesha! Myron!"

The cop's wife, Loraine, bellowed our names across the room, saving me from having to come up with a reason for my complaint. She was short and stout, like her husband Sam, but unlike her husband, she'd taken to dying her hair bright orange and dressing herself in African-style clothing. She bounded over to us with irrepressible enthusiasm, beads rattling, arms thrown wide, her smile so wide and genuine that it was hard not to smile a little in return. It was only up close that the faint webs of wrinkles around her eyes and on her cheeks gave away her age.

"Oh *gosh,* I'm so glad you both could come," she said, hugging Alesha so hard she actually looked at me with alarm. "Sammy will be so glad!"

"Where is Sam anyway?" I asked. "Is he hiding in some back room playing poker?"

Loraine eyed me strangely, then laughed and punched me on the shoulder. It was no dainty punch. Even through the thick sleeve of my leather jacket, her fist stung. "Myron, you're such a kidder! You know full well he's standing right over there. Go talk to him! He was really hoping you'd come."

She gave me a gentle push into the living room, a room decorated with weavings and paintings of much the same style as her dress. Two old cops in uniforms that had gone out of style decades ago parted to let me pass, and that's when I saw Sam standing by the gas fireplace, a can of Bud Light in hand.

I was shocked by his appearance. Gone was the heavy guy with the big beer gut, the ruddy complexion, and the broad frame to match his wife's. In his place was a rail-thin fellow with a spindly neck and pale, sallow cheeks. I hadn't seen him since he'd visited me in the hospital, almost two years previously, but it looked like he'd aged ten years in that time. Blond hair had gone white. Guys on the force used to jokingly call him Sam Clemens, Mark Twain's real name, because of Sam's bushy mustache and eyebrows, plus his penchant for wry observations about everyday life. But our Sam's heaviness always meant the nickname didn't completely fit. It was only now that he more closely looked the part.

He was talking to a short, stocky man I didn't recognize, one who looked much like the old Sam, though sans mustache. It was like a before and after shot. As I approached, Sam nodded at me. They were engaged in an animated conversation about the upcoming midterm election, one sipping beer whenever the other was talking. Sam, who loved politics almost as much as he loved his badge, said he was sure the Democrats were going to retake the house, and the other guy kept shaking his head, saying, no, it wasn't possible, never going to happen.

"Well, we'll see!" Sam exclaimed, then waved at me with his beer. "Terry, this here is Myron. I was his first partner when he made detective."

"And I'm sure he lived to regret it," Terry said.

They both laughed, a good and honest laugh among good and honest friends, and I found myself joining in. It was a welcome feeling. I'd forgotten how much I liked Sam. We'd only been partners a year before a close call with a knife-armed meth head prompted him to transfer to the quieter streets of Tigard, but it had been one of the best years of my life. I'd learned a ton from Sam about how to carry myself as a detective as opposed to a uniformed cop, how to ask the questions that gave you the answers you needed, and, most importantly, how to keep feeling like you were making a difference when all evidence pointed to the contrary.

"Sam's the best detective there is," I said.

"Aw, stop, you're making me blush," Sam said, but I could tell by the shine in his eyes that he enjoyed the compliment. "Terry here thinks I'm a loudmouthed asshole, like most everybody else in this sleepy little spit of a town, and I've got to maintain that reputation."

"Just because you're the best detective there is," I said, "doesn't mean you weren't a loudmouthed asshole."

"Ain't that the truth," Terry said.

"Damn straight," Sam said. "Man, it's good to see you, kid. Can I get you a beer?"

"No. Thank you, but ... No."

"Cutting down on the sauce, huh? Good for you."

"Maybe I'm just not thirsty."

"Sure, okay, whatever you say. I'm drinking Bud Light, so it's not like I'm drinking real beer anyway." He laughed and took another sip. "Yep, tastes like warmed-over piss, but I have to say, you do get kind of used to it. Liver cancer."

"Huh?" I said.

"It's all right," he said. "I can see the question all over your face. You been wanting to ask the moment you saw me. What the hell happened to me, right? Well, it was liver cancer. We've beat it back pretty good, so hopefully it's licked."

"Oh shit, Sam, I'm sorry."

He grinned. "Don't be! I'm alive, ain't I? And so are you, pal! If you're walking around aboveground, you can't ask for much more than that."

They both laughed, but this time, I couldn't see the humor in it. For one thing, his comment about being aboveground meant something completely different to me, because I knew that wasn't all you could ask for at all, that everybody got the same deal even after they died. For another, I felt like a complete failure for being totally oblivious the past few years to Sam's medical situation. Yes, I'd had my difficulties, but that was no excuse. Sam had visited *me* in the hospital, hadn't he?

He'd been there for me. I hadn't been there for him. Now I had to live with that.

"Is that why you're retiring?" I asked.

Sam shrugged. "Seemed like as good a time as any. Thirty-seven years on the force, man. Seemed like time to do something else."

"Like drink Bud Light," Terry said.

"You joke, pal, but your time will come soon enough, mark my words."

"Nah," Terry said. "I plan to just keel over right after I collar some escaped convict or something. Then I get to go out a hero. Think of the parade they'd throw in my honor!"

They both chuckled at this, but as Sam brought the beer up for another sip, almost as if he were shielding his face, I could see the sadness in his eyes. Being a cop, and especially a detective, had meant everything to him. He'd lived and breathed it. I doubted he ever would have retired unless his health forced him. If his knees had given out on him, he might have become a desk jockey, but I never saw him retiring altogether. He'd gotten a bit spooked by the stabbing, for good reason, but I hadn't thought of his transfer to Tigard as a cowardly move. It had more been an acknowledgment that his old body just couldn't keep up with the rigors of Portland's more hectic pace.

Thinking all this, I felt profoundly sad. Death took everything that mattered to us eventually, sometimes all at once, sometimes a little at a time. All that was left afterward were lots of ghosts, not just the human kind, but faint echoes of our former lives, reminding us of all that we had lost.

"Whoa," Sam said, "don't look so down there, Myron boy. I'm not in the ground yet."

"Oh," I said, embarrassed he'd read me so well, "I wasn't—"

"Just live it up, man. That's all. Live it up while you can. If you got something you're good at, do it as long as life will let you. You might think I got a bunch of regrets, but I don't. I knew what I loved and I kept doing it until Father Time told me it was time to take a break. I can live with cancer, but regret? Shit, no."

He looked at me knowingly, wiping the beer off his mustache. I knew what he was getting at, I knew he was talking about me holed up like a hermit rather than getting back to work, and I found myself irritated at him for meddling. He didn't know about my situation. He didn't have to live with a world full of billions of ghosts and not be able to tell them apart from the living. But this was followed immediately by a wave of remorse and shame.

This was Sam, dying of cancer, giving me some advice. This was my old partner, just trying to show me the way one more time.

I was trying to think of something to say when Sam's son joined us, a broad-shouldered young man in a nicely pressed Army uniform, his cap cupped under his arm. I hadn't seen him in years, but his face was so similar to his father's, except for the lack of mustache, that I probably would have guessed he was Sam's kid even if I'd never met him. He was tan and fit and smiling broadly. His buzz of blond hair had been cut so close that I saw the gleam of his scalp.

"Hey, good to see you, Kort!" I exclaimed, both genuinely glad to see him and relieved that I didn't have to continue the depressing turn the conversation had taken. "When did you get back from Afghanistan?"

Kort's smiled even brighter, the gleam of his teeth almost as bright as the medals on his chest. "Last year," he said. "I'm heading back out again tomorrow. Decided to re-up."

"Wow," I said, "your dad must be very proud."

I turned and smiled at Sam, and that's when I realized something was very wrong. Both Sam and Terry were staring at me with some mixture of horror and morbid fascination. None of them so much as glanced at Kort. Why would they? It was now apparent that I was the only one who was seeing him.

"What did you say?" Sam asked.

I tried to think of a way to explain my mistake, to pretend I was talking about something else, but I'd said too much. Kort seemed particularly oblivious to my plight, but then, he hadn't always been the brightest of kids. I wondered if he even knew he was dead.

"Who the hell are you talking to?" Sam asked. In a flash, his face had gone from white to bright red.

"I don't know," I mumbled.

"You know Kort died last November, right?"

"Um, well, I think I heard—"

"Shit-ass Taliban wearing a suicide vest. Fucking killed him in his sleep. My boy didn't have a chance."

"I'm sorry," I said.

"It's not some fucking joke."

"I didn't mean—"

"What the hell is wrong with you?"

I didn't have an answer, at least not one he would believe, so I said nothing. The conversations in our vicinity had gone suddenly quiet, people turning in our direction, gawking. Kort, the smile gone, looked incredibly pained. Sam's eyes turned watery.

"Hey, hey," Terry said, patting Sam on the shoulder. "Myron didn't mean nothing. You know he's had a hard time, too."

"Dad," Kort pleaded, "I'm right here."

"Not a joke," Sam said, taking another swig of beer, not looking at me.

"Dad," Kort said.

Now the kid was crying. This was even worse than being subjected to Sam's anger. We stood there in awkward silence, but then a couple of burly guys I didn't know who just came in joined us, oblivious to what had just transpired, starting right in on some inside joke about a blonde and a small-town sheriff at a gay bar. I took the opportunity to drift away, into the thick of the crowd, my gaze locking with Sam's for just a second before he looked hurriedly away. It felt like being shot.

We must have hit the fashionably late arrival time, because hordes of people flooded into the little house. There were cops, and plenty of them, some I recognized and many I didn't, but there were also just about every variety of man, woman, and child as well. I saw men in Navy uniforms that dated back to World War II, young women in bell-bottom jeans and perms that floated around their heads like halos, and a couple of barefoot children carrying bags of marbles and rolled-up Archie Bunker comics.

They mingled together, the living and the dead, talking and laughing, slapping backs and shaking hands, the noise rising to a dull roar. Most of them were talking about Sam—men he'd served with, people he'd helped, neighbors, people from church, most alive, many dead. The air grew hot and thick, filled with the smell of beer and sweat and dozens of mingling perfumes. I bumbled and jostled my way to the far wall, sandwiched between a grandfather clock that was no longer working and a bookcase filled mostly with thick tomes on all the major wars of the world.

I looked for Alesha, but couldn't find her. I thought I heard her laughter, but there were just too many people in the way. My collar was drenched with sweat. My tongue felt as dry as desert sand, and I thought about trying to navigate the sea of bodies to the kitchen, but I couldn't get my legs to move. I was safe along the wall.

"You," a gruff voice said.

I turned and there, leaning against the grandfather clock, was a black man in prison orange duds, lean as a pole, cornrows in his hair. He was thin and angular like a switchblade. When he sneered at me, I saw that several of his front teeth had been capped with gold. He looked familiar.

"You were with the asshole," he said.

His breath reeked so badly of cigarettes that I had to turn my face away. I told myself that if I didn't speak to him, he wasn't there. Not really. Not in any way that mattered.

"Hey, I'm talking to you," he said. "I knows you can see me 'cause you was looking right at me."

"Go away," I mumbled.

"Nah," he said. "Not until I figure out some way to get back at you and your fat-ass partner. Put me away for nothin', man, for slapping around some bitch. Not my fault she fell off the balcony. And then what happens? Some white-trash cracker knifed me when I'm in the shower 'cause I wouldn't be nobody's bitch."

I remembered him now—Jermaine something. I'd only been a detective for a couple of weeks, still afraid I was going to screw up so badly that everybody would know they'd made a mistake promoting me, when we were working Jermaine's case. We found him hiding in Forest Park, after an estranged girlfriend of Jermaine's told us that he would often hide in the park as a kid after shoplifting. Old habits died hard—or didn't really die at all, in Jermaine's case. It wasn't like he'd become a different person as a ghost.

For the first time, I saw the blood staining his uniform on the left side, below the rib cage.

"Cat got your tongue, dickweed?" he said.

I looked away.

"You scared of me now, ain't ya? What you gonna do, shoot me? Can't do nothin' to me now."

I pushed off the wall and merged into the crowd of bodies. Jermaine, snickering, followed.

"Yeah, I think I'll haunt your ass," he said. "I'm going to stick with you forever, cocksucker. You can run, but you can't hide. Get your skinny ass back here, boy."

He laughed, a loud honking laugh that got heads to turn—ghosts, all of them, staring at me as if *I* was the freak and not Jermaine. I swerved around a few more people, picking up my pace and leaving Jermaine's laughter behind, saw the narrow hall, and jetted down it. Pictures of Kort, from dimpled baby in diapers to proud young man in uniform, decked the walls.

The first door was the bathroom, but it was too obvious. The next bedroom was Kort's, and there was no way I was going in there. The last door led to an office of sorts, though along with a Mac computer on an old metal desk, there was also a sewing machine, an ironing board, an exercise bike, and a freestanding rack filled with dresses just as obnoxiously colorful as the one Loraine was wearing. I ducked inside and closed the door.

The noise from the party was a low murmur. An air freshener plugged into the wall filled the room with a minty-fresh odor, though it wasn't quite powerful enough to cover the overpowering stink of cat piss. I reached in my jacket for my Glock, but of course it wasn't there. I hadn't worn it since the accident, not because I couldn't but because I didn't trust myself with it. What good would it do against a ghost anyway?

I'd hoped he hadn't seen me, but only a few seconds passed and there Jermaine was, loping right through the closed door. He flashed me his gold-capped smile.

"There you are, boy," he said.

"Leave me alone," I said.

"Oh, is that any way to treat an old pal like me? We gonna be joined at the hip, brother, so you better get used to it. I'm gonna be there when you put your head down at night and when you take a piss and when you tryin' to make sweet love to a lady friend. Jermaine will be right there the whole time, your special guardian angel." He laughed and slapped his knee. "Look at me, I'm like Richard Pryor or something."

"I know people," I said.

"Oooooh. I know people, too."

"I know powerful people. You know Frank Warren at the NAANCP?"

Jermaine blew air through his lips, producing a wet smacking sound. "Those people? They got *nothing* they can do to me. Face it, pretty boy, you stuck with me."

He crossed his arms and smiled. I was in new terrain. I didn't know how to get rid of him. The nightmare my life had become had seemed bad before, but now I saw how much worse it could be. If a ghost wanted to follow me around all the time, how was I going to stop him if I couldn't even touch him? It wasn't like mean words would make somebody like Jermaine leave me alone.

Or would they?

Words couldn't affect Jermaine, but maybe it wasn't Jermaine I needed to target.

"Your mama still like raspberry iced tea?" I asked.

"What?"

"When we went to talk to her, she offered us raspberry iced tea. She said it was her favorite drink."

Confusion clouded his face. This obviously wasn't the way the game was supposed to be played. It may have just been my imagination, but Jermaine's bloodstain seemed to grow larger.

"What you talking about?" he said.

"I'm talking about your mama."

"Well, you better quit."

"Or what? You know, she lives on those disability checks, doesn't she? Kind of struggles month to month. Might be tough for her if she lost those checks. Be tough to see her on the streets."

I could almost see the icicles in the air between us, his gaze was so cold.

"You can't do nothin' to her," he said.

"Oh, you might be surprised. Cops have friends all over the place. I even got friends at the Social Security office."

"Like hell," Jermaine said, but I saw the doubt in his eyes.

"Want to find out?"

He said nothing.

"Figure I'll pay her a visit first," I said, "make sure she really knows all the awful stuff you've done, Jermaine. That will take a while, I'm sure. Hope she has some of that raspberry iced tea."

I could see him dismembering me with his eyes, the fires of his rage burning fiercely hot, but he didn't do anything. He didn't say anything, either—just went on looking at me for a long time until, with an aggressive snort, he turned and walked right back through the door. I watched and waited, and when I was sure he wasn't coming back, slumped into the wooden swivel chair by the desk.

The party was a steady hum beyond the door, all those people living and dead mere feet away, but it could have been on the other side of the world for all I cared. It was all too much. I'd had enough. Every time I thought maybe I could pick myself up, find a way to deal with my issues, something happened to set me back. I felt like a jigsaw puzzle where none of the pieces matched. Or maybe I was like the room where I found myself—filled with junk placed together because none of it belonged anywhere else, and yet without the junk, there was nothing but an empty room. I was an empty room. Take away all the junk, all my problems and troubles, and I was a hollow man. There was nothing left of me worth saving anymore.

I don't know how long I'd been sitting there when I heard the door creak open. I looked up and saw Alesha peering into the room.

"What are you doing in here?" she asked, smiling coyly.

"I don't know," I said.

She laughed. "You really shouldn't be in here, you know."

I nodded. She must have seen the anguish on my face, because she swallowed and closed the door behind her.

There must have been something about the way she was standing, but I was struck by her vitality, by how vibrant and alive she was, this sinewy, beautiful young woman with the breathtaking eyes and the polished black skin. She may have only been seven or eight years younger than me, but the distance between us seemed much more vast now, ages come and gone, civilizations risen and fallen, eons of struggle and suffering. I'd always felt older than Alesha, but not like this.

"What happened?" she asked.

"Nothing," I said.

"Doesn't seem like nothing."

I shrugged.

"You want to talk about it?" she asked.

I shrugged again.

"You're not giving me much to work with here," she said.

"Maybe there isn't much to worth with," I said.

"That doesn't even make sense."

"Yeah, well."

She looked at me as if waiting for me to say more, but I didn't have anything more. It took all the energy I had to engage in even this much conversation. I gazed at the carpet, focused on a piece of dryer lint. With a sigh, she came over to me and leaned against the desk, hands gripping the edge. Her legs, in those taut designer jeans, were inches from my own. She was so close I could smell her lilac perfume. When we spoke, something about the proximity required us to speak in a whisper, and it felt so much more intimate than before.

"Is it a panic attack or something?" she said.

"Sure," I said.

"What do you mean, sure? You mean that's it?"

"I mean I don't know."

"Come on, Myron. I'm here. I'm listening."

"I just didn't think it would be this hard."

"What would be this hard?"

"Living."

When she didn't answer, I looked at her. Because I'd been slumped over, elbows on my knees, the act of straightening and turning slightly in her direction brought our faces remarkably close together. I saw the tiny imperfections in her skin, a divot here, a mole there, every mark and scar a placeholder on the aged map that made her face her own. These imperfections did not mar her beauty; they made her beauty more unique. This was Alesha. This was my partner, my friend, my confidant. My silhouette loomed large in her wide black pupils. Her lips, full and bountiful, parted slightly.

"Maybe you're just lonely," she said.

She reached out and ruffled my hair, then caressed her thumb across the scar on my forehead from the shooting. It was probably an impulsive act, done without thinking, but this simple gesture unlocked some deep, buried frustration. Until she touched me, I didn't realize how much I'd been craving that kind of intimate human contact. I was a thirsty man who'd forgotten the taste of water. I started to speak, but the words collapsed under the weight of all my frustrations and never made it out of my mouth.

"Myron," she said, "I know it's been hard ... I know, losing Billie. We've never talked about it ..."

I kissed her.

It wasn't her. It was me. After all the years of furtive glances, inadvertent touches, and offhand comments filled with double meanings and sexual innuendo, I kissed her first. Her lips were just as soft and pliant as I'd imagined them to be. She reacted with surprise for only a second, jerking back, her eyes wide, but then she kissed me even more hungrily than I'd kissed her. She cupped her hands behind my head and leaned into the kiss. I tasted red wine and salty wheat crackers. Her nose, pressed against my cheek, was surprisingly cold, but her fingers in my hair and her lips pressed against my own burned hot. One kiss turned into many, a series of desperate little kisses, our breath warm on each other's faces.

She was leaning into me, her other hand pressing against my leather jacket for balance, and I knew if I didn't stop it now, I never would. The need was too strong. I pulled away. She followed at first, not understanding, and I clutched her by both shoulders and pushed her back. She was breathing a little fast and her face was alive with desire.

"What?" she said.

"I can't," I said.

"Why?"

"I just ... can't."

The hurt in her eyes was almost unbearable. I was wounding her. I was cutting her deeply, and it was worse than anything else I could have done to her. When she spoke again, in a whisper, she seemed so delicate, not at all like the brave and stubborn Alesha she presented to the world. It was as if she was made of sand and the slightest breeze would blow her away. Her hands fell limply to her sides.

"Is there something wrong with me?" she asked.

"God, no."

"Don't you want me?"

"More than anything."

"Then ... what?"

Her eyes searched my own. My hands still clutched her shoulders, her leaning into me, trusting me with her weight, and for just a second, I thought about pulling her into me. Embracing her would have been easy, and so right in this moment filled with long-suppressed desire but so wrong for what was in my heart, and so hard to live with if I really cared about what was best for Alesha. To her, I was not just another disposable boyfriend. If I let her in now, I would only disappoint her later—and her disappointment would be all the more crushing.

But was that really why I wasn't giving in? No. If I was being honest, there was really only one reason, and Alesha, who'd always been there for me when it mattered most, deserved to hear it.

"I'm still in love with my wife," I said.

If the fire in her eyes hadn't died before, it was totally extinguished now. She leaned back, nodding more to herself than to me, pulling only a few inches away, but the gulf between us felt much greater. Still perched on the edge of the desk, she turned and faced the door. She touched her hair and her face self-consciously, smoothed her shirt, took a breath, and straightened her back. After a moment's pause, she propelled herself toward the door without even giving me a glance. This cold dismissal was far worse than if she'd screamed profanities at me.

I'd been so afraid of wounding her that I hadn't realized that she could also wound me.

"Alesha," I said.

She stopped, her back to me, her hand on the doorknob. I heard a woman laugh in the living room, a sharp, piercing laughter, and it was a tether yanking us back into the world. For a moment there, it had just been us, a universe made for two. Alesha waited. I knew she was waiting for me to say something, but I didn't know what to say. There was no making it better. Anything I said would only make it worse. After a time, it was Alesha who spoke.

"She's dead, Myron," she said. "She's dead and she's never coming back. Until you accept this, you'll never be able to move on with your life."

Then she went out the door and left me alone in the room—in a universe made for one.

Chapter 19

"That Ford Explorer of yours is registered to some badass dudes," Alesha said.

That was her greeting, entering through my open office door, a big grin on her face, two cups of steaming Starbucks coffee in her hands. I knew she was bringing coffee—when she came by in the morning she always brought coffee—which was why I'd left the door open for her, forcing myself to put up with the dying goat yodeling from the Higher Plane Church of Spiritual Transcendence down the hall. It was Saturday, which usually meant I was free from the auditory torture, but apparently no such luck today. Or maybe it was Sunday when the place went dark. I could never remember. Their Sabbath probably rotated depending on the alignment of the stars.

The low sun shining through the rain-streaked window filled the room with shifting, wavery light. It was no longer raining, but it had rained Friday night, and the droplets of water remained on the glass as reminders of the party that was. It had rained long and hard, and I'd lain awake for hours in bed listening to it crackling on the roof, hoping at any moment my wife would return, always disappointed when she didn't. Two days gone now.

I rose and took one of the coffees from Alesha, then shut the door. The cup had a sleeve, but it still felt scorching hot. Alesha was dressed in her gray trench coat, jeans, and open-toed sandals. Off duty. I couldn't help but notice that she'd painted her toenails black with tiny gold zodiac symbols.

"What do I owe you?" I asked.

"You always ask," she said, "and I always tell you to go to hell."

"And yet if I didn't ask, I'd feel like a mooch."

"And yet if you didn't ask, you'd have to accept my generosity without making a big fuss that you were willing to pay for it anyway. So I'll say it again: Go to hell."

Still grinning, she settled into one of the office chairs. I took a seat behind the desk, waiting for her to spill the beans on what she knew. As usual, when she had something good for me, she took her time. I sipped the coffee, and, as usual, it was so scalding that it brought tears to my eyes. Since I never seemed to learn this particular lesson, I took my pain like a man and forced my wince to come out as a smile.

Alesha let her gaze wander around the room, settling, as it often did, on the wall above my computer. I didn't need to follow her eyes to know she was contemplating the special framed painting I'd hung there when I'd first rented the place.

"Okay," Alesha said, "I know I've asked this before, but why do you have a blank white picture up there again?"

"I told you, it has sentimental value."

"But it's blank."

"Let's get back to the badass dudes," I said, since there was no way I could explain to her that the painting wasn't blank for *me*. "How badass are we talking about?"

"Very badass," Alesha said.

"Are we going to play twenty questions again?"

She snickered. "I just like making you work for it a bit. You know, not all private detectives have somebody like me on the inside who can feed them information. I want you to be appropriately grateful. I might need some favors myself some day."

It was one of those offhand comments that would have meant nothing to somebody else but had the kind of double meaning we both recognized. She realized it as soon as she said it, holding my gaze for few extra beats before her smile wavered just a little and she looked away.

"Believe me," I said, "you know how much I appreciate your help."

"Duly noted," she said. Then, brightening: "Anyway, the Ford Explorer is registered to an enterprising businessman named Manuel Loretto—or rather, a corporation that he's tied to but not really tied to, if you get my drift. Came to the United States illegally when he was seven. His parents were deported, but he stayed with his aunt, eventually became a citizen. When he was sixteen, he dropped out of high school to work in a cannery in Salem. When he was eighteen, he started his first business—one of those street-side burrito vans. By the time he was twenty, he opened his first Mexican restaurant in Woodburn. Now, at forty-five, he's got his fingers in all kinds of pies, mostly catering to Hispanics—laundromats, auto-repair shops, even real estate offices."

"A true American success story," I said. "Very inspiring. I'm not seeing why it's relevant."

Alesha took a sip of her coffee. If her coffee was as hot as mine, she didn't show it. "It's relevant because one of the pies he's got his fingers in is the drug trade."

"Ah," I said.

"I'm telling you, the folder on this guy is a mile thick. The DEA has been trying to nail him for years. He's got so many layers between him and the street gangs that actually peddle the meth, crack, and other stuff at the street level that his fingers never actually get dirty. But amazingly, his businesses all seem to do much better than you'd think. Even in a weak economy, he was making money hand over fist."

"Imagine that. What about the picture I emailed you of those guys in the car?"

"No luck there yet," Alesha said. "I'm sure they're some of his operatives. The well-dressed one was probably a low-level *lugarteniente*."

"A what?"

"Forgot your high school Spanish, huh?"

"It's a little rusty."

"It means lieutenant. The way Loretto's operation works, like most of these things, he's got a bunch of lieutenants in charge of different things. They're all vying to move up the ranks."

"Okay," I said. "Another question. Is there any reason you can think of that a guy like that would be snooping around Karen Thorne's condo Thursday night? It's in the Pearl District, very posh."

"Huh," Alesha said. "Not really the crowd Loretto's gang runs in. Kind of hard to see how they might be mixed up in Karen's murder. How do you know he was in Karen's condo?"

"Because I was there," I said.

"And you saw him?"

"Let's just say I know he was there before me."

"Uh-huh. And you're not going to tell me how you know this, are you?"

"Not just yet."

"Right," she said, "when in Myron-ese means not just ever."

"Alesha—"

"No, no, it's okay," she said, though I could clearly see it wasn't. "You've got your sources to protect and that sort of thing."

"Exactly," I said, though the real reason I couldn't tell her was a little more complicated.

I knew it was the same guy who'd gone to Karen's apartment building because I'd swung by there Friday night on my way back from Janice's house. When I showed Perry, the friendly neighborhood ghost clerk, the cell-phone picture of the Hispanics I'd snapped in Vancouver, he'd identified the younger, more sharply dressed man as the same one who'd left the building when I was still unconscious on the floor upstairs. I wasn't about to tell Alesha that my source was a ghost.

"Got an address for Mr. Loretto?" I asked.

"Sure," she said. "Lives in a huge house in Lake Oswego. I doubt he'll talk to you without a warrant, though. Place has got more security than the White House."

"You never know. Some people find me irrepressibly charming."

"I'm serious, Myron. Don't play games with this guy."

"Duly noted," I said. "Can I have the address?"

She wrote it on a yellow sticky note. I knew the address. It wasn't that far from where my parents used to live, though I was sure his house was an order of magnitude more impressive.

"If you're going to talk to him," she said, "you should at least have me tag along."

"Hmm. In this case, I think it might be better if I didn't have a cop with me."

She sighed. "Fine. Just promise me you're not going to get yourself killed, okay?"

"Cross my heart and hope to die," I said.

"Not funny. Seriously, this guy isn't like the low-level whack jobs we usually deal with. He's smart, he's ruthless, and he's very, very powerful."

"Okay, okay."

She took another drink of coffee, studying me carefully. The yodeling from down the hall had thankfully fallen silent. No cars passed on the street outside. The quiet created a sense of intimacy in the room that wasn't there before, changing the tenor of the moment. Alesha looked away.

"All right," she said, "I better get going. You may like to work on Saturdays, but I like to have a break now and then."

"Late for your astrologist?" I said.

"Hairstylist, if you must know."

"So the state of your hair is more important than the state of the stars?"

"No, I just like to have nice hair first. I'm seeing her later today."

She winked at me. Taking her coffee, she rose and walked to the door. As if on cue, the yodeling from down the hall started up again.

Alesha grinned at me.

"Do you have to pay extra for the music?" she asked. "Or is it a fringe benefit?"

"What's the city ordinance on noise pollution again? And if I shoot them, can I claim self-defense?"

"Depends on how good your lawyer is," Alesha said.

I thought that was her exit line, but she paused as if she was thinking of saying something else. Billie strolled casually through the open door at just that moment, plunking herself down in the chair as if she'd just stepped out for coffee rather than been gone for days. She wore a purple beret, tilted so far to the side that it looked like it might slide off her head at any second, a baggy Jimmy Hendrix T-shirt, and Army fatigue pants cut off at the knees. She looked at the floor, not at me.

Alesha, of course, didn't see her, but she did see my surprised reaction.

"What?" she said.

"Hmm? Oh, nothing."

"Nothing," Billie said. "How nice. I'm nothing. Happy to see you, too."

"Didn't look like nothing," Alesha said. "Looked like you, I don't know ..."

"Saw a ghost?" Billie interjected, with a snicker.

"... sat on a tack or something," Alesha finished.

"I don't know," I said. "Just thinking about the case, I guess."

"Ah. Well ..." She swallowed. "We're still shooting pool tomorrow night, right?"

"Oh," I said. "Yes."

"You forgot, didn't you?"

"No, I didn't."

"Yes, you did. That's okay. We can reschedule for another time, no biggie."

"Alesha, I'll be there. Sharkey's at 8 p.m., right?"

"Sure, if you can make it."

"I'll make it."

She nodded and left. When I looked back at Billie, she was smirking. Someone smirking at you is annoying all by itself, but for some reason it's particularly annoying when that person is wearing a beret. Adding in that she'd been gone for two days, plus the mood music down the hall, and I wasn't in a gracious state of mind.

"What?" I said.

"You know she wants you," Billie said.

"Jesus."

"And you want her."

"Oh come on, Billie. That's not true."

"Uh-huh. I think he doth protest too much. It's not like it's a new thing. You guys have always had chemistry, even when I was alive. Honestly, I don't know why you don't jump in the sack with her now. It's not like I have much to offer you."

"You're my *wife*, for God's sake."

"Your dead wife."

"Billie—"

"Your dead invisible ghost wife. Aren't you tired of playing the part of the celibate priest? You used to be really good in bed. I really hate to see that go to waste. Some woman should get some good out of it."

I shook my head. "Will you quit? I can't believe you disappear for two days and this is what you want to talk about."

"I'm just saying, since you can't sleep with me, it might as well be with Alesha. Hell, she might even love you."

"That's crazy."

"You know it's not. She's practically telling you she loves you with every word out of her mouth."

"Oh, and you don't?"

"Don't what?"

I didn't say anything. I'd blurted the question without thinking it through, without really wanting an honest answer.

"Love you? You know I do," she said, though she didn't sound all that convincing. "That's not the point. The point is that you're a man with sexual needs, and she's an attractive woman who's obviously ready to take care of them."

"All right, I'm done with this conversation. I've got work to do."

I rose from the desk, grabbed my phone, keys, and wallet, and donned my leather jacket. Billie watched me, still wearing an annoying smirk, but when I took out the Glock and made sure it was loaded, her expression changed to one of concern.

"Where are you going?"

"Detecting," I said, placing the Glock back in my side holster. It was always a comforting presence.

"Uh-huh. And where, exactly, will you be detecting?"

"Why? You afraid I won't come back? Don't worry, I won't be gone two days."

"Myron, don't be like that. You know I need my space. I was always that way. I was that way before you even married me, so you knew what you were getting into. So just tell me where you're going, okay?"

I told her. I didn't necessarily have a great attitude doing it, but I told her. In fact, I told her everything that had happened since she left, from my bump on the head in Karen's condo all the way up to what I'd learned about Manuel Loretto. She was shaking her head before I'd even finished.

"You're not going into that guy's place," she said.

"I'll be fine," I said.

"Like hell. Even if you do get to talk to him, why do you think he'd tell you anything?"

"I'm feeling a strong sense of déjà vu."

"What?"

"I just had this conversation with Alesha."

She glared at me. "I don't give a rat's ass what you talked about with Alesha. *I'm* your wife, and I don't want you going."

"Oh, now you're my wife?"

"Damn it, Myron! Why is this case so damn important?"

"You *know* why it's important. Why do you even have to ask?"

She stewed in silence, shaking her head. I turned to leave, and she sprang to her feet.

"Fine," she said. "If somebody has to go in, then it's going to be me."

"What?"

"I'll snoop around while you wait in the car."

"It's too dangerous," I said. "What if somebody sees you?"

She gave me a what-are-you-thinking look.

"Oh, right," I said.

WE WERE HALFWAY to Lake Oswego before either of us said a word, the traffic light, the sun shining daggers on the glistening asphalt. As usual, my anger with her was short-lived; what I felt now was mostly a mix of gratitude and relief. What Billie was thinking I couldn't say, which was also no surprise. She'd taken off her beret and was turning it around slowly in her hands, her face thoughtful. I was watching the fuel-economy monitor on the console, something I found endlessly fascinating. For the trip, I was currently at sixty miles per gallon. I often treated it like a game, seeing how high I could push it, using all of the Prius's sensors to maximize its efficiency.

"So how's Mom and Dad?" she asked, when I'd finally gotten so used to the silence that her voice startled me.

"How do you know I saw Mom and Dad?" I said.

"Because you always see your parents when I go off on my own a while."

"I didn't realize I was so predictable."

"Only to me."

"Oh. Well, they're about the same. Mom's still convinced I'll come to my senses and have them come live with us at the house."

"Wouldn't that be lovely," Billie said.

We both laughed. It was good to hear her laugh. Billie may not have laughed often—she spent most of her time brooding, and brooding and laughter did not mix—but when she *did* laugh, everything seemed right in the world. Everything seemed right with us.

I was still laughing when a young man in a red Camaro passed on the right, gaping at me. He had every reason to gape. From his point of view, I was having a lively conversation with my empty passenger seat. I waved to him. He flipped me the bird. That was all right. I took satisfaction that he had no idea that he was carrying his own passenger, a young woman in the backseat whose entire face had been badly burned into a blackened mess. There were times I actually liked the weird ghosts. I comforted myself imagining that she followed this jerk around everywhere.

Manuel Loretto's house in Lake Oswego was even more impressive than I'd imagined, and I'd been imagining something plenty impressive. It was more like a fortress than a house, with the eight-foot wall of uneven stone surrounding a forested estate of at least twenty acres, the wrought-iron gate spiked with the kind of forked blades that might have been used in the Spanish Inquisition to extract confessions, and the turret at the gate where two guys in black uniforms and semiautomatic weapons stood watch on the turret's balcony. I drove past without stopping, catching a glimpse of a mansion through the trees, a mansion five or six stories high with a similar uneven stone facade as the wall and a turret on each corner.

"They say a man's home is his castle," I said to Billie. "I guess Loretto took it literally."

"And you thought you were just going to charm your way in there."

"It was worth a try."

"No, dear, it wasn't. Drive a little farther. I want plenty of distance between you and them."

It was more than a little farther, a half-mile at least through tall Douglas firs crowding the road, before we came to suitable place for me to park: a gravel drive between two other large but not quite as awe-inspiring houses, a real estate sign marking a three-acre plot for sale. I pulled in, out of sight from the road, and killed the engine. I rolled down all the windows, letting in a rush of cool, woodsy air. It smelled of fir and wet earth and fresh growing things.

In the old days, I used to go to the woods all the time, for exercise, for solitude and peace of mind, but I seldom did anymore. For some reason, some of the really, *really* weird ghosts seemed to be drawn to the forest. It was one thing to run into the strange ones in the city, surrounded by living, breathing human beings, and quite another to run into them when you were alone.

Billie donned her beret and stepped right through the door, then turned back and leaned down to the open window. "It's not like I can ask questions or open drawers," she said, "so I may be a while."

"Oh, darn," I said, "and I forgot the socks I was knitting at home."

"I'm only telling you because I don't want you getting impatient and marching down there looking for me. Remember, I'm a *ghost*. Just keep telling yourself that if you get worried. They can't hurt me. I'm a ghost."

"All right, you don't need to keep saying it all the time. I know you're a ghost, for God's sake."

She arched an eyebrow at me, which, combined with that beret, may not have been as annoying as a smirk but was pretty close.

"Do you?" she said. "Sometimes I wonder."

Before I could come up with a witty retort, she walked up the road.

I considered turning on the radio, but I wasn't in the mood for music. I rolled down the window, enjoying the cool breeze on my face and the sound of the morning rain dripping from the trees.

I thought about everything I'd learned about Tony Neuman so far and wondered how it all fit together. Five years ago, he'd been a crazy bearded man robbing a Starbucks who'd panicked and shot me in the face. More recently he'd passed himself off as a high-rolling day trader, but in reality he had a fake name and no discernable past. He may have killed his rich wife in the hopes of inheriting her fortune, he definitely slept with his wife's depressed housewife of a sister, and he possibly owed money to a Mexican drug kingpin named Manuel

Loretto. Add it all up and what did I have?

A headache. That's what I had. My old friend, that bullet lodged in my brain, was acting up again, starting with tiny tremors somewhere deep inside and escalating to a steady pulsing that I felt all the way down to my toes. To take my mind off the pain, I thought about using my cell phone to talk to other people of interest in the case, but I had no signal in the trees. I opted for counting passing cars. I made it all the way to seven before I lost interest. Nobody came out of the forest, ghosts or otherwise, but I did see through my rearview mirror a man wrapped only in a dirty white sheet pushing a shopping cart along the road, a naked woman in the basket with her legs sticking out the front. The man was mumbling to himself, and the woman was whistling "Material Girl" by Madonna.

We weren't even in a real forest and already I'd spotted a weird one. Fun times.

When I finally heard the crunch of Billie's feet on the gravel, nearly two hours had passed.

"That took a while," I said, when she floated in through the door.

"It was harder than I thought it would be," she said. "He's got ghost security."

"What?"

"At least two of the guys wandering around in there are ghosts. I don't think Loretto *knows* he's got ghost security, but they still seem pretty loyal to him. I think they died in a turf war dustup with a Russian outfit. At least that's what I'm guessing based on something they said."

"Nice. He's so powerful he's got both the living and the dead protecting him. So did you manage to learn anything useful?"

She took off her beret and smoothed her hair, then turned and looked at me with sympathy. "I had to sneak around a lot so they didn't see me, but yeah, I found out some interesting stuff. I don't think you're going to be very happy about it, though. Tony Neuman is dead."

"What?"

"I guess they found him holed up on the coast outside Seaside a couple of weeks ago. He owed them a bunch of money. Some kind of stock scheme he'd sold them on as a sure thing. I guess it wasn't such a sure thing, but they still wanted their money."

"And they killed him?"

Billie nodded. "I guess they'd killed Karen first. They told him if he didn't pay up by last July, they'd kill her as punishment, and they did. That's why he took off and hid."

"Not well enough, apparently."

"Nope."

"Where's the body?"

"Not totally sure. I got the impression he might have gone for a nice one-way boat ride out into the ocean, though."

"But why were they following me, then?"

Billie hesitated. She looked down at her beret, turning it slowly. "I don't know. I mean, I could only learn so much, just listening in on people's conversations, especially when half the time they were talking in Spanish."

"It's okay," I reassured her. "You did great. Really."

"Yeah. But I think … Well, I think they still believe Tony has the money somewhere. That he hid it or gave it to somebody or something. And when you showed up at the condo …"

"They thought maybe I knew where the money was," I said.

"Right. So they followed you."

"Hmm. So Tony was a sleazeball who assumed another man's name and slept with his wife's sister, but he didn't kill his wife."

"It doesn't appear that way," Billie said.

"I'm still left wondering why he shot me."

Billie reached for my hand, on the steering wheel, stopping just short of it before setting her own hand back in her lap. "I'm sorry," she said. "I know this isn't what you were hoping for. I know you wanted more closure than this."

"It's not about closure," I said thickly. "It's about justice."

"I'm sorry."

I looked out the window. I knew Billie wanted me to say it was over, that I was ready to put this case behind me, but I couldn't. There was still something that didn't quite add up. I couldn't say what it was, not yet, but I knew if I didn't at least make a stab at figuring it out, it would gnaw at me forever. There was some kind of deeper truth about Tony that was just eluding me. It was like smoke. I was grasping it, trying to hold on to it, but it was slipping through my fingers.

Closure. I didn't think I'd ever have closure, whatever that meant, but maybe Karen Thorne might. That was something at least.

Shafts of sunlight slanted through the firs, droplets of water sparkling on the leafy branches like tiny white pearls. I thought I saw a face amid all the green, another ghost, maybe, but it didn't appear again. Great. Now I was even *imagining* ghosts.

I put my foot on the brake and hit the power button, waiting for the Prius's console to beep to life. Maybe I couldn't quite let Tony go, and maybe I never would, but that didn't mean I had to obsess about him twenty-four hours a day. Tony was dead, after all. That might make him out of reach for most people, but not for me. I'd find him eventually. In the meantime, a little break from it all might do me good.

"I wonder what the weather's like in Honolulu," I said.

Chapter 20

FIFTY-EIGHT DAYS after Billie walked out on me, I awoke to find her standing at the end of the couch, accompanied by a young mousy woman in a yellow headscarf and a simple, full-length blue dress, the kind of conservative outfit worn by the Russian Orthodox Christians who'd been immigrating to Oregon in recent years. Billie was dressed in a sharp gray pantsuit, sunglasses perched on top of her head, looking all the world like she'd just stepped off a designer clothing photo shoot.

I blinked through my hangover, trying to focus on them in the bright glare of sunlight filling the living room, and sat up so fast my head began to spin.

The television was on, but the sound was muted. The perky hosts of some morning talk show, both wearing outrageous white chef's hats, were baking red and green peppers in a sizzling skillet. Realizing I was lying there in nothing but my boxers, I grabbed one of the empty chip bags and covered myself with it. In the process, I managed to knock over two of the empty beer bottles on the coffee table, their clatter as loud as cannon fire. Billie, surveying my sad state of affairs, wrinkled her nose in disgust.

"Jesus," she said.

The young woman frowned, though whether it was because of me or because of Billie invoking the Lord's name, I couldn't say. Now that I got a better look at her, I doubted she was more than eighteen, her face free of makeup of any kind, eyebrows growing slightly together, the skin around her eyes pink and raw as if she had been crying. I propped myself up on my elbows.

"Took you long enough," I said. My mouth felt as though I'd been chewing on dirt all night.

"You smell like you slept in the sewer," Billie said.

"Thank you. It's a new cologne I'm wearing, Scent of Dumpster. Like it?"

"I didn't think you'd let yourself go all to hell."

"Yeah, well, I didn't think you'd disappear for nearly three months. Guess we're even."

Billie nodded. "You're mad. I can see that."

"Your powers of deduction are amazing, Sherlock." I nodded to the woman. "Hello, I'm Myron. Sorry I didn't have time to tidy up a bit. I wasn't expecting guests, you see."

The young woman looked at Billie. "Maybe I go," she said. Her voice, tinged with a Russian accent, was just as mousy as her appearance, a tiny squeak.

"No," Billie said. "Look, I know you're mad, Myron. That's fine. We can talk about that later. For right now, I want you to put that aside. This is Antonia. She died of cancer three years ago, and she needs your help."

"I'm very sorry to hear that, Antonia," I said. "But I'm not a shaman. I don't know what you heard, but I can't bring people back from the dead."

Antonia looked confused, glancing from me to Billie and back again. "That's—that's not—"

"Her daughter was abducted five days ago," Billie explained. "Someone took her right out of her school playground in Woodburn.

She needs to get her daughter back with her father again. Think you can stop feeling sorry for yourself long enough to help her do that?"

I glared at her. "Sorry for myself?"

"This isn't about us, Myron. This is about what you can do to help Antonia."

"I don't see how I can do anything the police—"

"Please, mister," Antonia said. "The police, they know nothing. They are not looking in right places for little Katya. I have ideas. There is woman who always wanted child I think took her. I can tell you people, people no longer living, you can talk to, and they might help find this woman. They will help."

It took a while for me to filter all this through my jittery brain. Not liking my position being loomed over by the two of them, I rose from my personal landfill of chip crumbs, candy-bar wrappers, and unopened junk mail, wading through the clutter in the room to the television. My legs and arms crackled as if there were glue in the joints. I turned off the television, then spotted my fraying terrycloth robe on the floor and slipped that on my aching body. The robe may have stunk of mildew and scotch, but at least it gave me some measure of modesty.

"I don't know what you heard," I said, "but I'm not a detective anymore."

"I pay you," Antonia said.

I sighed. "It's not about the money. I just don't think I can—"

"Please," Antonia begged, "please, there is no one. I have money in jars in special place in field near where we live. My husband, he drink and he spend money, so I must save some. You can have this money. I tell you where it is. Please, mister. Your wife, she say you are a very good man. She say you have a good heart. Please help me. *Please.*"

Her face was so earnest, so genuine in her desperation, that I couldn't help but be moved. What if that little girl was my own? Something clicked into place deep inside me, some gear gummed up by too much booze and self-pity. I felt the fog that had clouded my mind the past year begin to lift. There was a glimmer of hope, at last. There was a rope before me, leading out of the pit where I'd fallen, if only I had the courage to grab it. I doubted things would get any easier for me, but I didn't need easier. I realized that now. I needed to feel like I mattered again. I needed *purpose*.

Antonia had tears in her eyes, but she wasn't the only one. When I looked at Billie, I saw that her own eyes were watery.

"A good heart?" I said.

She nodded, and when she managed to speak, her voice was rough and strained. "The one I wish I had," she said.

Chapter 21

AFTER COMING BACK from Manuel Loretto's place, I spent the rest of Saturday poking around the house catching up on chores, plus brooding about Tony Neuman and how I might go about finding him in a world filled with hundreds of billions of ghosts. I was good at brooding. There was a real art to it, walking that fine line of morose thoughtfulness without slipping into outright depression. I wasn't as good as Billie, who brooded at the pro level, but I still had some talent.

I went for a walk at dusk, the fall air crisp and cool, and saw the same Ford Explorer that had tailed me on Friday parked at the end of the street. Irritated, I started to approach them, but they gunned the engine and screeched around the corner. How long would they keep tailing me? I was going to have to get the word out to them somehow that their efforts were pointless.

On Sunday afternoon, I met Alesha at Sharkey's, a pool hall about halfway between my house in Sellwood and her condo in northeast Portland. We met there about every other week, and we liked Sunday afternoons because the place was generally deserted—at least of the living. A few ghosts always wandered around from table to table, mostly old-timers who'd spent hours playing the game and now watched the movement of the balls longingly.

Alesha was racking up a set when I got there, alone, at our favorite table in the corner. Sometimes she brought a boyfriend, but mostly she came alone. Smoking had been banned in all Portland bars for years, but the smell of cigarettes still clung to the green felt and the dark-paneled walls—walls so thin I could feel the November breeze flitting through the gaps in the wood. Billie was at home finishing a painting. When I'd left, there'd been a particularly annoying ring to the way she'd told me to go have fun. She said it the same way she might tell me to go to hell.

While we played, I told Alesha about what Billie had learned about Tony's fate. When I was done, she was already three balls ahead of me and had set the table up to make it hard for me to come back.

"Interesting," she said. "And how do you know all this?"

"Sources," I said.

"Right. And I take it that these sources probably wouldn't be willing to testify in court?"

"Let's just say their testimony probably wouldn't do much good."

Alesha picked up the chalk and polished the end of her cue stick. "No chance of putting anybody in Loretto's operation behind bars, then. Six, corner pocket."

No surprise, she banked it off the wall and into the pocket.

"I'm glad we don't play for money," I said.

"Yeah, whose idea was that again?"

"I forget. Tell me something. Do you really think Loretto's men would keep following me because they think I might lead them to the money?"

"With Tony dead?" Alesha said. "It's possible, I guess. They might think you were hired to find the money. Why, you have reason to believe they're still following you?"

"Yes," I said. "The Ford Explorer was parked down the street from my house yesterday."

"Hmm. You think they might be outside right now?"

"It's worth a check," I said.

We checked, peering carefully through one of the windows, and sure enough, the black Ford Explorer was parked across the street in front of the Subway and the H&R Block. I could clearly see the same two guys I'd snapped pictures of on Friday sitting in the front, eating sandwiches, and I said as much to Alesha.

"Since you know what they look like now," she said, "it's hard to believe Loretto would send the same guys."

"Somehow I doubt they told Loretto about our little meeting."

"Yeah, probably. That little oversight might get them in a heap of trouble if Loretto finds out, though. You know, they look awfully lonely over there."

That got me to smile. "You thinking what I'm thinking?"

"I'm thinking there's a back door to this place they probably don't know about."

We used that back door to gain access to the alley behind the buildings, circling around our friends in the Explorer, deftly crossing the street and approaching them quickly from behind. Two old Jewish men in tweed suits were arguing about how it was President Truman's fault we were going to war in Korea, and I veered around them, which got Alesha to raise her eyebrows at me. She took the driver's side, me the passenger side, and we both popped into the backseats at exactly the same moment.

Cursing, the two Mexicans dropped their sandwiches in their laps and went for their guns, but Alesha flashed her badge before they'd gotten far.

"Now, now," she said, "let's not do anything hasty. You'd hate to have all of Portland's finest hunting you down."

The big one with the blocky face swallowed what was still in his mouth with one big gulp. He looked as if he wanted to throw up. The smaller, snappier-dressed man wiped the lettuce off his lips. He did not look happy, but he didn't look scared either.

"We done nothing wrong, man," the smaller one said. "We just sitting here having lunch. It's a free country."

"Oh yeah?" Alesha said. "I assume you've got concealed-weapon permits for those pieces you're carrying?"

They said nothing.

"That's what I thought," she said. "Here's the deal. My partner just has a few questions for you. Tell him what you know, and I'll look the other way on those permits."

"We not saying fucking nothing," the big guy said. "You—you take us in, we call a fucking lawyer. *No hay problema.*"

"That may be true," I said. "But what if I get the word back to Loretto how you never told him how I took your pretty picture yesterday?"

They made a show of glaring at me, but I saw a flicker of fear in their eyes.

"You no fucking cop," the big guy said.

"That's right," I said, "and it's why I can do all kinds of things that cops can't or won't do. I could get you in all kinds of trouble. What if it got back to Loretto that your mistake allowed me to get enough evidence to put him behind bars for Tony Neuman's murder?"

I expected another show of fear from them, but they just looked confused.

"Why you think Tony dead, man?" the smaller one asked.

"A little bird told me," I said.

"Who?"

"You tell me. You're probably the one who dumped the body."

The smaller man shook his head. "I don't know what the fuck you talking about, man. Manuel Loretto is a respected businessman. He's no murderer."

"Look," I said, "give me something to work with or I'm telling him how you screwed up tailing me. You're better off working with us. Somebody's going to go down for killing both Karen and Tony, and unless you're careful, it's going to be you."

The bigger one shook his head. "Shit, this is fucking crazy, man."

"Shut up," the smaller one said. "We're not telling them nothing."

"Fine," I said. "Better pack your bags, because he's going to go ballistic when I send him the picture I took of you two."

"I don't get it," the smaller one said. "Why you think we following you if we already know Tony's dead? It don't make no sense."

"Stop bullshitting me," I said.

"Hey, man, we just want to find the dude. He's a friend and he been missing a long time. We just worried about him."

Alesha chuckled. "Your concern is very touching. How much did he rip off from your boss?"

"I'm not saying nothing else," the smaller one said. "You gonna arrest us, go ahead. But otherwise get out of the fucking car."

"I'm going to send him the picture," I said.

"You do that, man. You tell him what you told me and he just think you another *loco hombre blanco*. Anything else?"

"Stop following me."

"It's a free country, man."

"Stop following me or you'll regret it."

"What you gonna do? Shoot me?"

"I might. Remember, I'm not a cop."

"Boo-ya. Done?"

There didn't seem to be anything more to gain, so we reluctantly got out of the car. They left with all the speed of a hearse carrying a full load, easing down the street well under the speed limit, turning on their right blinker long before they disappeared around the corner.

Just another pair of nice, law-abiding citizens.

AFTER OUR FUN little encounter with Loretto's henchmen, Alesha and I bought our own Subway sandwiches and ate in a booth in the back, trying to puzzle out what we'd gleaned from talking to them. Rather than help clarify things, I had more questions than ever. While it was quite possible they were bluffing about looking for Tony Neuman, they certainly did seem sincere.

When I got home, I didn't tell Billie anything about my afternoon other than that I'd had a fun time playing pool with Alesha. She hardly noticed me, deep into one of her paintings. I still leaned toward thinking that Loretto's men were lying to me about Tony Neuman, but there was another more troubling possibility.

Billie may have been the one lying.

She might have done it to protect me, because she thought Loretto was more than I could handle, but she'd still lied to my face. It was a breach of trust that cut deep. I wasn't quite ready to confront her on it yet, though. I needed more information.

Monday morning, I woke when the sky was just starting to soften from deep black to a hazy gray, the sun nowhere to be found. Billie, who'd lain down beside me on top of the covers, as she did most nights, was already up and painting. She was working on an ocean landscape based on a photo I'd taped on the wall for her the evening before, one she'd taken years ago when the two of us stayed at a B&B in Pacific City. I asked her if she wanted to join me at the office when I relayed what I'd learned to Karen, and she said maybe later, that she wanted to go for a walk first.

It was just as well. I still wasn't quite sure what I was going to say to Karen. I wasn't sure what I was going to say to Billie either.

The Ford Explorer wasn't out front when I headed out in the Prius, the early traffic just picking up. It wasn't parked outside the office either. Elvis was just setting up shop with his hot-dog stand. I asked if he'd seen the Explorer around the past couple days and he said no, not that he remembered. I showed him the cell-phone picture of the two Mexicans and asked if he'd seen them either. When he said no, I asked if he could keep his eye out for them. He said he'd be more than happy to oblige.

An Asian kid delivering newspapers, riding by on a bike while I was speaking to someone he obviously didn't see, gave me a funny look. I smiled at him like a madman, really putting as much crazy into it as I could, and he peddled away very fast.

The one benefit of coming in so early was that no tsunami of screeching emanated from the Higher Plane Church of Spiritual Transcendence down the hall. My office was so quiet that the drumming of my fingers on the desk echoed off the walls. Karen wasn't due until ten, which give me nearly three hours.

It may have been early to make some phone calls, but I didn't care. First I tried Karen's sister, Beth, but there was no answer—on any of her three phones. I left another message for her. Worried, I called Bernie's cell phone, and he picked up on the first ring. I asked him if he'd heard from Beth lately and he said yes, he'd talked to her yesterday, they'd had lunch at Jake's downtown. I told him to have her call me if possible. It might help the case. When he asked me how, I told him it was too early to say. He wasn't happy when he hung up.

I tried Karen's mother, Margaret Thorne, next. I wasn't sure what she might bring to the case, but it never did hurt to ask. After a half-dozen rings, a woman answered hello, or at least some groggy approximation of it.

"Mrs. Thorne?" I said.

"Yes?"

"My name is Myron Vale. Do you have a moment?"

"What time is it? Do you know how early it is?" She sounded like she was waking up fast, and what she was waking up to was not a happy person. "I'm not interested in whatever it is you're selling."

"I'm a private investigator," I said. "I'm investigating your daughter Karen's death."

There was silence on the other end. I heard what sounded like a bird twitter in the background, followed by a flutter that might have been wings.

"Who hired you?" she asked, a new wariness in her voice.

"Your husband. Ex-husband, I mean."

"Why are you investigating? Does Bernard actually think ... Well, of course he does. He always did watch too much *Columbo*, and these days, well, he's more paranoid than ever."

"Why would you say that?" I asked.

She was silent. I sensed that I was onto something, and that maybe getting in touch with her when she was still too muzzy-headed to remember to keep her guard up had been a smart move.

"I think I've said too much already," she said.

"Please, Mrs. Thorne. Don't hang up."

"I don't even know you. I don't know what your motives are here. I really should go."

"Wait," I said. "Even if all your help does is convince Bernie that Karen's death was all her own fault, wouldn't that be a good thing? I know she had a serious drinking problem."

"Well, you could blame that on him, too, couldn't you?"

"I don't understand."

She sighed. "Drinking, drugs, she was just trying to be like her daddy. There, I said it."

"You're saying Bernie Thorne is—"

"A drug addict. He's taken just about anything a person can take over the years. He's very high-functioning, you understand. But I finally put my foot down. It was either the drugs or me, and, well, you can see what he chose. He had more love for little piles of white powder than his wife."

"Cocaine?"

"Mostly, yes. I think he tried just about everything, though. Meth, crack, you name it. In his own way, he was very careful about his addictions. He was careful about alcohol because he didn't like what it did to the brain. He knew what some drugs could do to him if he wasn't careful. He said he understood the lure of meth, but he didn't like what it did to the body. I think he thought of cocaine as a rich man's drug."

"Do you know how he got it?"

"What kind of question is that?"

"I just thought—"

"I was not part of that world, Mr. Vale. I wanted no part of it. I have no idea who his dealer was."

"Did he sell any himself?"

"Bernard? No! He would never take that kind of risk. That was part of the problem. A man in his position had a hard time finding a way to get what he needed without consorting with the wrong sort of people."

"What did you think of Tony?"

"Karen's husband? I only met him at the wedding. I'm afraid Karen and I had a bit of a falling out during the divorce. But he seemed like just the sort of man who would appeal to Karen—very handsome, very suave, and very phony. Now, is that it? I've said far more than I should, but as much as I despise Bernard, I hate to see you wasting his money. After all, he cuts me a very nice check every month. My daughter died because she was loaded, and she decided to drive while doing it, nothing more."

"It's shocking you don't all get along better," I said.

"What?"

"Never mind. Can I call you again if I have more questions?"

"I'd rather you didn't," she said, and hung up.

Mulling it over, I swiveled around in my chair and watched the street out the window. Elvis was serving hot dogs to two lumberjacks wearing red plaid shirts and muddy overalls. An Office Depot truck rumbled past, spitting black clouds from its exhaust pipe. The mailman stopped at the bar across the street, dropping a couple of envelopes into the slot in the door. Another mailman, an older man with snowy white hair and dressed in a uniform several decades out of style, followed close on his heels. It was another day in Portland—the world of the living and of the dead coming to life.

If Bernie Thorne was a drug addict, then where would he get his drugs? The obvious answer was that he was getting them from Manuel Loretto's operation and that Tony Neuman was his supplier. That's how the puzzle made sense. Tony was probably a supplier to lots of rich people, acting as the perfect middleman between the street gangs and the upper-class folks who would never stoop to getting their stuff from someone in the gang itself. But Tony screwed Loretto over somehow, tried to get a lot of money fast by killing Karen, but his plot failed, and now Loretto wanted to find him.

Maybe it was to get his money or drugs back. Maybe it was just for revenge. It was probably for both.

Was Tony still alive? That was the question. I had a hard time be-lieving that if Loretto's people had found him already, they wouldn't have been able to squeeze out of Tony where the money or drugs were before they killed him. It's not like their powers of persuasion were limited by the Geneva Convention. They also must have believed he was still around Portland, or at least that there hadn't been any reason to think he'd fled the city.

I thought about calling Bernie to confront him about the drug thing, but I wasn't sure what I would gain from it—at least not yet. He would probably just deny it. It was also possible that Tony was dead, and *Bernie* had been the one to do it—maybe because of a deal gone wrong between them, maybe for revenge because Tony had killed Karen. But if that was so, then why did Bernie hire me to find Tony?

Of course, he hadn't, had he? Even if he was the one paying me, Karen had hired me, and I'd managed to convince Bernie that this was the case. If he'd resisted helping me and his daughter, that would only have made him look suspicious. He also desperately wanted to talk to his daughter using me as the medium. That might have been motiva-tion enough to send me on a wild-goose chase. He wanted to please his daughter, after all. But he must have known that my investigation could lead right back to him. It was hard to believe a man so cautious about how he got his drugs would take that kind of risk—or that he would have stooped to murder.

I was still watching the street when someone cleared a throat be-hind me.

"Hope I'm not too early," Karen said.

Her voice sounded sultry and slightly slurred. I swiveled around, fingers steepled and one leg crossed on my knee, and was surprised, once again, how stunningly beautiful she was. She stood just inside the door, a stylish black trench coat wrapped tightly around her body, her long legs bare except for her shiny red stilettos, her blond hair flowing in long luxurious curls over her shoulders. If anything, the trench coat didn't make her body less appealing; it offered just enough curves to hint at what lay beneath.

Her face, except for a touch of red lipstick that matched the shoes, seemed bare of makeup, but I knew from all my years of watching Billie in front of the bathroom mirror that Karen's simple, creamy complexion didn't mean she was wearing no makeup; it just meant she'd mastered the art of it. Her eyes were the greenest things in the room.

I was blessed to have two highly attractive ladies in my life, Billie and Alesha, but Karen Thorne was like the Sistine Chapel of beautiful women. Even if it was art so perfect it was beyond comprehension, I couldn't help but appreciate that something like it existed in the world—or, in her case, once did.

"I kind of liked it when you opened the door," I said. "It was a neat trick."

She shrugged. She was tilting a little on her feet. "I'm a ghost. I guess walking through walls is, um … what ghosts do."

"Had a little something to start off the day, huh?"

"What?"

"Forget it. Take seat. There's lots to talk about."

I motioned to one of the chairs. She wobbled her way to the chair and settled uneasily into it, crossing her legs one way, then the other, hugging her body tightly with both arms.

"I guess you didn't find Tony?" she asked.

"Not yet," I replied.

"Do you … do you think you might?"

"Hard to say. There are a lot of unknowns right now."

"Oh. I thought—I thought you said there's lots to talk about."

"There is. I want to talk about some of those unknowns. Let's talk about your father first."

"My father?"

"Yes. It's better if I just get to the point, so I'm sorry if this sounds harsh. Do you know if he does drugs?"

She stared at me. I was waiting for the indignant reaction, the protesting that a man like her father would never do such a thing, but I got a nod instead.

"Yes," she said.

"Yes, he does drugs?"

"I ... I didn't think so before. But now that I've been staying with him, I see him doing lines of coke sometimes. At first I thought maybe he was just doing it because he was so sad I was gone, but ... Well, he's obviously been doing it a while."

"Where is he getting his drugs?"

"I don't know. His supply is just about out. He seems pretty worried about it. I overhead him talking to some man on the phone about it and he got very angry. He slammed the phone down."

"What man?"

"I don't know!"

"Do you think it's possible he got his drugs from Tony?"

Now I *did* get the indignant reaction I'd been expecting. She bolted upright in her chair and glared at me. "Tony! No way! He would never deal drugs. He was too smart to stoop to something like that. I *told* you, he was a respectable investor."

"Yes, you did tell me that. Did he do drugs?"

"I don't know. Maybe."

"So he did."

She shrugged. "I saw him snort coke a couple times. Just once or twice."

"Uh-huh. How about you? Did you join him?"

"No way! I mean, I did weed a few times in college, but I didn't like that sort of thing."

"Oh, that's right, booze is your addiction of choice."

Her eyes welled up, and she struggled to keep the tears contained. "Why are you being so mean?"

"I'm not trying to be mean. I'm just getting the sense you're not telling me the whole truth, and it irritates me."

"I'm telling you everything, I swear!"

"You didn't tell me about your blood-alcohol level when you crashed. You didn't tell me your father is a drug addict."

"He's not a drug addict!"

"You're sure?"

"He—he just does it once in a while. To relax. He's not an addict."

"Just like you're not an alcoholic?"

Her lower lip was trembling. I knew I was being hard on her, but I needed some answers. If she was holding out on me, I needed to know. I thought for a moment about telling her what Billie had discovered, that Tony was already dead, just to see her reaction, but it seemed pointless when I didn't believe it to be true anymore.

"Where is your father getting his drugs?" I pressed again.

"I told you, I don't know!"

"Did the man he was talking to sound Mexican?"

"I didn't hear! Maybe. I don't know."

"Where was Tony five years ago in November?"

"What? How should I know?"

"He never told you what he was doing back then?"

"He said—he said he was working in New York. At an investment firm. I don't—I don't remember the name …"

"Probably because it wasn't real. I have reason to believe he was in Portland. Did you know your sister Janice was sleeping with Tony?"

"What?"

"You heard me."

"How could you—how could you say such a—"

"She admitted it," I said.

This was a lot for her to take in, too much, and I saw her face closing up as if an iron mask had slipped over it. I'd hit her with a barrage of questions, many without even thinking through what I was after, and she was shutting down on me. She looked at me but didn't see me. She was so still that when the tears dribbled down her face, the movement startled me. I reached for the tissue box on the corner of my desk, then caught myself.

"Nobody loves me," she whispered.

"Oh, that's not true," I said. "Your father loves you very much. Your mother too."

She laughed derisively. "Right."

"People are complicated. They can love us and still do mean things to us."

"If you say so."

"Look, I'm sorry for coming off so hard. I'm a bit of an asshole sometimes. It's a fatal condition, I'm afraid, but I do need to try harder to keep the symptoms under control."

She wiped away the tears. "No, no, you're the only friend I have right now, Myron. I appreciate you being honest with me. Nobody in my whole life has ever been honest with me. Maybe … Maybe if they had, things wouldn't have turned out the way they did. Please don't give up on me. On this, I mean. I need to know who killed me and why. I want the truth. All of it."

"I'm not giving up," I said. Briefly, I thought about telling her my own special connection to Tony, since she claimed to want the whole truth, but decided it was an unnecessary complication. There would be a time for it, but not now. "There's lots more detecting to do. I want to talk to your other sister, Beth. Having a hell of a time getting in touch with her."

"Her cabin," Karen said. "She stopped by to visit with Dad yesterday afternoon. She said she was going to her cabin afterward to do some writing. But I don't know why you should bother. Beth lives in her own little world. Trying to talk to her in any real way is like trying to talk to somebody in outer space. Janice and I can get her to open up a little, but I don't know anybody else who can."

I hesitated. What I was going to say was awkward, but I needed to say it anyway. "So you don't think she could have had an affair with Tony?"

"Jesus. Beth? No."

"Why not?"

"Have you seen her? She's not exactly Tony's type."

"Uh-huh. You mean she's not attractive enough?"

"She's attractive! She's just … a special kind of attractiveness."

"Right. Can you tell me how to find her cabin?"

She told me. It was a good hour away, in the foothills of Mount

Hood. I had her repeat the directions three times, to make sure I didn't get lost. I didn't want to get lost in the forest. I didn't want to go out there at all, really, but it had to be done.

"I went out there, you know," Karen said. "She wasn't there, but I thought maybe he'd be hiding there. Because he knows she doesn't use it all the time, and she doesn't rent it out. He wasn't there."

"Well, your sister may know something. You never know."

She shook her head, a bemused look in her eyes. "Beth and Tony. Wouldn't that be something? And then *both* my sisters would have betrayed me."

"Yeah. Well, I better get going. I'll let you know by SRS if I find out anything meaningful. Otherwise, check back on Friday morning, okay?"

I stood, gathering up my wallet, phone, and other things. She stood as well, but she looked confused and nervous, holding herself tightly, glancing around the room as if she was afraid someone or something was going to jump out at her. I put on my jacket and she watched me, moving slowly to the center of the room. She had kind of a sad-puppy look to her, and I felt bad running out on her so quickly. I tried to think of something comforting to say.

"You're not alone, okay?" I said. "I know it seems bleak right now, but I've seen a lot of ghosts. That first year is always the hardest, no matter how you died."

Her eyes were wide and bright. I thought she might cry, but instead she took a step closer to me, close enough that she had to lift her chin to look me in the face, close enough that I caught the scent of her floral perfume, magnolias and roses.

"I appreciate you," she said. "I mean, I appreciate everything you're doing. I want you to know that."

"Just my job," I said.

"You're a good man, Myron."

"Thank you. I'll put you in touch with my mother."

"If only I'd met a man like you. Maybe—maybe things would have been different."

"Karen—"

"Shh."

She put a finger up to my lips, and crazy as it was, I could actually feel it there—not as strong as an actual touch, with a bit more of an electric sizzle behind it, but close enough to the real thing that I might have mistaken her for a real person if I didn't know otherwise.

"You must be very lonely," she said.

I swallowed, and the lump in my throat felt as a big as a golf ball. "I manage."

"I know what it's like to be lonely. I've been lonely my entire life."

"Well …"

"You know," she said, dropping her voice to a seductive purr, "we could help each other with the loneliness. That's a problem we can solve, the two of us."

"Karen, we should really—"

"Let me show you," she said.

I had been so focused on her eyes—they were hypnotic, that particular shade of green—that I was only barely aware that her hands were working on the sash of her coat. With a shrug of her shoulders and a little shimmy, she slipped out of her trench coat.

And there she was, completely naked except for those red stiletto heels.

It goes without saying that there are plenty of people in the world who look better with their clothes on, even very attractive people, and I would have wagered good money before she stripped bare that Karen would be one of them because it was hard to imagine her looking *more* beautiful, but I was surprised again. Kate Upton, Bo Derrick, Rita Hayworth—take your pick of pinup girl from any generation, and I doubted they would have looked any better naked next to Karen Thorne. It wasn't just the full, supple breasts, the womanly hips, or the taut calves; it was the way it all fit together, all those slopes and curves in between, the way it all worked together as one thing, like a well-designed city.

"Well, what do you think?" she asked.

"I'm trying not to," I said.

"Think?"

"Look," I said.

"Ah. Don't worry about that. I'm not shy."

"It's not you I'm worried about. Why don't you put your trench coat back on?"

"I have a better idea," she said. "Why don't you take off your pants?"

Before I could reply, Billie stepped through the door into the room.

Everybody did their best audition for a mime parade, freezing in place, facial expressions exaggerated to comical effect. It was one of those moments when life too perfectly matches a sitcom for anyone to actually believe it happened—even if it wasn't *really* happening, not to anyone else but me. If anyone else walked in, they'd only see my shocked and vaguely guilty expression, and not the shocked and strangely bemused expression on my wife's face or the shocked and highly embarrassed expression on Karen's. They'd wonder why I was acting so crazy, which, of course, was how people looked at me most of the time these days. It would only be more so.

Billie was wearing her white gi with the green belt fastened tight, what she wore to her Kempo practices, which she often went to on Mondays. It only added to the strangeness of the moment.

"Oh no," Karen choked.

"Well," Billie said, having no trouble really giving the naked woman in front of her a scrutinizing look up and down, "if I'd known you were going to be here today in your birthday suit, I would have brought a drawing pad. I need to brush up on my nudes."

She was grinning. I'd expected some kind of outraged explosion out of Billie, or at least some hint of jealousy, and I was oddly disappointed by its absence. Poor Karen's husky confidence disappeared in an instant, and she blushed the mother of all blushes, a real whopper that exploded bright red in her cheeks, spread down her neck, and went even lower, much lower. I'd never known someone could blush that low until I saw it happen.

"Maybe you should put on that trench coat now," I whispered to her.

"Oh," she said, and snatched up her coat. She struggled with it, having a hard time getting her arms in the right places. "Oh dear. I've got to … I've got to go."

"I'll bet," Billie said.

Karen finally got the darn thing on—I have to admit, I felt a fair amount of disappointment—and was hustling toward the door when Billie put up a hand, stopping her abruptly. There wasn't a drop of rage in Billie's hands, but Karen still looked like she was afraid Billie was going to strangle her.

"Please," she said in a tiny voice.

"It's okay," Billie said. "I know you're in a vulnerable place. You just got some bad news, after all."

Karen blinked rapidly. "Bad news?"

"Well, of course. About your husband being … well, you know."

When Karen only offered still more blinking in reply, both women looked at me.

"You didn't tell her?" Billie asked.

"Tell me what?" Karen said.

"Not time yet," I said.

Billie, who'd shown little sign of anger at catching me with a naked woman in my office, now crossed her arms and glowered at me.

"Oh really?" she said.

"Will somebody *please* tell me what's going on?" Karen said.

I looked at Karen, and in my sternest voice, channeling some of the anger I was feeling toward Billie, I said, "There's nothing going on. I will be in touch when there is. Leave now."

That was all the encouragement Karen needed. Meekly, she made her exit, leaving me and Billie and a lot of tension filling the air between us. She was crossing her arms, glaring. I joined her in the effort. As if on cue, a deep, gravelly baritone started belting out some kind of Indian folk song down the hall.

"What the hell is going on?" she said. "Why didn't you tell her?"

I knew I had to choose my words carefully, so she wouldn't just disappear for three days this time. "I'm just waiting for all the information to come in," I said.

"What information, Myron? It's over! Tony Neuman is dead!"

"I know you said that."

"I said that? What's that supposed to mean? "

"Billie—"

"Are you saying I'm *lying?*"

"I don't know."

"Yes, you do. There's only one reason you didn't tell Karen her husband is dead, and it's because you think I lied to you about what I found out at Manuel Loretto's. You don't trust me. You think I'm lying."

"Well, did you?" I shot back.

"What reason would I possibly have to lie? I'm on *your* side."

"You didn't answer my question."

"Can't you just trust me on this?"

"Still no answer. Did you lie to me?"

"I don't believe this!"

"Did you?"

"I'm done! I'm done with this!"

"Did you lie, Billie? Did you lie to me?"

"*Yes!*" she screamed. *"And this time it was for a good reason!"*

It was as if an F-15 had flown low overhead, leaving a sonic boom in its wake. Whether the sound of her shout was real in the literal sense or not, I still felt its vibrations in the floorboards and in the walls and in every piece of furniture and junk that filled my little office. She was glaring and breathing hard, her face coated in a sheen of sweat. I was so dumfounded that it took me a few seconds to get out any words.

"What do you mean, this time?" I said. "When—when did you lie before? Is that priest involved in this somehow? Does he know something bad's going to happen to me?"

"Myron," she said, rubbing her temples.

"Is it something else? Is it about why you killed yourself? We've never really talked about it. Answer me, damn it!"

Now it was me who was shouting, and my voice boomed even louder. She shook her head and closed her eyes, standing like that for a few long seconds, then turned and abruptly walked out of the room. She was gone so quickly that I couldn't even tell her to stop. I wasn't ready to let it go at that, the fear and anger coursing through me in equal measure, so I stormed to the door and threw it open.

She was gone.

There was, however, someone else in the narrow hall, a tiny Indian man dressed in a simple brown cloak. He was approaching from the church door on the right, bare feet on the threadbare brown carpet, and I saw other similarly dressed people of various nationalities watching from the doorway. The tips of his fingers clasped in the sign of prayer, the man bowed slightly.

"Greetings, brother," he said. "Would you mind keeping it down a bit? We're trying to sing a few hymns, you see."

Chapter 22

THE MONEY WAS hidden in a grove of pin oaks at the edge of a farmer's field in Woodburn. I traipsed through the tall grass under the setting sun, Billie and Antonia beside me, the headache that had been hounding me for days finally fading under the welcome arrival of a cool breeze. It was the first glimpse of cooler weather I'd seen in weeks. The first few days of July had brought with it a merciless heat wave, and the heat, as I'd learned over the past two years, was one of the triggers that brought on the headaches. The throbbing in my skull had been with me so long that I'd almost forgotten what it was like without it.

"Just up there, by a big stump," Antonia said.

She was dressed in the same outfit as when I'd met her six weeks earlier, the simple blue dress and the white headscarf. Billie wore skin-tight black shorts, a sleeveless black T-shirt, and Birkenstocks. The grass sliced at my bare arms and crunched under my shoes, but it did not bend in the slightest to Billie and Antonia. As annoying as the grass was, I found myself wishing the whole world was covered in tall grass. It would make it much easier for me to tell the ghosts apart.

Fully within the trees, the grass was thinner, festooned with weeds and exposed roots, all of it dappled with the shadows of oaks in full dress. The shadows shimmered and shifted in response to the breeze. I heard the whinny of a horse far off in the distance, but otherwise a reverent silence hung over the grove. In the old days, before the shooting, it was just the kind of place I would have come to on my own, and stayed a while. There weren't even any ghosts around, except for the two I'd brought with me.

I spotted the stump right away, at the edge of a ravine that probably filled with water in the winter but was filled with nothing now but the crisp remains of last year's leaves. Antonia, her face still swollen red from all the crying, walked ahead of me and pointed at a spot one foot to the right of the stump. I stepped up beside her, testing the ground with my foot. It was so soft I hardly needed the hand shovel I'd brought with me.

"Look," I said, "I'm going to try to reason with you one more time. I *really* don't want to take this money."

"Please," Antonia said. "If you don't take, very much hurt me."

"Your husband doesn't have a lot of money. It should go to him."

Antonia shook her head adamantly. "He only waste it on drinking. Please. You *must* have money. You brought Katya home. You brought her to her father. He may drink too much, but he is still good and loves her so. It is the only way I can thank you."

"For God's sake, Myron, just take it," Billie said. "You came all the way out here, didn't you?"

"All right, all right," I said.

It took only a moment to dig up the Folgers can, buried as it was only a few inches under the surface. A station wagon with a bad muffler rumbled past and we all tensed, but it didn't stop. I brushed off the dirt and removed the plastic lid. Inside, in yet another, smaller plastic container, was a thick wad of bills tied with a rubber band. Flipping through the cash, it was a mix of denominations, but mostly twenties.

"It's too much," I said. "There has to be at least two thousand dollars here."

"Two thousand, one hundred, fifty-nine," Antonia said, intoning the words as precisely as a Jeopardy contestant. "And it is all yours, Myron Vale."

"You really sure about this?" I said.

"Myron," Billie warned.

"Okay, fine." Then, looking at Antonia, I said more softly, "Thank you. Really. It's not necessary, but thank you."

She looked like she might cry again, but she blinked a few times and kept them in check. She reached out with her right hand and hovered it over my chest.

"A good heart," she said. "Your wife very right. Now I go. I walk home to be with my husband and daughter."

She walked out of the grove, gone before I'd even thought to offer her a ride. I looked at Billie, who was shaking her head at me. I had the hand shovel in one hand and the money in the other.

"What?" I said.

"You're not going to put that money back, are you?"

"Nope."

"Good."

"Someone might find it, then. I'm going to open a college savings account for Katya instead."

Billie sighed. "How am I not surprised? But you know, you're going to have a hard time making a living as a private investigator if you never accept any payment."

"Who said I'm going to be a private investigator?"

"Aren't you?"

"No way. This was great, glad I did my part, but it was a one-shot deal."

"I see."

She started out of the grove, back toward the Prius. I followed.

"I mean it," I said.

"I know you do," she said.

"Then why are you smiling like that?"

"Because," she said, smiling even wider, "I know something you don't know."

"What's that?"

"You don't believe a word you're saying."

Chapter 23

DRIVING OUT to Beth's cabin at noon, I was in an odd state of mind. Still reeling from that last conversation with Billie before she again walked out on me, my thoughts were whipped up with anger, but my body was still pumped up with lust from the sight of Karen's magnificent naked body. It was a strange brew of emotions and impulses, careening me just on the edge of chaos. I'd never felt more out of control or more alive.

It was no way to work. I grabbed a burger on the way out of town, hoping a little food in my stomach might settle me down. It helped a little. The long drive helped a little more. The cabin was located just outside Government Camp, in the foothills of Mount Hood and a good sixty miles from my house on US-26. Before I'd gone far, however, I noticed a distinctive black Ford Explorer in my rearview mirror, three or four cars back, and I took a brief detour through the little town of Sandy to lose them. That helped focus my mind as well.

No longer hungry, no longer followed, I continued up US-26 under a gray-blue sky that was like an amateur's watercolor, all the colors blurring into a muddy mess. As the city fell away, and then the occasional farmer's field and pasture, a smattering of firs and pin oaks began to line the four-lane road, growing thicker in number as the Prius slowly gained elevation. By the time I passed the little towns of Brightwood, Welches, and Rhododendron, the highway dropped to two lanes and there were slender-trunked Sitka spruces mixed in with the firs.

I tried not to look in the trees, but I couldn't help but notice the ghosts close to the road—or what I assumed were ghosts, of course. Two Native Americans in deerskins trotted along the shoulder, each carrying bloodied tomahawks in one hand and scalps in the other. A burly, bearded man was skinning a black bear on a rise. An old man, naked, tan, and wrinkled like a prune, was pointing a revolver at his own head and weeping. Two teenage girls dressed in denim were trying to wave down cars with no luck. I almost stopped until I saw that one of the girls had maggots crawling out of her eyes.

The strangest ones were the not-quite-humans loping through the shadows, prehistoric people with tiny foreheads, wide noses, and jutting jaws. I'd only spotted a few over the years, usually from a distance, and they always made me wonder how far back this ghost thing went. I'd never seen a ghost of an animal, including those closely related to humans, like chimpanzees and monkeys. Did that mean they had no ghosts? Or did it mean I only saw the ghosts of humans and their predecessors because their DNA was most closely related to my own?

I did my best to force these thoughts from my mind. This was just the rational side of me trying to make sense of something that wasn't rational.

Just outside Government Camp, a dusting of white appeared here and there in the trees, but most of the ground looked sodden and wet, the rains having washed away the early-October snow. Lots of muted greens and reds and browns. As remote as Beth's cabin was, it wasn't too hard to find, just north of the Zigzag River a few miles from town, a cozy little place with a covered porch supported by four wooden beams. It was at the end of a long gravel road rutted with puddles, nestled in among the spruces and firs, far removed from any other house. With a warm yellow glow in the paned windows, a wood shake roof littered with fir needles, and a forest looming dark and endless behind it, the cabin seemed like something out of a fairy tale.

A red Prius was parked under the tiny carport, which brought a smile to my face. A woman after my own heart. Beth herself was just emerging from the cabin, a bulging white trash bag in hand, when I parked my own Prius behind hers.

She stopped just before the steps and stared at me, tennis shoes impossibly white, her Nike windbreaker zipped up to her chin. The jacket was the same color as the fir trees, which made me wonder if it was deliberate. The photo of her in Bernie's office hadn't done her justice. While she was shorter and blockier than her sisters, with something of a hooked nose and brown hair that fell severely straight on both sides of her face, she had her own kind of beauty.

Getting out of the car, I stepped into mountain air that nipped at my bare face. Taking a deep breath through my nose, the air smelled strongly of fir and was noticeably thinner in my lungs.

"Somebody after my own heart," I said to Beth.

"What?" she said.

"You drive a Prius," I said.

"Oh. Right. You must be Myron." She had a clipped, no-nonsense way of speaking, as if she was always in a hurry to get to the next sentence.

"Ah. My reputation precedes me, then. Who called you?"

"Janice," she said.

"And after I paid her all that money and everything to keep quiet."

"What?"

"Just a joke."

"Oh, right. I have garbage here."

"So I see," I said.

She watched me for a little longer, as if waiting for me to see some deeper meaning in her comment, then nodded curtly and headed to the carport. As she passed, I caught a whiff of the garbage—rotten milk, spoiled meat, and other unpleasantness. I wasn't sure what she wanted me to do, so I waited while she deposited the bag in a brown plastic can behind her car and headed toward the cabin. I caught some movement in the trees behind her, but it was a tall black man with a deer draped over his shoulder, dressed in a deerskin cap and with a rifle musket slung over his shoulder, just passing through without looking our way. Beth moved like she spoke, crisply and with purpose, and she took no notice of the black man. Another ghost, then.

"I have to get back to writing," she announced, without stopping or even glancing my way.

"I just want a few minutes of your time," I said.

"I don't want to think about Karen's death. It just makes me sad."

"Tony's not here, is he?"

That got her to stop, abruptly, with one foot on the step. She whirled around, face aghast. Since she'd barely showed a hint of emotion since I'd arrived, such a blatant display of it was a bit of a surprise.

"Karen's husband?" she said. "Are you *crazy?*"

"He's not?"

"Of course not! Why would he be here? I detested that man and how he turned Karen into a drunk, weak-kneed, simpering nymphomaniac. I would *never* let him hide here. How could you say such a thing?"

"I've just learned that Mr. Neuman has a certain way with women."

"Well, not with me! He ruined my sister and just may have killed her, too."

"So you think she was murdered?"

"I do. My opinion was in the minority, though. I hope you catch him, but I'm afraid I can't be of much help. I don't know what I could tell you that you haven't already learned from Dad and Janice. Now, if you'll excuse me, I'm in the middle of working on a sonnet and I don't want to lose my train of thought."

She shook her head as if she was trying to shake off her encounter with me and proceeded up the steps. Her reaction hadn't seemed faked it all—I'd obviously touched some kind of nerve—but I still really wanted to see the inside of the cabin. Or at least to see how hard she would work to keep me out of it.

"It's been a long drive," I said. "Mind if I use your restroom before I go?"

"The gas station on the highway has a public restroom."

"Please. I was also hoping for a glass of water. I know I'm imposing."

She sighed, her back to me. I felt a strange thrill, as if she was about to confess that Tony was inside, but then she turned slowly and nodded.

"All right," she said, "but only for a moment."

"Thank you," I said, trying to keep the disappointment out of my voice.

"I'll have you know, though, I have a gun."

"What?"

"Inside the cabin. I bought it a couple years ago."

"Okay."

"For protection," she added. "I had an incident a couple weeks ago, a couple of Mexicans came up here asking if Tony had ever been here or ever given me anything. They were not nice men. They wanted to come inside. I told them no. They asked again and I pointed the gun at them. They left and didn't come back."

"Did they say what Tony would have given you?"

"No, but when I came back a week later, one of the windows was broken and it was obvious they'd searched the whole cabin."

"I'm sorry to hear that."

"I'm just glad I had the gun when they came the first time."

"Right. Well, I don't think you have to worry about me. You can ask your father or sister if you're not sure."

"I already have."

She said this the same way my mother once told me that she'd already talked to my fourth-grade teacher when I protested that she could call the school if she really wanted to know if I was listening in class. *I already have.* Beth regarded me silently for a while, long enough that I felt the need to smile, which only increased the awkwardness, or at least mine, then she turned toward the house. She didn't ask me to come in or even wave for me to follow, but she did leave the door open.

Overwhelmed by her sense of hospitality, I followed her into the cabin. My jacket was unzipped, and I kept my hand where it had easy access to the Glock, just in case. I eased into the room, ready for Tony to jump me, but it didn't happen. The cabin was a cozy affair with deeply stained oak paneling, a low-nap taupe carpet almost as smooth as hardwood, and a high ceiling with exposed beams that made the place seem bigger than it was. A fire crackled in the large stone fireplace, the room's most significant and attractive feature.

Since Beth immediately plunked herself in front of a laptop at a picnic-style kitchen table, I closed the door. It was so warm inside, I already felt myself sweating.

"Bathroom's down the hall," she informed me.

She certainly didn't seem to be acting as if someone was hiding in the cabin. Still, I stayed ready as I used the facilities and glanced in the two bedrooms next to the bathroom, finding nobody inside. Neither of the rooms had closets. When I returned to the main room, she was still at the computer, but a glass of water sat on the far end of the table.

"There you go," she said.

The galley kitchen was through an alcove and fully in view. I didn't see anyone in there either. It was possible Tony was in some nook or cranny I'd missed, but I doubted it. I picked up the glass and found it cool to the touch.

"How much do I owe you?" I asked.

She squinted at me. "Is that another joke?"

"You don't seem to be smiling, so I guess not."

She went back to her computer. The humming of the laptop seemed loud in the silent room, and when I took a drink, I was embarrassed at the sound of my own gulping. The water was ice cold and there was a slightly mineral aftertaste. I put the glass down and waited for her to look at me, but of course she didn't.

"Are you sure there's nothing you can tell me that might help?" I asked.

She sighed.

"I know," I said, "I'm being a bit annoying. It's a habit I'm trying to break. I've been told he might have owed some people money. Do you know anything about that?"

"No," she said.

"I heard he might have been selling drugs."

"Doesn't surprise me."

"Why is that?"

"He just seems like he'd be into that sort of thing."

"But you don't know if he was or wasn't?"

"No."

"Did you know Karen changed her will because she was afraid Tony might be thinking of killing her?"

"No."

"Did you know Janice was having an affair with him?"

This, finally, got her to look up from her keyboard. With her hair flanking her face, it was as if she were lifting a hood. I saw a glimmer of surprise, then her eyes narrowed and took on a cold, reptilian quality, focusing not on me but on something beyond.

"Well, that doesn't surprise me either," she said.

"Why is that?"

She frowned and stared at her computer. "I think I've said enough."

"All right."

"It's just that being with a man was never about love for her. It's always about winning. So of course she has to take Karen's man, too. That proves she's winning."

"I see."

"Our whole family is very competitive."

"But not you?"

"I really think you should leave now."

"Okay."

"But of course I'm competitive. It's the way the Thornes are made. But I found the best way to be competitive is to play my own game. I have my own vision of my life, and I don't require their approval to manifest it."

"Manifest," I said. "Nice word, seldom used."

"Another joke," she said.

"You're a tough crowd."

"I don't laugh much, I know. Now, if you'll excuse me, I really must return to my work."

This time, her goodbye had a note of finality to it. I still waited a few extra beats, just to see if she'd talk again, but no such luck. She concentrated on her screen with the intensity of a high school student taking her SATs. I thanked her, received a grunt in reply, and showed myself out.

The air had cooled noticeably. Standing there on the porch, checking the time on my cell phone, my breath fogged in front of me. I barely had one bar on the phone, blinking in and out. It was not yet three o'clock, but the gray, gauzy quality of the light and the deepening shadows of the tree trunks made it feel later. There was something bothering me, something about my encounter with Beth that didn't add up, but I couldn't put my finger on it.

Approaching the Prius, I saw that there was a man sitting in the backseat. I reached for the Glock, closing my fingers around the handle. The glare of the light, weak as it was, made it hard to see who was inside until I got close. It was a middle-age man with thinning gray-blond hair, dressed in a bright blue military jacket with a red collar, a style that hearkened back to the Revolutionary War.

I opened the door. The man didn't look at me until it must have dawned on him that I was staring right at him, then he flinched. The buttons, the white pants, the shiny black boots—it was definitely military dress from a much earlier era.

"Ghost?" I said.

He had a long nose and small mouth, giving him a youthful appearance, but his skin had the cracked and weathered quality of old bark. "You—you can see me?" he stuttered.

"I'm gifted that way. Get out."

"I was just ... I've never driven in one of these. I thought—"

"This isn't a Toyota dealership," I said, "and I'm not doing any free test drives."

With a shrug, he stepped out of the car, right through the side. He wore a long ceremonial sword. It wasn't until he was out in the open air, when a slight breeze ruffled his hair, that I saw the bullet hole on his right temple, a tiny charred oval with only a trace of blood around it.

"There's something familiar about you," I said.

"I hear that frequently," he said.

The clothes. The face. Even the manner of his death. It came back to me in a flash. "Meriwether Lewis," I guessed.

He bowed his head.

"No William Clark?" I said.

"I'm afraid the captain and I had a bit of a falling out. A bit of a disagreement on whether the war in Iraq was worth fighting after 9/11."

"I see. That's a very modern debate."

"Once a man of the military, always a man of the military."

"Right. So what are you doing up here?"

"Exploring," he said.

"Still? Hasn't it all been pretty much explored by now?"

"Not by me," he said.

"Right. Can I show you something?" When he nodded, I took out Tony's picture, the one I'd gotten from Karen's apartment. "Have you seen this man around here?"

"I don't believe so, though I have just come from the north."

Disappointed, I put the picture away. "Well, thanks anyway. Say, did you really commit suicide?"

"That's a rather personal question, don't you think?"

"Sorry. You still want a ride?"

His face brightened. "Yes, of course. I'm fascinated by the hybrid technology."

"You traveled eight-thousand miles, most of it on foot, and you're impressed by a Prius?"

"Actually, I'm most impressed by the Segway scooters, but the Prius is certainly intriguing. I do try to keep up on all the modern modes of transportation."

I gave Lewis a ride back down the gravel road, answering his questions on the way. He was most curious about when the gas motor kicked in versus the electric one. If I hadn't been so bothered by my conversation with Beth, I would have asked him some questions about his adventures with the Corps of Discovery, but the troubling thing gnawing at me kept crowding out other thoughts.

Just before we reached Government Camp, I pulled to the shoulder and let him out. He tapped the hood.

"A good vehicle," he said. "They've progressed much since the first horseless carriage."

"What will you do now?" I asked.

"Oh, make camp for the night. I prefer sleeping outdoors. A man really doesn't need anything more than a few trees to block the wind and the stars overhead to be happy."

I wished him well and he marched off into the woods. He'd just vanished into the trees when I finally realized what was bothering me—and I had Lewis's comment partly to thank.

The garbage.

The cabin hadn't smelled like garbage.

Stopped on the side of the road, with my Prius's electric engine as silent as a sleeping baby, my mind raced over what this meant. If Beth had only just removed the garbage from the house, as smelly as that bag had been, there should have been some trace of the stench when we'd gone inside. More importantly, she'd only arrived the previous night, so she hadn't even had time to create that much trash. Those two things meant not only that somebody else had produced the garbage but that this person also wasn't staying in the cabin.

This person was most likely staying in the woods nearby.

Like Lewis, Tony Neuman was probably camping under the stars. Unlike Lewis, Tony was using the cabin as his base and Beth as his contact with the world. The problem was, I had no idea where he would be hiding in the miles and miles of national forest that surrounded us. My best bet would be to watch the cabin and hope that Tony showed up at some point, or that Beth went out to meet him.

There was no time to waste, because she could have been on her way to see him already.

I couldn't just drive up there, though, or she'd see me coming long before I got there—not to mention Tony, who might be monitoring the road himself. I'd have to walk, and preferably in the forest. The good news was that the cabin was probably only a half a mile up the road from Government Camp. Even through the forest, I could get to the cabin in minutes if I hustled.

Just off to the left, there was a 7-Eleven, and I parked at the back of the lot, trying to use the building to hide the car. A man dressed in a black parka, cracked ski goggles on his head, was sitting by the door and weeping into his hands. A young couple went inside without even glancing his way. I started to get out of the car, then remembered who I was dealing with and decided I should at least tell somebody where I was.

The cell phone had two bars, but the call went through and Alesha picked up on the first ring. I heard ringing phones and laughter in the background, the familiar sounds of our police bureau.

"Yes, Kimosabe?" she said.

"I think I found him," I said.

"What?"

"Government Camp. He's hiding in the woods behind Beth Thorne's cabin. Here's the address."

I gave it to her, and I heard the scratch of her pen on the other end.

"And you know this how?" she asked.

"No time to explain. I don't know exactly where he is yet, but there's a good chance I'll find out in a moment. Cell phone's iffy up here, so I just wanted you to know where I was if you don't hear from me soon."

"Myron, wait, you're not going to—"

"No time. One last thing. I'm pretty sure he's the one who shot me."

"What? Myron—"

I hung up.

Chapter 24

THE MEETING RAN long, and the gray, overcast afternoon was sliding into an early dusk by the time I pulled into our driveway. The light was so poor that the street lamps lining the street were already aglow, casting their pallid light on the oak leaves, which had just begun their autumn shift to yellow and crimson. When I saw how dark our house was, I felt a pinch of guilt.

Once inside, I heard the *whisk-whisk* of a paintbrush coming from down the hall. Walking through the shadows, I found her in her studio working on the same painting she'd been working on for the better part of a week. She always worked with her easel near the window and turned toward the light, but even so, it was so dark in the room I don't know how she could work. I could barely see her face. I could barely see her body either, and I wished I could, since she appeared to be working in the black lingerie she'd worn last night. The glimpses of white flesh and sloping curves tantalized me.

There were moments, as fleeting and as wonderful as they were, when I forgot that my wife was a ghost. This morning I'd had one of those moments. I'd blown her a kiss and was out the door with a smile on my face, forgetting how helpless she was in the house without me.

"I'm sorry," I said, "I should have turned on more lights before I left. Didn't know I'd be this long."

"It's okay," she said, "you've had a lot on your mind lately."

"Do you want me to turn on the overhead light?"

"No. I'm used to it. What did Frank want?"

"What else? My help."

"He's got a case for you?"

"It's not a case," I said.

"Okay."

"Don't call it a case. I'm just doing him a favor. Somebody stole some inheritance money, leaving the widow broke. The deceased husband wants to make sure she gets her money back. I'm just putting some missing pieces together for them."

"Sounds like a case," she said.

"It's not," I insisted.

"If you say so."

"It's really not."

I couldn't see her face, but I could imagine how smug her smile was. She dabbed at some yellow paint on the palette she was holding, a palette I realized would be way too heavy for her to use her limited ability to levitate to keep in the air like that. I hadn't realized this until today.

"You're not using a real brush, are you?" I asked.

"It's real," she said.

"I mean, nobody will be able to see it but you and me."

"And other ghosts."

"And other ghosts, right. Can I see it yet?"

"Nope. I told you, it's a surprise. But I can tell you where we're going to hang it—now that you're starting your fourth case."

"It's not a case. None of them were cases."

Saying nothing, she applied a little more paint. I sighed.

"Where are we going to hang it?" I asked.

"In your office," she said.

"I don't have an office."

"Not yet."

"You don't mean an office in the house, do you?"

"Nope."

I watched her paint a little while, marveling at the enigma that was my wife. She'd always been an enigma to me, never knowable directly but always obliquely, like having to guess at what a painting looked like by watching the person painting it instead of seeing it yourself. For some strange reason, it was why I loved her.

"Let me get this straight," I said. "You're painting a picture to hang in an office that I don't have yet, for a job that I don't want?"

"No, I'm painting a picture for an office that you're going to rent for a job you haven't figured out you already have."

"Uh-huh. And it will look just like a blank canvas to every other living person but me. Only the ghosts will be able to see what it is."

She looked at me, and I could just make out a hint of her smile, the shine of her teeth floating suspended in the darkness like the Cheshire cat's.

"That's exactly the point," she said. "They'll know right away they've got the right detective."

Chapter 25

As a boy, some of my fondest memories took place in the woods. After baseball, hiking had been my father's true love, and even before I could walk, he was packing me along the Pacific Northwest's many trails in a harness on his back. I'd breathed the rarified air of Mount Rainier and looked down upon the sapphire waters of Crater Lake before I could even speak my own name. Most of these treks had been day trips, since my mother did not share his abiding love of the outdoors, but I cherish those brief jaunts with Dad far more than the longer, more expensive vacations Mom dragged us on to Disneyland or Hawaii or the Caribbean, where the tension that existed between my parents only seemed to grow with each passing day.

Taciturn by nature, not given to public displays of emotion of any sort, my father changed somehow in the woods. Something about the fresh forest air and the treetop call of the birds and the pliant earth beneath his feet unlocked some part of my father's personality that would not reveal itself anywhere else. He talked to me. He told me things. He opened up in ways he never did elsewhere.

It was in the woods I learned how much he still missed his brother, someone he never talked about anywhere else, or *with* anyone else. It was in the woods I learned about the dyslexia he'd battled as a child and why it still made him reluctant to read aloud in front of anyone. It was in the woods I'd learned his greatest fear—not that he would die in the line of duty but that he would live long enough to become a burden to those he loved.

I wondered, sometimes, if he would be restored to his former self when he died. I hoped he would be, though there was no way to know. I hoped he would be so that we could walk in the forest together, and I might have my father back again.

So it was with both excitement and trepidation that I veered away from the gravel road and into the forest near Beth Thorne's cabin. Many ghosts awaited me, and quite a few were in my own mind.

It was not yet four o'clock, but the light was already failing. Fir trees loomed large and foreboding, the tall trunks nearly lost to shadow, the few bits of colorless sky I could spot through the dense canopy graying into blackness. An owl hooted a warning. Now and then I spotted house lights through the forest, which I tried to use as my compass, never getting too close for fear of being seen. The ground was a soft carpet of fir needles and moss and mud spots that mucked against my tennis shoes.

My breath fogged the air, and blown back by a faint wind, warmed my own cheeks. I checked the Glock, made sure it was loaded. My fingers already felt numb, hard to move.

I glimpsed a few ghosts at first—a black boy climbing a tree, a woman in a tent of a dress berating her much thinner husband—and then, the farther I got from the highway, many more. I saw an old man playing golf with a toddler, helping him with his swing. I saw a pair of bearded lumberjacks sawing away at one of the tallest of the firs, but of course making no progress. I saw a group of young men in mountain-climbing gear sitting in a circle and drinking beer. I saw, flitting in and out of shadow, darting from one tree to another, the hazy forms of the primitive people, bent and shuffling, communicating with each other through grunts and hisses.

Sometimes the ghosts walked beside me. Sometimes they spoke to me, asking my name, asking if I could see them, asking for help or favors or even just a smile. Sometimes their numbers grew to a crowd, enough that I was afraid something terrible might happen if I acknowledged them—which I never did, not even in the slightest way.

Once I even thought I saw the priest, standing on the other side of a ravine and watching me. Even for him, I didn't stop.

I was on a mission now. I was going to find the man who'd shot me, the man who'd cursed me with my strange affliction. I would not let the unpredictability of ghosts or my own fears stand in the way.

Occasionally, I heard voices and laughter from the distant cabins, but I could never be sure if they were from the living. I hustled as fast as I could, legs burning, shirt sticking to my back, though it still seemed to take a lifetime to reach Beth's cabin. I passed it once and doubled back too far before finally coming upon it again. I was struck again by how her place resembled a fairy-tale cottage, the light in the windows beating back the encroaching darkness, the witch inside with Hansel and Gretel.

The underbrush was spare enough that I was afraid of getting too close, but the light was so poor that if I didn't get closer, I didn't know if I'd even see anyone coming or going. Tree by tree, I darted nearer, until I found the biggest fir with the widest trunk, crouching behind it.

Then I waited. Although it was hard to tell from my distance, I did not see movement in the windows. I wondered if I was too late and felt depressed at my own slowness—out of shape, rusty from too much time sitting in a chair, distracted by demons no one else could see. I waited some more. Hours must have passed. I checked my cell phone and was surprised to find it had only been forty-five minutes from when I'd called Alesha.

There was movement just off to my right, a man's shape, and I grabbed the Glock and pointed it at him. It was a muscular man in a white toga. He loped on without acknowledging me. I kept the Glock out, just to be safe. Tony Neuman was out here. He could have been watching me, even now. I heard raucous laughter somewhere in the distance. A woman screamed even farther away.

Could that have been Beth? Or was it merely another ghost?

Crouching there in the cold, the moisture in the dirt seeping into my shoes, I felt the old despair setting over me. A good detective relies on sharp senses, keen intelligence, and a fair amount of instinct. When one or more of these is compromised, what good is he?

The curtain of night fell slowly upon the forest, the tops of the trees losing their distinctiveness to the sky. I wished I'd brought a flashlight. The whisper of the breeze was a voice mocking me for my foolishness. The windows of Beth's cabin cast their light farther and farther, the shadows of the panes even reaching to the tree where I crouched. I began to shiver. I was beginning to lose hope when finally I saw a shape pass the window.

I tightened my grip on the Glock. The movement had been too fast and too far away to make out who it was, but within seconds the door creaked open and Beth emerged. As she locked the door behind her, I saw her distinctly in the porch light; she was dressed in a gray wool knit hat pulled low over her ears, a bulky black parka, and dark jeans. She had a heavy black duffel bag slung over her shoulder. Thankfully, despite her perfect camouflage, she'd made the odd choice to also wear her bright white tennis shoes, which acted like a lighthouse beacon in the dark sea of the forest.

She stood on the porch for a long time, watching, scanning the trees, and I remained absolutely still. It was so quiet, except for the faint breeze, that even a single snap of a twig might alert her to my presence. I didn't even hear any ghosts. I wondered if they were watching, too, as if this was all just an interesting spectacle to them. Finally, Beth marched north into the trees, toward the mountain, in a steady, monotonous gait that I could have picked out in a crowd. The crunch of her footsteps sounded as if they were coming right next to me.

I watched the white of her shoes, flitting in and out of the trees. I couldn't lose the shoes. When she'd gone as far as I dared, when the sound of her own footsteps was lost to me, I began to follow. I concentrated on the path, navigating toward spots on the ground, dry dirt and soft beds of needles, that muffled my footsteps.

We walked for a long time, and now and then I lost her briefly only to pick her up again. I was careful not to gain on her. More than once the white sneakers stopped, and I could sense her studying the forest, listening. I stopped along with her, heart thudding away in my ears, the sweat on my back freezing immediately to my skin. It was during one of these stops that my head began to pound.

It couldn't have come at a worse time—my old friend, starting slow and gaining steam, that throbbing at the front of my skull where the .38 had made its home. All the symptoms reared their ugly heads: the nausea, the whoosh of wooziness, the bleariness in the eyes. I blinked and tried to follow her, lurching from one trunk to another. For a while I even managed to keep the fuzzy whiteness of her shoes in sight. Then it was gone.

Leaning against a trunk, gritting my teeth at the pain, I scanned and rescanned the forest, praying the shoes would come into view, but it was hopeless. I'd lost her. I was a crippled, useless joke of a detective, and I'd lost her.

I closed my eyes and leaned my forehead against the tree, the bark as cool as ice. Tony Neuman's face, those chiseled cheekbones, those dead gray eyes, flared up in my mind, and I felt both helpless and enraged.

He wouldn't get away.

Not now. Not when I was so close.

As if in reply to my silent vow, I heard the murmur of chanting in the distance.

With no other ideas, I followed the sound, tripping more than once on an unseen root or rock. Soon I came upon a clearing, where what little starlight that made it through the thick night air showed me a circle of six Native American men, their heads bowed, chanting in their own language. Their faces were painted white, feathers were braided into their hair, and most of their faces were bloodied, their wounds deep black gashes in the near darkness.

I cleared my throat. They all looked at me, eyes flying wide with fright.

"I won't hurt you," I said. "Do you know who I am?"

Nobody moved. Nobody spoke.

"I'm Myron Vale, the ghost detective."

The bigger of the men cautiously rose to his feet, his face as bone white as a skull's. "I know you," he said solemnly. "I hear your name spoken."

"I need your help," I said. "If you help me, I'll help you when you need it. There is a man hiding in this forest, a living man. The woman who lives nearby in a cabin brings him things. Do you know where he is?"

The big Native American man hesitated, then spoke to his comrades in his own language. They spoke back. He nodded and turned back to me.

"Why do you wish to find this man?" he asked.

"He shot me," I said, pointing to my scar.

"And you wish ... revenge?"

"Justice," I said.

"Ah."

"I'm good to my word. If you ever need my help, I'll be there for you. You can ask any—"

He held up a hand. "We know your word is good—as good as any white man's can be. You have simply never offered it to us before."

They conversed some more, then rose swiftly as one, the man who'd acted as their translator pointing the way. They hollered and whooped a battle cry, and I cringed, fearing I was losing the element of surprise, then remembered that neither Beth nor Tony would be able to hear them.

As we set out into the forest, they flanked me in a V, the man who'd spoken to me at the front, the other braves spreading out to the sides with their tomahawks at the ready. The pulsing in my head was still there, and my vision was still blurred and my balance unsteady, but with them as my guide we made swift progress. We angled to the right, and though the way ahead seemed flat, we must have been going up ever so slightly, judging by the increased strain in my calves. It wasn't long before I heard the murmur of a river.

We crested a rise, the Native Americans crouching behind the trunks of the firs there, waving me forward. Joining them, I peered below, and the first thing I saw was a campfire perhaps a quarter-mile ahead, set back a short ways from a river that shimmered like a carpet of polished onyx. I felt moisture in the air. I saw the outline of a dome tent near the fire, as well as a couple of coolers. I saw the shadows of two people, one taller than the other.

When I turned to thank my companions, I found I was alone.

With the river, the wind, and the distance from the campfire, I was too far away to make out any conversation. Glock in hand, I crept along the rise until I was just above the campfire, close enough that I caught a whiff of wood smoke on the wind. They had their backs to me, and with the firelight and the openness of the sky above them, I could clearly see Beth's white shoes. The man wore a camo jacket and had a rifle slung over his shoulder. They were whispering, then the man leaned over and cupped Beth's face with both hands, kissing her.

It was my moment. Glock aimed at him, safety off, I walked into the clearing from behind. The ground near the campfire was a mixture of pebble and dirt. Finally, my headache had subsided, my balance steady, my vision clear. I was halfway to them when the man broke off the kiss and veered toward me, bringing his rifle to bear.

"Don't," I said.

When he kept bringing the rifle up, I blasted an empty beer can on the ground near him. Dirt and rocks sprayed the air, and the can skittered high before plopping in the river. The shot made my ears ring, and the boom rolled over the trees and receded into the distance. My old police instincts kicked into gear, and I rushed forward, keeping the Glock trained on the man.

"All right, all right," he said, holding his rifle to the side.

I felt both a surge of victory and a tremendous sense of relief, because not only did I recognize the man's chiseled face in the firelight as Tony Neuman's, even under a baseball cap, even with a scraggly dark beard, but I recognized the voice as the same one that had haunted my dreams. *Nobody move! This is a robbery!* There was no doubt now, and as I stopped within a few steps of him, I saw those same dead eyes peering back at me. Beth's face was as white as her shoes.

"Drop it," I said to Tony.

He did, the rifle clattering on pebbles. He was thinner than in his photos, his face gaunt, the muscles in his neck defined. The fire crackled, shadows dancing around us, the smoke whipping up into the darkness.

"How—how did you find us?" Beth asked.

Tony snorted. "How do you think? He followed you."

"But I was so careful."

"Not careful enough, you stupid bitch."

"I'm—I'm sorry."

"Just shut up!"

Witnessing this little exchange, and seeing the adoring way Beth regarded him, even after being treated so poorly, made my stomach turn. I'd built this man up so much in my mind and now, facing him in the flesh, he was small and cruel and hardly worthy of all the animosity and fear I'd directed his way. I'd put dozens and dozens of guys like him behind bars. Maybe he was a little smarter, a little more handsome, but he was cut from the same cloth. Just another loser.

"How much is it going to take?" he asked me.

"Excuse me?"

"You're obviously a smart guy—talented, resourceful. I'm sure we can come to an arrangement here. What's your price?"

The anger he'd displayed toward Beth was gone; his voice was smooth, seductive almost. It was such an abrupt transformation that only a fool would fall for such fake sincerity—and yet, part of me *wanted* to fall for it. In the span of a few seconds, he'd showed me the two sides of himself: the lowlife thug he really was and the talented thespian who'd never met someone he couldn't con. I finally had an inkling how he got not one, but three rich Thorne girls to fall for him.

"I don't want money," I said.

"Everybody wants money. It's only a question of how many digits make your heart beat faster."

"I don't want money from *you*."

"Oh, I see, holier than thou, huh? Fine. I don't believe you, though. I've never met someone who couldn't be bought, and believe me, I've met *lots* of people."

"Well, good for you. I just want to put the guy who shot me behind bars."

It was as if I'd fired off another round, the way this sentence got them both to turn rigid. Beth glanced from Tony to me and back again.

"What is he talking about?" she asked.

"I have no idea," Tony said.

"I think you do," I said. "You've come a long way from robbing coffee shops, but you're still the same lowlife who put the .38 in my brain."

"You're insane."

"A lot of people would agree with that," I said, "but that doesn't make me wrong."

"You have no proof. You have nothing that will stick—not on that, not on Karen, nothing. You take me in, and there's no way they'll arrest me. I'll be back on the street in minutes."

"That's probably true," I said, "and I'm sure Manuel Loretto's people will be waiting at the curb when you walk out of the station."

He glared. The wind picked up, the flames shimmering, the tops of the firs bowing and leaning.

"You wouldn't do that," he said.

"I wouldn't be so sure."

"You were a cop once. Cops don't do that sort of thing."

"I stopped being a cop the minute you shot me," I said.

"Wait a minute," Beth said. "How did you know he was a cop once?"

Tony hesitated. "You must have told me."

"No, I didn't. I didn't even know it."

"Yeah, Tony," I said, "how did you know I was a cop once?"

He bore into me with his lead-ball eyes, the thespian mask falling away. Above us, tucked back into the forest, I heard the chanting of the Native Americans. Far behind Tony and Beth, gathered at the river's edge, a group of hairy primitives stopped to drink water.

"Tony?" Beth said.

He turned to her, sadness in his eyes, and brushed her cheek with the thumb of his left hand.

Then, before I could do anything, he'd spun her around in front of him and locked her neck in the vise of his left arm.

"Tony!" Beth gasped.

"Shut up!" he screamed.

I advanced a step, the Glock still trained on him. There was no clear shot with her in the way, but I'd remedy that in a moment. Unfortunately, I hadn't even managed to take another step when his right hand appeared with a revolver, pointed directly at the side of her head.

"Drop your piece," he said.

I did no such thing, keeping the Glock aimed at his head.

"Drop it or she dies," he said.

"Let me guess," I said. "A Smith & Wesson .38?"

"I'm counting to three. One ... two ..."

"Tony!" Beth screamed.

"... three."

I put down the Glock. I felt like a fool for not frisking him earlier and a high-minded idiot for putting Beth's life ahead of my own, but I didn't see I had any choice in the matter.

Tony tilted his head back and roared with laughter. "I knew it! Once a cop, always a cop!"

He pointed the revolver directly at me and shoved Beth roughly to the side. She tripped and sprawled on the rocks, crouching on all fours and sobbing. Grinning malevolently, Tony took another step toward me, the gun only inches from the end of my nose. Then he lifted the gun so it pressed against the scar on my forehead.

"Think you can survive *two* bullets in there?" he said.

"Go ahead," I said. "You'll put me out of my misery, and I'll haunt your ass for all eternity."

He made a *oooooo* sound and broke off, snickering. "I see. Believe in ghosts, do you?"

"It's one of the few things I believe in anymore."

"That's great. That's fantastic. You're one crazy-ass person, Myron. I always wondered what that nutty wife of yours saw in you, but I can see it now. You're two crazy-ass peas in a crazy-ass pod."

"What?"

He shook his head. "Life is funny, isn't it? Who would have thought we'd come face to face again? I've been watching you over the years, but I never thought you'd recognize me. Here's a little something to put in what's left of your brain. Might as well have it be your last thought. It's cruel, I know, but I can't resist. Bet you didn't know that wife of yours had an abortion, did you? I know she told you it was a miscarriage, but it wasn't. And here's the other thing. It was *my* child."

My face must have been quite a sight, because he erupted with gales of laughter. Beth, who'd been sobbing this whole time, fell utterly silent. I was swimming in a sea of rage and confusion, not wanting to believe any of it, but sensing some truth in it that had eluded me, a missing piece or two in the jigsaw puzzle of my life that was falling into place even if I couldn't quite grasp the whole picture.

Questions, dozens of them, sprang up in my mind, but before I could say anything, a shot rang out.

The bullet hit Tony in the shoulder, a ripple of clothes and flesh. He yelped and staggered back, still on his feet, still holding the revolver.

"Drop it!" Alesha shouted from the trees.

I couldn't see her. Tony, bent over and holding his side, turned his revolver toward the sound of Alesha's voice. Another shot boomed through the forest, but this bullet missed him and hit the fire, sparks flaring into the black. Beth screamed and rushed toward Tony. Judging by the way she was turning her body, I guessed she was trying to protect him, but Tony must have thought she was attacking him, because he shot her in the stomach.

Alesha fired again and this time winged his thigh. He bellowed with rage and lurched away, along the river. Beth was on the ground, curled in a ball near the fire and keening.

I snatched up the Glock. "Alesha! She needs help!"

"Coming!" she called, voice closer.

I ran after Tony. Alesha yelled at me to stop, but I wasn't letting him get away. He was a dark shape in front of the wrinkled tarp of the river, lurching and stumbling over the bigger rocks near the water's edge. He wasn't moving fast, and I gained on him quickly.

"Stop!" I shouted.

He whirled around, bringing the revolver to bear. I fired, only wanting to wing him, but far from the fire and immersed in darkness, I had no choice but to aim for the chest. It hit him dead-on and he fell backward, the revolver arcing high behind him and Tony himself landing with a splash at the river's edge.

His arms and legs jerked spasmodically. I charged into the river and dropped to my knees next to him, ice-cold water soaking my legs and feet. He stared upward, his eyes hooded by shadows, a gurgled gasp escaping his lips. Still alive. He was still alive. I grabbed him by his camo jacket and pulled his face up to mine, close enough that I saw the blood staining his teeth and felt his breath hot on my face. Even in the darkness, I saw the pupils of his eyes narrowing to tiny dots.

"No!" I yelled at him. "You don't get to leave. *You don't get to leave!*"

I wanted answers. I wanted justice. If he died, I got neither unless he chose to give them to me. I shook him violently, trying to will him back to life, but he was already going limp. His lungs produced one last rattling breath, then there was no more. Alesha was talking to me, hand on my shoulder, pulling me away from Tony and back toward the shore. Reluctantly, I let Tony's body splash into the water.

"Beth—" I said.

"Already dead," she said.

Then I saw him standing on the far shore, dressed not in his camo jacket but an orange vest, tinted glasses, and blue jeans with duct-tape patches that glinted like silver. The steadily moving current between us might have only been a hundred yards across, but it might as well have been a mile. There was no reaching him. It was too dark and he was too far away to see his face, but he waved casually, as if to an old friend, and I knew he was mocking me. He was a ghost and he was mocking me, because he and I both knew there was nothing I could do to him.

That's when something emerged from the river.

It was a dark oval shape a dozen yards from the far shore. I thought it might be an otter or a beaver until it kept rising and I saw that it was a head—Beth's head, judging by the severely straight hair. Tony's hand stopped midwave. Her shoulders came next, then the rest of her, walking out of the river as if she'd traversed it on the bottom— which she probably had. Black parka, dark jeans, and finally the white tennis shoes rose out of the depths as she marched toward him.

Abandoning all pretense of mocking me, Tony turned and sprinted toward the forest behind him. Beth followed, arms raised like some kind of zombie. When he disappeared into the trees, she wasn't far behind. I caught occasional glimpses of her white tennis shoes flashing through the trees. Hands gripping my shoulders, Alesha was murmuring to me, asking if I was all right, asking me if I'd been hurt.

It didn't help when I started laughing hysterically.

Chapter 26

SIGNED THE LEASE, paid first and last, picked up the keys—and there we were a few days before Christmas, Billie and me, standing in the tiny room that would serve as the home base of Myron Vale Investigations. It was just after two in the afternoon, but the window was small enough and caked with enough dust that not much of the winter light even made it into the room. I flicked on the overhead lamp, revealing the chipping plaster walls and the fraying blue remains on the floor of something that might have once been carpet.

"Well, electricity still works," I said. "That's a relief."

"You had your doubts?" Billie asked.

"For what we're paying," I said, "I wasn't even sure the floor would still be here."

Even empty, the room seemed as small as a coffin. I made a mental note not to call it a coffin to Billie, who'd already warned me about my sour attitude. It wasn't sour so much as chagrined. She'd been right, of course, even if I couldn't bring myself to admit it to her face. Already there'd been too many clients to use the house as an office, too much traffic both of the human and the ghost kind that I wanted to keep separate from my personal life. And Billie needed her space to work. She promised she'd come to the office every day, but she did need to paint. She'd go crazy, she insisted, if she didn't. *Crazier.*

"Well," she said, "where do you want to hang it?"

I set her painting down in front of me, a painting wrapped in a black plastic garbage bag. She'd forced me to close my eyes when I put it in the bag, and like a good husband, I'd dutifully done so.

"Can I look at it first?"

She batted long, dark eyelashes at me. She was dressed in a black turtleneck, black hip-hugging jeans, and a black leather belt with a giant silver buckle. My little ninja. It was my favorite sweater, the one she'd worn when I'd met her at the Portland Museum of Art so many years ago. Billie had a beautiful body, naked or clothed, but there was something about the way that sweater clung to her curves that drove me crazy.

"You have to promise you'll hang it no matter what," she said.

"Why? You know I'll like it. I always like your paintings."

"I'm a little more nervous about this one. It's . . . different."

"The suspense is killing me here," I said.

"Okay, fine, go for it."

Like a kid at Christmas, I eagerly unwrapped the painting and held it up so I could get a good look at it. She was right, it was certainly different, but not in a bad way. In the center was a logo of sorts, a glowing gold medallion with the letters *MV* in the center in a stylistic font, as if scratched instead of written. Behind the logo was the city of Portland at night, a view from the Morrison Bridge, the gauzy lights of the buildings mirrored in the Willamette River. The scene was both impressionist and realistic at the same time, capturing not only how it looked but also how it felt.

"Wow," I said.

"You like it?"

"Gives me chills," I said, and I didn't mean it in a Hallmark greeting sort of way, but genuine chills. I couldn't believe how much effort she'd put into it, to create something so personal to me. If she'd asked if I'd wanted a logo, I would have refused, probably saying the idea was silly, but now that I saw it, I was in awe. Which was probably why she hadn't asked. "Where should I hang it? Conveniently, there's already some picture hooks on the walls."

"You decide. But somewhere people can see it when they come in."

I considered it. When people came through the door, they'd be looking at the window, which was the same place I planned to put the metal desk I'd picked up from Goodwill that afternoon. The wall just to the left, though, would be clearly in view of my potential customers, and it had the added benefit of hanging over where I most likely would put my computer. I hung it there and stood back to admire it.

"Well?" I said. "What do you think?"

When she didn't answer, I turned and found her standing by the window, gazing at the street below. In the pale afternoon light, she was a study in monochrome, black eyeliner, pearly white skin, black clothes—even the white walls around her completed the picture. Concentrating as she was, face lost in contemplation, she was both close to me and unreachable at the same time. Not wanting to break the moment, not wanting to disturb that perfect thing about her that I could never express in words, I found myself just watching her until she finally spoke.

"Elvis is down there," she said.

"What?"

"Come look."

I did. Sure enough, on a street that was alive and bustling even on a winter day, with all manner of people in all manner of dress, there was a guy who looked just like Elvis working a bright yellow hot-dog stand on the corner. It was the heavy Elvis from his later years, a bit bloated in his white polyester suit, but there was no mistaking that plume of dark hair and sideburns down nearly to his chin. He was serving up a hot dog to a dusty-faced man in a miner's cap, smiling and laughing like he didn't have a care in the world.

"Think he's the real deal?" Billie asked.

"I don't know," I said, "but I'll have to talk to him and find out. He's certainly having fun."

The two of us stood watching him for a time, me sneaking in glances at her beautiful face, our hands nearly touching—if they could have touched. I wanted to hold her hand. She'd never been much of a hand holder in her living years, but she'd put up with it for my sake. It was one of those little things that I missed. It was good, though, just standing close to her.

Things still weren't right between us, but we were getting closer. We were closer to a good place than we'd been since the shooting and the many rocky years before that. It was only her suicide that lingered like a curtain between us. I knew until we parted that curtain and faced the truth of our lives, without any dissembling or deception at all, that our relationship could never fully heal.

She gave me her own fleeting glance, her eyes full of worry as if she'd been reading my thoughts, then looked back out the window. She swallowed and leaned closer, the shadow of the window frame casting a dark bar across her eyes that resembled a blindfold.

"I want to tell you something," she said, "but I'm afraid."

"You don't need to be afraid. You can tell me anything."

"I wish that was true."

"It is, Billie. You know it is."

"It's a very bad thing. I don't know ... if you could ever forgive me."

"I can forgive anything. I love you. You know how much I love you."

She glanced at me. There was so much anguish on her face that it alarmed me. This was not a woman who wore her emotions on her sleeve. This was a woman after my own heart, a woman who bottled up all that torment inside. On some deep level, it made her impossible to really know, but it also completed me in a way I would never understand. She peered out the window, her breath fogging the glass. I knew her breath wasn't really fogging the glass, just as I knew the painting wasn't anything more than a blank canvas, but what I knew and what I saw were not the same and might not ever be again. I don't know if I'd ever be okay with that, but I was finally beginning to accept it.

"I've been thinking about this story," Billie said softly. "I don't think I ever told you about it. It was about this … this beautiful princess who did all these terrible things. She didn't mean to, it was just the way she was, but she lost everything and everyone she cared about because of her wickedness. Her family died. Her castle crumbled. She ended up alone in the forest, living in a cave, full of remorse. Then one day a handsome prince riding on horseback saw her drinking from a stream and fell in love. But she wouldn't have him. She said if he knew all the terrible things she'd done, he could never love her."

"Billie," I said.

"Shh. Let me finish." Her voice had taken on a warbly, strained quality. "This prince … he said he couldn't live without her, so she made him a promise. If he could find a way to erase all the terrible things that had happened, so she could be the princess he wanted her to be, then she would marry him. And the prince … this prince, he searched and searched and finally found an old witch who made him a potion that would do as he asked. If the princess drank the potion and kissed him, all the terrible things would be erased. The old witch warned him that there was a cost, there was always a cost, but the prince was already riding away."

Billie turned to me, wearing a wan smile. I heard some strange sounds coming from down the hall, something like the bleating of sheep mixed with harps not in tune, but I was too enraptured with Billie to care.

"What happened?" I asked.

"He brought her the potion," Billie said, "and explained what it would do. She was skeptical, but she drank it anyway. It made her feel warm inside, full of love and joy. Grateful for this second chance, she leaned in to kiss the prince—and that's when she knew the terrible price she must pay. She knew all those terrible things would really be erased, but only from her own mind—not for real. And that wasn't even the worst part."

"What?"

"The worst part was that when they kissed, the horrible memories that haunted her every waking thought, all those awful things she'd done, would pass into him. She would forget, but he would remember exactly who and what she was. She knew the prince. She knew if she told him that this was the price, he would have begged for her to kiss him anyway. He would have told her he would love her no matter what she had done. He would have told her that there was nothing that could force him from her side."

She fell silent, blinking long eyelashes at me, as if waiting for me to answer some question she hadn't even asked. The bleating sheep down the hall were growing increasingly louder. Maybe they were actual sheep. Maybe, if all their racket kept up, we would be having lamb for dinner.

"Well?" I said.

"Well, what?"

"Well, what did she do? Did she kiss him anyway? Did she leave? Don't tell me they just went on with that being the status quo, never kissing. That's not how it ends, is it? Come on, I need some hope here."

She opened her mouth as if to answer, then stopped abruptly and looked out the window again. "You know, this is a pretty interesting neighborhood. I think I'll go wander around a bit, exploring."

"Billie," I pleaded.

"I bet there's even a graveyard. Those are always a good place to think. Never find any ghosts there. Who wants to hang around a bunch of rotting corpses?"

She walked toward the door. I couldn't believe it.

"Billie, come on," I said. "You're killing me here. What's the ending of the story?"

"I don't know," she said.

"What? What do you mean, you don't know? You mean you don't remember it? You told me this story and you didn't even remember the ending? You can't do that!"

At the door, she turned and looked at me over her shoulder, both sadness and impishness in her eyes. That was the Billie I knew, impish and sad. I would take her that way for all eternity if she let me. I really didn't care about the truth, when it came down to it. I just cared about her.

"No," she said, "I mean I haven't thought it up yet. I'll be sure to tell you when I do."

Then she walked through the door.

Chapter 27

It wasn't until dawn on Tuesday that I finally made it back to Portland from Government Camp. There was the hike up the river to where the cell phones could get reception, the waiting for the police and the medics to trudge into the wilderness, the barrage of questions, a hike back to the sherriff's office, more questions, lots and lots of questions, an intervening call from Alesha's department chief, and, finally, many hours later, the drive back home.

The sky over the oaks was still a hazy charcoal black except for a purple ribbon low on the horizon. Pulling the Prius into our driveway, I took a sip from the coffee I'd gotten at a little market on the way down and winced at how cold it was. It seemed like I'd only picked up the coffee minutes ago, but it must have been much longer. I'd barely been conscious of driving, I'd been so lost in thought.

Or just lost.

Mrs. Halverson, the old woman who'd died the previous winter, was out in her white terrycloth robe and pink slippers at the mailbox, waiting for the postman. Unfortunately, my odd ability hadn't been affected at all by Tony's death; I still saw ghosts everywhere. Getting out of the car, the air was wet and heavy. It was going to rain and it would be a cold rain. November rains were always cold. There would be Karen Thorne to deal with, and her father, maybe a few other loose ends like Manuel Loretto, but those things could wait. Right now I needed answers from my wife.

Still not knowing what I was going to say to her or how to say it, I ascended the steps to the porch. After hesitating with my hand on the doorknob, I entered the house. I'd left lights on in every room, but she was nowhere to be found. Not in the living room. Not in her studio. Not in the bedroom. Nowhere. I searched the garage and the backyard just to be sure, but she was truly gone.

I felt the first cold grip of panic taking hold of me. I couldn't have her disappear on me. Not like this.

Not content this time to wait around for her to show up, I hopped in the car and circled the neighborhood, checking the route I knew she often walked. No suck luck. Feeling increasingly more desperate, I headed to the office, gas engine roaring, tires squealing as the Prius rounded each corner. A group of young men in World War II Army uniforms, some with bandaged arms and legs, were crossing MLK Boulevard, and I barreled right through them. Fortunately they were ghosts and not on their way to some strange masquerade ball. I watched them shaking fists at me in my rearview mirror.

I reached the office in less than ten minutes. No Elvis at the corner. Must have been his day off. I saw the soft glow of the desk lamp in my office window, but of course that didn't mean she was there; I left that one all the time just in case she stopped by when I wasn't around. Weaving around a couple of pigtailed girls carrying tin lunch pails and five guys smoking weed, I sprinted into my building and up the rickety stairs to my office. She wasn't inside.

I stood there for a moment, catching my breath, heart racing and face coated with sweat. Where would she go? There were dozens of places that came to mind, and surely another couple dozen I didn't know about, but one jumped to the top of the list.

A brisk walk through the chill air and I was relieved to find her the same place I'd found her a week ago, after Karen Thorne had shown me that photo of Tony Neuman—sitting on the bench in the little park next to the Gothic church. The shadow of the steeple cut across the middle of the park, dividing it like a knife. Billie wore a tan, wide-brimmed fedora, bent low and shadowing her eyes, a leather jacket with lots of pockets, khakis, and ankle-high hiking boots. A pair of binoculars hung around her neck. A young man and woman with two kids, Tommy Hilfiger types in polos and white pants, as if they'd just gotten off a plane from Martha's Vineyard, were playing over by the aluminum slide. It seemed a tad early to be taking kids to the park, but I saw the bright red backpacks and matching lunch bags and figured it was a quick stop on their way to school. Probably a posh private school, by the looks of them.

I sat next to her, the metal as cold as ice. Billie went on staring at the ground, neither of us saying a word for a long time, the children's laughter ringing off the church's stone walls.

"The man is a ghost, you know," she said finally. "The women and children are alive, but the man is a ghost."

"Yeah?" I said.

"I just figured I should tell you."

"Good to know," I said. The woman with the kids glanced at me, and I reminded myself to keep my voice low.

We sat in silence. I watched the family. At first, I couldn't see any sign that the father was a ghost—they seemed to act as one unit—but then I saw how the children and the woman never looked at him. He cheered them on and clapped as they went down the slide, but he got nothing in return. He was a spectator, nothing more.

I cleared my throat. "Billie—" I began.

"Tony killed me," she said.

"What?"

"It wasn't a suicide."

She still wasn't looking at me, her knuckles white as she gripped the edge of the bench. I'd been prepared for a lot of things, prepared for an ugly truth that had been buried for years, but not for this.

"Wait," I said. "You're saying … I don't understand …"

"I've been thinking about where to start," she said. "I don't know if that's a good place, but I want you to know that first. I didn't kill myself. I was unhappy, but I didn't kill myself. I wouldn't do that. I'd never do that."

She lifted her head back, her eyes closed and the morning sun hitting her fully in the face. I waited for her to explain.

"We were in a bad place," she said. "I'm not making excuses. What I did … What I did was horrible. *Horrible.* But when we couldn't get pregnant, things just went bad between us. We were both kind of walking our own path, you know? I was lonely. I was so very lonely."

"I was always there," I insisted. "I never left. I never once left."

"Then Tony came along," Billie continued, as if she hadn't heard. "Only he didn't call himself Tony. He went by the name Greg Ostertan, and he was a photographer who traveled the world. That was his story. He was very kind. At least he seemed kind. I didn't know he was a con artist. I—I guess I didn't want to know."

"So he was right. You did have an affair with him."

"Yes."

"How long was it going on? A year?"

"I—I don't know. Maybe."

"And he got you pregnant?"

She winced. "It wasn't something I wanted."

"Oh, that's a relief. So the miscarriage … ?"

"I had an abortion. It was actually—actually twelve weeks, not ten. I knew it was his. I thought, you know, we wanted to have a baby so much … But I just couldn't. It wasn't yours. Ours. I couldn't."

"I see."

"I never even told Greg about it. Until later."

"That's supposed to make me feel better?"

She was crying now, silent tears streaking that alabaster skin of hers, but this time I felt no desire to comfort her. I steeled myself to ask the question I'd been pondering all the way back from the mountain.

"Did you two plot to kill me?" I asked.

She whirled around and finally looked at me. "No! It wasn't like that!"

"Then what was it like, Billie?"

"Somehow—somehow Greg, I mean Tony ... He found out about your life-insurance policy. He arranged that whole thing at Starbucks. I didn't know about it until after it happened. Not at first, either. When I saw you in the hospital that first time, I had ... I hated myself. I hated everything I'd done. Tony tried to come around, and I told him I never wanted to see him again. He gave me some space, but when the weeks passed and you still weren't ... you weren't getting any better ..."

"Oh, God! I was in a coma and you slept with him again?"

"Myron—"

"Jesus!"

I was shouting. Alarmed, the woman across the park gathered up her kids and hustled them to the exit. The man, lingering after them, looked at me coldly. I didn't care. I didn't care if anyone heard, dead or alive.

"I can't believe this!" I cried.

"I know," Billie said, her voice retreating to a whisper even as mine grew in volume. "I'm horrible. I know how horrible I am."

"But he killed you anyway?"

"He started ... He started saying how much he wanted to take care of me. He wanted to marry me. Then he started saying some strange things about how you—if somebody should, you know, put you out of your misery. That it would be a kind thing, if I just found a way to pull the plug. He said if it was done quietly, that doctors will sometimes do this, then the life-insurance money would take care of me. And then I kind of figured it out. He'd shot you so I'd get the money. He didn't plan on you living. I—I confronted him. He denied it, but I could tell by the look in his eyes that it was true. I told him—I told him I was going to the police. I was going to tell them everything."

It all made sense now, in a terrible, twisted sort of way. "So he killed you and staged it as a suicide."

She nodded.

"He should have just pulled the plug on me himself," I said bitterly.

"I thought about that. I've had a lot of time to think about it, over the years. I think he must have thought it was too risky. And that if there was foul play, the insurance company may not pay out."

"Smart guy, that Tony. Or Greg. Or let's just call him your boyfriend, to keep it straight."

"Please, Myron. Please don't."

"Don't what, Billie? Be mad? You had an affair with a man who shot me, the man who made me the way I am, and you let me live with a lie that last five years when you knew the truth. Don't you think I should be, I don't know, an itsty-bitsy teeny-weeny bit mad about that? *Don't you think?*"

She bowed her head. We sat like that for a time, me fuming, her limp and defeated, the morning sun slowly creeping into the park, glinting off the slide, turning the moss on the church's stone walls from black to green. My fingers, gripping the bench's side rail, were numb. A cool breeze brushed against my neck. A morning bus grumbled and screeched its way down the street.

"I'm very sorry," Billie whispered.

"Well, that's good," I said.

"You'll never know how sorry. I just ... I wish I could take it all back."

I snorted a laugh. "Me too."

"I—I don't expect you could ever ... forgive me. So I'm not—I'm not going to ask. I just want you to know how sorry I am. And how much I love you. I don't know if you'll ever believe it again, but I never stopped loving you."

Her voice broke on the last words. I couldn't look at her. If I looked at her, I might cry, and I was not going to let myself cry. I was too mad to cry. A couple of cowboys, spurs clanging on the sidewalk, strutted by us, so cocky and sure of themselves that I wanted to shout at them. I wanted to make sure they knew they were dead. They were dead and gone and there was nothing they could do about it.

"I thought up an ending to my story," Billie said.

"What story?"

"You know, the one I told you when you first got your office. The one about—about the princess who did the terrible things."

I sat in silence. I remembered it, though I wasn't really in the mood for a story. I was more in the mood for punching a stone wall.

"You see," Billie said, her voice scratchy and weak, "that princess … When she figured it out, when she knew that if she kissed the prince, all those terrible things she'd done would pass to him, she couldn't do it. She knew he might stay with her anyway, but she also knew he would never again see her the way he did as he leaned in for that kiss. And the worst part was, she'd never know. That was what really stopped her. She'd see that things were different in his eyes, but she wouldn't know why. So she didn't kiss him."

"How tragic," I said, not even trying to hide my sarcasm.

"That's not the end. You see, he wouldn't—he wouldn't take no for an answer. He said he'd stay with her anyway. Not knowing how else to scare him away, she went ahead and told him all the awful things she'd done. All the people she'd hurt. And as she feared, she watched the love seep from his eyes. But even then, he wouldn't leave. So she did the only thing she could."

"And what was that?"

"She left."

As these words hung in the air, I felt the panic return, a terrible clench of panic mixed with the most profound sadness I'd ever known. It was as if a pit had opened in the ground beneath me, swallowing me whole. I knew, then, why Billie was wearing those clothes.

"It was the only way," Billie said. "It was the only … It was the only way to make him move on with his life."

"No," I said.

"If the princess left, then the prince … he could find a new princess."

"It doesn't have to be like that."

"He could make a new start. He could—he could find the love he really deserved."

"Billie," I said.

She rose from the swing, straightening her hat, her back to me. I stood. We were still alone in the park, but Portland was coming to life now, the rumble of traffic reaching us over the rooftops, kids carrying backpacks on their way to school, a garbage truck beeping and groaning on its daily route. The city was indifferent to our little plight. Neither the living nor the dead cared.

"Where—where will you—" I began.

"I don't know," she said. "South America, maybe. Or maybe Africa. I'd like to see something new."

I saw her wipe at her face, then she turned and faced me, straightening her back, putting on a stoic front even as her eyes were red and her face flushed. There was an instant, no more than a flicker, when I thought I caught a glimpse of the stone wall behind her, one of those fleeting moments when I could *tell*. She was there and she wasn't. She was my Billie, my wife, my lover and confidant. She was the woman who'd said yes and the woman who'd betrayed me. She was everything to me, everything I'd ever loved or wanted in a woman, but some part of me knew she wasn't there at all.

"Goodbye, Myron Vale," she said. "Thank you for loving me."

"Wait," I said.

"Myron—"

"I thought of a different ending," I said. "To your story. I think—I think you'll like it."

She waited, eyes watery, pupils dark.

"This princess," I said, "she told the prince all the terrible things she'd done. You're right about that. And the prince, he was angry. He'd never been so angry. He didn't understand why she would do what she did. But ... but he still didn't want her to go. He thought maybe they could fix it, somehow." My throat was growing tight, but I pressed on anyway. "He didn't know how he could—how he could survive without her anymore. He said, if she stayed, maybe they could get through it. And if they got through it, what they had, maybe it would be better. It would be better because it would be true. It would be *true*."

"Oh, Myron," Billie said.

"And the princess stayed. And things got better. And they—they lived happily ever after."

Billie, blinking away her tears, regarded me with admiration or pity, I could not tell. The wound of her betrayal still burned within me, but I forced it from my mind. I told myself I was strong enough to get past it. I needed her too much to let her go. She stepped closer, inches away, and reached up and brushed her hand down the side of my face. I thought I felt the slightest caress of her touch, but it may have all been in my mind. *Of course* it was all in my mind.

"I like your ending better," she said, tilting her head back and rising onto her tiptoes.

"I'm glad," I said.

"Close your eyes."

I did. As she leaned in, I felt her warm breath on my lips, and I could not believe the sensation was not real. I felt the heat of her body close to my own. Why could my mind sense these things but not her touch? My hands started to rise, to embrace her, but I kept them at bay, wanting to live with the illusion just a little while longer.

"You forgot one thing," she said softly.

"What's that?"

"For the rest of time, she could never kiss him."

When I opened my eyes, Billie was gone.

Chapter 28

AFTER ONE LAST admiring look at the empty office—as shabby as it was, there was something so official about having an office that I couldn't help but feel a little pride—I locked up and headed down to the street. The sidewalks were packed with the usual crowd, old and young, present and past, everybody's breaths misting in the frigid air. A woman in a bikini rolled by on roller skates. Had to love that. Across the way, a homeless man sitting on the steps of the facing building was playing "Silent Night" on a harmonica.

I buttoned my jacket, shoved my hands in my pocket, and leaned against the brick facade. What could I do, but wait for Billie? I'd spent so much of my life waiting for her, even in the old days, that I didn't even get frustrated by it anymore. It was just part of life. Like the rising of the sun in the morning. Or my father's fading memory. Or ghosts.

I'd been waiting a while when I spotted that Elvis guy through the crowd, the one working a hot-dog stand. I wandered over to him, leaning against a *USA Today* stand and watching him work. He really enjoyed it, I could tell. When there were no customers, he smiled and gave me a friendly wave, no trepidation in it at all. Cautiously, I approached him.

"You know what I can do?" I muttered, quiet enough that nobody else alive would be able to hear.

"You bet, pardner," he said. "Word's already gotten around."

"You're not afraid of me?

"Hell no. I ain't afraid of nothing—except Priscilla back when she was chasing me with a frying pan."

"So you're the real deal, huh?"

"If I said I wasn't, would it matter?"

"I guess not."

Grinning, he rotated one of his hot dogs. I could hear them sizzle and smell the grease, my stomach grumbling at it all. I hadn't had breakfast yet.

"A man is what he believes he is," Elvis said. "What other people believe—well, that's like the audience at a live show. They matter, sure they do, without them there ain't no reason for a show at all, but they ain't the one doing the singing." He lifted a hot dog with his metal tongs. "Want one?"

"Wish I could," I said.

"Ah, right. So why you moping around here all hangdog? Afraid Santa ain't coming for Christmas?"

"I'm just waiting for my wife. She should be back in a minute."

"I see. Well, I know all about waiting on the missus. You can wait here with me anytime you want, pal. Always happy to keep you company. What you doing in these parts, anyway?"

"Renting that office," I said, nodding toward the building.

"Yeah? What's your line?"

I sighed. "Private investigator."

"Sounds like a good fit, from what I hear. You don't sound too happy about it, though."

"Just getting used to the idea, I guess."

A little blond girl with a red rash spotting her face stopped to get a hot dog. Elvis served it up with a smile, and the way he moved, it was just like he was on stage. As heavy and out of shape as he appeared, he still had a grace to his movements I never would. When the girl was gone, he motioned for me to come a little closer. A businessman getting a newspaper out of the stand was gawking at me, but I leaned in anyway.

"Yeah?" I said.

"Want to know the secret of happiness?"

"Sure."

"Two things," he said. "First, find something you're good at and do it as much as you can. And even more important, find somebody to love who will love you back."

"That's it?"

"That's it, pardner."

"That doesn't sound too hard," I said.

He smiled in that hound-dog way of his, both coy and knowing, full of charm and tease, his eyes revealing a man who'd witnessed both the best and worst that life had to offer.

"It's not hard at all," he said. "It's real easy. In fact, it's so easy that just about everybody manages to screw it up."

Chapter 29

I WAS IN my office when Alesha called. Feet up, cup of eggnog spiced with cinnamon and brandy perched on my lap, I watched the cell phone vibrating on my desk, the screen glowing her name.

The room was dark except for the phone and my monitor's screen saver of dancing green lines. Other than the faint hum of the computer's fan and the muted hubbub of a party down the hall at the Higher Plane Church of Spiritual Transcendence, my office was an oasis of silence. Even outside, Burnside was strangely quiet for New Year's Eve. Though in a way it made sense, since at fifteen minutes to midnight, most people were already where they wanted to celebrate.

Even me. I was where I wanted to be—alone.

It was the third time Alesha had called in the last two hours. I knew what she wanted. Last week, she'd invited me a New Year's Eve thing at a girlfriend's place, and in a moment of weakness, I'd said maybe instead of no. She took that as a yes and asked me when I wanted her to pick me up. To get her off my back, I told her I'd meet her there. Hence the phone calls.

When the cell stopped ringing, I took a sip of the eggnog and turned back to the monitor. I hovered with my hand on the mouse, then sighed and put my hand in my lap again. I'd spent the last hour looking at flights to Hawaii, but I just couldn't muster the energy anymore.

After Billie left, I'd wrapped up things with Karen and Bernie, but I hadn't done a whole lot in the month and a half since. Not surprisingly, Karen had been a little shaken up about the whole thing. Just finding out that Tony had, indeed, killed her to try to get her inheritance was one thing. To find out that he'd been skimming off the top from the Mexican mafia while he dealt drugs for them, and had slept with both of her sisters along the way, was a whole other planet of personal pain and humiliation. I sat with her a lot for a couple of days until she put herself back together enough to get on with her life. Or afterlife, in her case.

She was relieved to find out Beth was haunting Tony. It saved her the trouble of doing it herself.

At Bernie's request, I acted as the otherworldly translator so he and Karen could have a nice heart-to-heart. He'd come clean about his drug addiction and vowed to give it up as a dedication to her. Who knew, he might have even meant it. He was certainly grateful anyway, doubling my fee.

Which was why I'd been looking at airfare to Honolulu. With enough room in my bank account to breathe easy for once, I could afford to walk barefoot on a sun-drenched golden beach for a few weeks. But as much as I wanted to be alone *here,* it was hard to imagine being alone *there.* I was in a kind of limbo. Not crazy, at least. Not ready to once again be fitted for a sleeveless jacket. But in limbo.

Or purgatory. I'd been thinking about that word a lot lately. I often wondered what kind of book Dante would have written if only he'd walked a day in my shoes. Maybe the old man handing out the Gideon Bibles had been right. Maybe God was real. Maybe this *was* purgatory. Maybe the reason everybody was here, and not in heaven, was that nobody deserved any better.

I was sitting there mulling this over, and waiting for the pop and boom of fireworks to reach me from the Willamette River, when I heard scratching on my window. There were no tree branches near-by, so it was a curious sound. I rolled the chair over and pulled the blinds—and was surprised to find a black cat sitting on the other side of the frosted glass, gazing at me with yellow eyes. The bar sign across the street painted red highlights in his dark fur, giving him an eerie halo.

"Well, hello," I said. "Where did you come from?"

Yet I realized as soon as I'd asked the question *exactly* where this cat had come from, because I'd seen him before. He had a distinctive starburst of white fur over his left eye. He was sleek and muscular like a tiny panther, with eyes narrowed and focused with unbridled inten-sity. My mother had been terribly afraid of him—maybe because he'd possessed the remarkable ability to see both living and dead people. Kind of like me.

"Patch," I said.

As if in response, he blinked at me.

"You've come a long way, pal. That's a long trek for a little guy like you."

Patch scratched at the glass again. I opened the window—it was an old wooden window and it took some doing—and he stepped in-side.

In two graceful hops, he went from the window to the arm of my chair to my desk. He perched himself on the corner and immediately set to cleaning his paws, as if this was his usual spot and his usual rou-tine. Afraid he might be uncomfortable if I closed the window, I left it open, and the chill winter air tickled the hairs on the back of my neck. I could smell the coming rain. A few blocks over, I heard the crackle of fireworks from some eager early bird.

"I don't know anything about taking care of a cat," I said.

He paused in his cleaning to look at me.

"It's not that I have anything against cats, you understand," I said. "I'm not pro or con. Billie was allergic, so that kind of closed that door."

He blinked a few times.

"I guess it'd be all right if you stay," I said. "But I better look up what kind of stuff I need to know. Things you need, that sort of thing."

I started to turn to the computer when Patch placed his paw on my cell phone and looked at me.

"Oh," I said. "You think I should call Alesha?"

He cocked his head to the side.

"I don't know. Do you really think she'd want to leave a cool party to help me with some furry visitor out of the blue? Sorry, you're pretty cute, but you are just a cat. She'd probably just be irritated that I've been blowing her off so much lately. I've pretty much been a jerk."

Patch was a picture of perfect feline stoicism, showing neither approval nor disappointment at what I'd said. I realized that I was sitting in my office on New Year's Eve talking to a cat, that this would be grounds for merciless and lifelong teasing if word ever got back to my old pals at the bureau, but I didn't care. I didn't care what anyone else thought except for Alesha. I wanted her help, I realized. I didn't know what would happen between us, if anything, but I did know that other than my four-legged companion here, Alesha was probably the only other friend I had.

I reached out and petted Patch on the head, and he rose to meet my palm, launching immediately into a seriously impressive purr. It may have been the loudest cat purr I'd ever heard. In fact, it may have even been loud enough to wake the dead.

It was five minutes to midnight. An image of Alesha with another man rose up in my mind, glasses of champagne raised, the air twinkling with confetti, both of them leaning in for the first kiss of the New Year.

I reached for the phone.

Acknowledgments

THERE MAY BE WRITERS who produce books all on their own, without the help of anybody, but I am most assuredly not such a person. I'd like to single out a few people who've been instrumental in assisting me in getting *Ghost Detective* fit for publication.

First, to my good friend Michael J. Totten, fellow writer in the trenches, intrepid world traveler, and frequent hiking companion: Thanks for the early read, thoughtful suggestions, and unqualified enthusiasm for the book. We've both come a long ways from those early college years hanging out in coffee shops, pal.

To Elissa Englund, my fantastic copy editor: A big hearty thanks for helping me whip the manuscript into shape. You're a pro's pro. Any typos or errors that remain are entirely my own fault.

Katarina and Calvin … I didn't realize I was half a person until I became a father. I feel so fortunate to have such beautiful, bright, and good-hearted children. Thank you for believing in me, despite my many failings. I'll keep striving to be the father you deserve.

And now, again, and forever, to my first reader and love of my life, Heidi: I didn't have any success as a writer until I met you. I doubt there's any coincidence in that. Thanks for everything, hon.

About the Author

Scott William Carter's first novel, *The Last Great Getaway of the Water Balloon Boys,* was hailed by *Publishers Weekly* as a "touching and impressive debut" and won the prestigious Oregon Book Award. Since then, he has published ten novels and over fifty short stories, his fiction spanning a wide variety of genres and styles. His most recent book for younger readers, *Wooden Bones,* chronicles the untold story of Pinocchio and was singled out for praise by the Junior Library Guild. He lives in Oregon with his wife and children.

Visit him online at *www.ScottWilliamCarter.com.*

48197205R00175

Made in the USA
Middletown, DE
13 September 2017